"I PUSHED YOU INTO KILLING HIMSELF."

Dr. David Jorgenson stated the words bluntly. "Is that what you're suggesting?"

A deathly silence fell between them. Kris stared at her hands clasped in her lap. She didn't answer his question—a question he knew he shouldn't have asked. Neither of them was ready to deal with the consequences of what her reply would certainly be.

"I'm sorry. I should never have said that."

Kris shook her head slowly. "This isn't the way I thought this interview would be," she murmured. "I thought I knew exactly how you would be."

"You're not what I expected, either. Look," David said suddenly, "I think we'd both do better talking in a different environment, one where I didn't have to keep an eye on the clock for my next appointment, somewhere we could be more relaxed. What I'm saying is . . . will you have dinner with me tonight . . . ?"

Books by Meg Hudson

For Virginia and Jack

Meg Hudson

THE DAY BEFORE DAWN

Harlequin Books

TORONTO • NEW YORK • LONDON
AMSTERDAM • PARIS • SYDNEY • HAMBURG
STOCKHOLM • ATHENS • TOKYO • MILAN

Published February 1988

First printing December 1987

ISBN 0-373-70295-7

CHAPTER ONE

SHE STOOD at the top of the hill, her back to the big brick hospital, and scanned, with deceptively dry eyes, the sprawling submarine-base complex that stretched all the way down to the river. Withered leaves driven by the cold November wind scuttled around her ankles. Overhead, swollen charcoal clouds appeared ready to release their rain burden at any second.

Kris concentrated on the maze of rooftops dominating the hillside below her, oblivious to the leaves, the wind, the clouds. Jay had lived in one of those buildings. He had walked along those streets, those sidewalks.

Down by the river, the *Nautilus*—the first atomic submarine—was enshrined in an impressive memorial, retired to her permanent berth just outside the main gate of Submarine Base New London. Kris imagined Jay's excitement upon his arrival here in Groton, Connecticut, imagined him visiting the memorial, pictured the glow in his eyes as he took up residence in "Submarine City." Mistakenly, so mistakenly, he had thought the submarine service the most marvelous thing in the world.

She felt the familiar catch in her throat. More than a catch. It was like a lock, suddenly bolted. Even after six months, she felt it every time she began thinking about Jay. And it hurt just as much as it had in the beginning.

She squared slim shoulders, brushed back shoulder-length, nutmeg-brown hair. Then, before she could change her mind about what she had to do, she turned, walked determinedly across the parking lot and pushed open the naval hospital's wide main door.

The lobby was paneled in pine. Framed photographic portraits of austere naval officers in dress uniform were strategically positioned along the walls. At the reception desk, three yeomen in navy blues were laughing over a private joke.

One of the young men—about Jay's age, Kris guessed—looking up, saw her and switched the grin on his face to an official smile. "May I help you, ma'am," he greeted her.

"I have an appointment with Lieutenant Commander Jorgenson."

"Take that corridor straight ahead, first turn to the right, then halfway down the hall on the left. Number A-25."

Kris nodded, forcing herself to concentrate on the directions, trying not to let herself think about how much this young submariner was like Jay. Not so much in looks as in manner. That same vulnerable youthfulness, eagerness...

"Thank you," she said, managing a smile, but avoiding looking directly into his bright blue eyes.

Her legs felt matchstick frail as she started along the corridor he had indicated. She felt fragile, clear to her spine. For a second she paused, a sudden urge to flee making her quiver. This was a bad time becoming steadily worse. Now that she was actually here, she wanted desperately to leave.

The door she sought was open. Beyond it, a tiny reception area was empty. Again she hesitated. It was as if she'd been given an unexpected chance to turn and run.

At that moment, a man loomed in the doorway of the adjoining office. "Miss Sothern?" he asked soberly. He had a deep voice, the hint of a Down East accent. He was standing in front of her, not behind her. Yet her retreat was cut off.

"Yes," Kris managed. Her voice sounded quavery to her.

"I'm Dr. Jorgenson. Come in, won't you?"

He stood aside to let her enter the office, then motioned her to a chair. It was a small, sterile room painted in pale gray, the metal desk, file cabinets and chairs a slightly darker version of the same dull tone. As Kris sat down stiffly, she wondered if Jay had ever sat in this same chair. Her eyes wandered, trying to escape her memories. She focused on a framed photograph on the desk, a picture of an attractive blonde flanked by two young children. The doctor's family?

Then her eyes traveled to the face of Dr. Jorgenson himself. He'd taken his seat behind the desk and was glancing at an open file folder spread out before him, so Kris had a chance to observe without being observed.

His looks surprised her. It occurred to her that he was the first psychiatrist she had ever come face-to-face with. She'd spoken to an admiral—a former navy psychiatrist himself—at the Navy Department in Washington. But this was her first visual confrontation with a member of the profession.

Dr. Jorgenson's appearance did not fit with her preconceived image of him. True, people seldom looked as one imagined they would. Obviously, no physical pattern had been designed to fit psychiatrists only. Still, this man looked as if he should be standing on the deck of a ship at sea, not confined to an office as gray as the rain now falling beyond the single, uncurtained window.

He was big. Not merely big, but burly. Thick-chested, broad-shouldered. She'd noted immediately that he was not in uniform, but was wearing rumpled white duck slacks and a matching coat. Now she saw that the seams of the coat were strained by his shoulders.

His face, in repose, was heavy like the rest of him. Certainly, she wouldn't call him handsome. His chin was square, his nose looked as if it had been broken at least once, his mouth was full yet slightly crooked. He frowned as he scanned the contents of the folder and, at one point, impatiently brushed back a strand of the thick dark hair that had fallen over his forehead.

Watching him, Kris felt her stomach knot the way it had been knotting much too often these past few months. Her throat locked again as she suddenly realized that the information he was studying so intently must be about Jay. She stared at the folder, mesmerized, and was startled when Dr. Jorgenson asked abruptly, "Are you all right, Miss Sothern?"

She had to moisten her lips to answer him. "Yes."

"Would you care for a cup of coffee?"

"No, thank you."

"How about something cold to drink? A Coke?"

Her throat was dry, her lips parched. "Please," she said.

He left her alone in the office, the folder still spread open on his desk. Everything inside Kris yearned to reach out, grab and read. She wished she knew how far away he had to go to get the Coke, how long he'd be gone.

He wasn't gone very long. He came back carrying two frosty cans and two paper cups. He poured Coke for both of them and handed her a cup. Then he sat down behind the desk again, moving easily for such a big man, appearing very much in command of himself. In contrast, Kris felt as if she were falling apart.

"I had a call from Washington earlier in the week," he said without preamble. "From Admiral Carrington, to be specific."

She hadn't expected that. Not so quickly, anyhow. She set her cup down, afraid she'd spill the contents if she tried to hold it any longer.

Without waiting for her to answer, Dr. Jorgenson continued, "It appears that you've been making... well, some extremely serious accusations. The admiral suggested that I meet with you to hear exactly what you have to say before we proceed on an official basis. I take it you were agreeable to his suggestion or you wouldn't be here."

"I..." She groped for words. "Yes," she said finally. "Admiral Carrington suggested I meet with you and... yes, I was agreeable to that."

"I understand you live across the river in New London."

"Yes."

"Are you from this area, Miss Sothern, or did you move here only recently?"

"I've lived in New London about a year. I... I work at Hawthorne College."

"You're a teacher?"

"No. In administration. I'm in the admissions office."

"I see." He was scanning the folder again. Now he looked up and, for the first time, Kris met his eyes directly.

His appearance had disconcerted her, but his eyes gave her a decided shock. They were compellingly beautiful. Gray as the falling rain, with a sensuous silver sheen and fringed by thick lashes as dark as his hair. They didn't go with the rest of him, Kris thought chaotically. They didn't go with the rest of him at all!

He had been speaking to her impersonally, his manner polite but stern, his statements terse and edged with a steely coldness. She couldn't blame him. If her accusations proved out, his career was on the line—both as a naval officer and as a doctor. She knew that. There was no doubt he knew it, too.

She was here to vindicate her brother's death, as committed to fight as a duelist would have been in an earlier age. For months now, the desire for revenge had been growing within her, gnawing away at her conscience. It started as a burning frustration. Then she'd slowly gained the strength, mustered the determination, to begin action with the phone call to Admiral Carrington. Finally…she was here, facing the man who might as well have killed Jay with his bare hands.

The last sip of Coke Kris had taken rose in her throat, bitter as bile. She felt her head begin to swim, watched her surroundings become unfocused. Heard, from far away, Dr. Jorgenson saying sharply, "Miss Sothern!" Then she felt his hand shake her shoulder. She heard something snap, and she gasped at the potency of the capsule of ammonia spirits he was waving under her nose.

"Sorry," he apologized, as she sputtered and tried to push him away. "But you nearly passed out on me."

Kris managed to sit up straight, her elfin chin tilting defiantly as she forcefully pulled herself together. She was a small person. Having this man towering over her made her feel all the smaller. She tugged at the invisible veil of her dignity, draped herself in its protection.

Dr. Jorgenson sat down behind his desk again and flashed her an amazingly infectious grin. "I thought I was going to have to find a bed for you," he admitted, "and the hospital's pretty full. Anyway, you have some color in your cheeks again. A moment ago, they were like wax."

He went on, his tone more gentle. "Look, Miss Sothern, I can see how rough it was for you to keep this appointment today. We can put off going any further, if you want, till you feel up to telling me what's on your mind. You're close enough to Groton that getting back over here shouldn't pose any problems for you. I have a busy schedule for the next few weeks, but I promise I'll find a time slot for you whenever you call me."

"No," Kris said.

He'd already closed the file folder and was pushing it to one side. "No?" he echoed.

"That's what I said, doctor. It won't be any easier to come back. It will never be any easier."

"That's not so," he reprimanded gently.

"Yes, it is so. Oh, I realize you're a psychiatrist and you could probably go into all sorts of statistics about the effect of time in assuaging grief, but those kinds of statistics deal with normal grief. This isn't normal grief, doctor, because Jay didn't die normally. Jay was pushed into dying."

The silence that fell between them was a deadly bomb ready to be detonated. Into it, David Jorgenson asked carefully, "Am I correct in assuming you think I'm the person who pushed him? The admiral seemed to have garnered that impression from you, I might add."

He saw her throat work, and he felt a pang of pity for her. That was disconcerting. He hadn't expected to feel sorry for Kristine Sothern. Rather, from the moment Admiral Harold Carrington had called him about her, he'd considered her a menace, someone he wanted to get in and out of his life as swiftly as possible. A person with a potential neurosis that could be dangerous.

"If you can deal with her in private and prevent this matter from going any further, it will be to everyone's advantage," the admiral had told him in an agreed-upon off-the-record conversation. They were talking doctor to doctor, rather than superior officer to junior officer. David had had the good fortune to evoke the admiral's personal interest early in his navy career. That interest had persisted.

"Miss Sothern has acquired a serious chip," the admiral had continued. "The boy was her only brother and they were very close. She needs to blame his death on someone. Six months have passed and she still hasn't come to grips with the truth, won't accept the truth. So she's built her own fantasy to fight the pain of losing him. I think you know what I'm saying."

"Yes, sir," David had answered, knowing exactly.

"If we have to begin going through channels with her...well, frankly it will become one hell of a mess. You only have half a year left in the navy, Jorgenson. With the record you've built up, you can write your own ticket in private practice. I don't want to see that blown away by a woman who's chasing make-believe ogres because she can't cope with what happened. So pull out all the stops with her, understand? Make her see reason."

"Yes, sir," David had replied again, not knowing, even remotely, how he could make the sister of a dead submariner—a young man he couldn't even remember—see reason.

Now, looking across at Kris Sothern on this dreary cold November afternoon, he still wasn't sure how to proceed. Meeting her, though, had convinced him of one thing. She was an entirely different character type from what both he and the admiral had imagined.

It wasn't just her physical appearance, although that, in itself, was enough to put a man off guard. She was so slight, so lovely. A study in brown, today. Silky brown hair, brown doe's eyes set in a small, heart-shaped face. Her tan wool coat and cocoa-colored dress were mismatched enough in tone to make it seem that she'd just grabbed something from her wardrobe without thinking beyond getting dressed.

David Jorgenson had the impression that he could pick Kristine Sothern up with one hand and carry her under his arm as if she were a child instead of a woman, probably in her late twenties. He'd nearly had to test that theory when she'd come close to fainting a few minutes ago. Even now, he wasn't sure that she still wouldn't pass out. The color in her cheeks seemed to be fading again.

She hadn't answered his question—a question he knew he shouldn't have asked. Neither of them was ready to deal with the consequences of what her answer almost certainly would be. An affirmative. *Yes, I think you pushed my brother to his death.*

Idiot! he chastised himself. If she didn't think that, she wouldn't be here!

He said, "I'm sorry. I take that back."

She was staring at her hands, clasped in her lap, studying her unpainted but perfectly manicured fingernails. She looked up at him, her soft brown eyes dazed. "What are you sorry about? What do you take back?"

"We were moving too fast, too soon, that's all. You...well, why don't you tell me why you've come here, what your feelings are? If you're sure you want to. Today, I mean." Listening to himself, David decided he sounded like a med student on his first rotation. He tried to backtrack. "What I meant to say was..."

Kris shook her head slowly, stopping him. "This isn't the way I thought it would be," she murmured.

"What isn't?"

"Meeting you, Commander Jorgenson. It's not the way I thought it would be at all. I had this interview with you pictured." The faintest of smiles whisked over her lips. "I thought I knew exactly how you'd be."

"And I'm not what you expected?"

"No. No, you're not."

"Well, then," David conceded, relaxing ever so slightly while warning himself it would be stupid not to continue a certain vigilance with her. "You're not what I expected, either. So on that score, we're even."

Kris turned and stared out the window. "I thought you'd be older," she allowed. "More...didactic in your attitude."

"Didactic?"

"Yes. I expected you to have a witness here recording everything I said."

"We're not in court, Miss Sothern," David commented, not bothered by the put-down. "I might add that a psychiatrist's office is akin to a confessional...or should be. Whatever you say within these walls won't go beyond them, unless you wish it to."

"And at the end of what I have to say, do you grant absolution, Dr. Jorgenson? Is that what you're suggesting?"

"Far from it," he answered sincerely. "I doubt anyone is more aware than I am that I don't have that kind of power."

"But you do have the power of life and death. You hold it in your hands."

"No, I don't agree with that." *Damned right you'd better stay vigilant,* David warned himself again.

"You knew my brother quite well, didn't you, doctor?"

She shot the question at him, and David Jorgenson's guard immediately went on red alert. So, the moment of truth was at hand. He had been leaning forward. Now he pushed back his swivel chair, stretched out his long legs and wished he hadn't given up smoking! His face was inscrutable as he said carefully, "The fact is, Miss Sothern, I didn't know your brother at all."

Her eyelids flickered as he watched her closely. Had he shocked her? He suspected he had, but despite his professional expertise, he couldn't really tell.

He said, "I should amend that by saying I don't *remember* your brother, though I've been trying very hard to since I received the admiral's call. I can imagine how that must strike you. It must sound as if I'm indifferent to the men I deal with."

"It does, yes."

"Look, Miss Sothern," David went on patiently, "literally hundreds of men have passed through my office in the two and a half years I've been assigned to the sub base. I've been interested in each and every individual, but it's impossible for me to recall every name, every face—with very few exceptions."

"And Jay wasn't such an exception?"

"I'm sorry, no. He wasn't."

Again, he couldn't read her. He saw her eyes shift to the material on his desk. "I suppose whatever's in that folder concerns Jay?" she observed.

"Yes. I requested transcripts of all his records starting with his enlistment in the service. I had them sent over from my office when I knew I'd be meeting with you here at the hospital this afternoon. This particular folder contains material dealing with his performance in boot camp." David hesitated, then added, "He did extremely well."

Kris didn't comment on that. After a moment, she said, "You must have records of his time at the submarine school here."

"Yes."

"And since his return to this base after his last tour of duty at sea?"

"Yes."

"I suppose it's all considered classified material?"

"Well...these *are* official records, of course. I wouldn't go so far as to say they're classified, but they are not open for inspection, no."

"Then if I wanted to see them I would have to have a lawyer subpoena them, something like that?"

Here it comes, David decided grimly.

Levelly, he said, "I doubt there is anything in your brother's records we would keep from you, Miss Sothern. True, I can't hand them over and let you read them for yourself. But I stand more than ready to answer any of your questions."

"Then perhaps you can tell me why you pronounced him fit for submarine duty?" Kris demanded, not hiding her bitterness. "Not only in the first place, while he was still here in school, but later. Last spring, to be precise, when he returned from leave and was immediately okayed for his third tour of duty on a submarine.''

"You're making it sound," David said slowly, "like this is something I did personally.''

"Well, didn't you? You must have realized..."

He waited for her to finish the sentence, then saw that she wasn't going to. She'd been ready to fling another accusation at him, he would have bet on that. As he would have bet that she'd had second thoughts. He wondered why. Suddenly, her silence seemed as dangerous as her talk.

He said carefully, "As far as I can determine from the records, your brother did very well on his first two tours at sea. Both were routine three-month tours. He was subsequently checked out, physically *and* mentally, before being assigned to another tour. According to the records, I was the psychiatrist who checked him..."

"Yet you insist you don't remember him?"

"I'm not insisting anything, Miss Sothern," David said patiently. "It's a fact that I don't remember him. I only wish I did." He meant that and hoped his sincerity came through.

When she didn't comment, he flicked open the folder and glanced down at it. "According to this," he said, "your brother enlisted in the navy when he was eighteen. He was just out of high school?"

"That's right."

"From the beginning, it says, he wanted to be a submariner."

"Yes."

"Were you in favor of that?"

"It was what Jay wanted."

"It had to be," David agreed. "As I'm sure you know, the submarine service is comprised entirely of volunteers. They're an elite group of people, the submariners, a great, wonderful bunch of people. You should be proud your brother was one of them."

Her brown eyes pinned him to an invisible target. He wanted to wriggle away from her steady gaze. He had the crazy sensation that he could feel her pain. It hurt when she murmured, "I curse the day Jay ever heard of a submarine, Commander Jorgenson. Certainly you, as a psychiatrist, should understand that."

He waited for her to continue. When she didn't, he said steadily, "It was his decision, Miss Sothern. This isn't a professional consultation, of course, but I think you should try to accept that. No one forced your brother to volunteer for the submarine service. Obviously, it was something he wanted—must have wanted intensely, in fact."

"Oh, yes," Kris agreed, her voice so quiet that David had to strain to hear her. "Definitely it was something Jay wanted. He'd had this fascination with submarines ever since he was a little boy. Other kids wanted to be astronauts, wanted to travel into space. Jay wanted to explore beneath the sea in a submarine. I don't think he ever missed a submarine movie or a program about submarines on TV. He had his own library of submarine books and dreamed of the day he could see the *Nautilus* in person."

"You came to this area after your brother had finished submarine school and was assigned to a ship? That's to say, a submarine."

"Yes."

"Evidently you had no problem getting a job at Hawthorne College?"

"I was working in a similar capacity in a small college in Lancaster, Pennsylvania. That's where we're from,"

Kris admitted. "I got the job at Hawthorne through a friend of a friend."

"You took it so you could be near your brother?"

"You make that sound abnormal, doctor. I don't know why. I wanted to live in this area as long as Jay was based here so he'd have a home to come to in between his times at sea."

"Did your brother live with you before he joined the service, Miss Sothern?"

Her face tightened. "Yes, he did. Are you indicating there was something wrong with that?"

Easy, he reminded himself. Take it easy. Aloud he said, "No, not at all. You and your brother lived with your family in Lancaster?"

"I was Jay's family, Dr. Jorgenson," Kris said, staring down at her hands again. "There were just the two of us. Our parents were killed in a train wreck when I was eighteen and Jay was nine. Nearly eleven years ago, now. We had no close relatives. Anyway, neither Jay nor I wanted any help from anyone. I was just out of high school, so I went to work full-time and took college courses at night. Jay worked after school and on Saturdays. We both kept our Sundays free so we could spend time together. We lived in the house we'd inherited from our parents. The mortgage was paid off, but it wasn't easy. An apartment wouldn't have been any easier, so..."

She broke off, flustered as she realized how she'd been talking to him. Babbling about things she had no need to get into.

"Did you sell your home when you moved here?" he asked.

"Yes. There was no point keeping it once Jay enlisted. I knew he'd never be coming back to live in Lancaster."

"And you weren't too happy about that, were you?" David queried automatically. "No, wait, there's no need to protest. Your feeling was entirely understandable." He added slowly, "It's always hard to let go of the people we love. Don't think you're alone in that respect, or that there was anything unusual in your not wanting your brother to enlist. You were...let's see, twenty-seven when he enlisted?"

Kris glanced up quickly. "Yes, that's right."

He caught the note of surprise. But if asked, he could have recited, practically verbatim, almost every word she'd said to him. He supposed his training was partially responsible for that kind of retention. Still, he was honestly interested in the small things people confided. He'd learned time and again, professionally, how the insignificant remark easily passed over might hold the clue to a problem.

Certainly, Kris Sothern had told him things she'd had no intention of talking about. At the same time, her small size, her gestures and expressions, so quintessentially girlish, created a provocative distraction. David couldn't help but wonder about her personal life. Had she devoted herself entirely to her brother all those years? Had her sense of responsibility toward a boy nine years her junior been that acute? How much had Kris Sothern sacrificed for her brother Jay?

David Jorgenson brought his thoughts back to the one fact that mattered the most at this juncture; Jay Sothern had been more than merely "right" for the submarine service. Judging from everything that had been recorded about his performance, he'd been a natural.

Somehow, David thought grimly, he had to convince Jay's sister of that. Obviously, she was suspicious of him, and hostile. It would be easy for her to feel embarrassed if she decided she'd confided too much in him. Still, he had to convince her that something entirely apart from his life as a submariner had caused Jay Sothern, at the age of twenty, to take his own life.

This meeting had not gone the way either of them had expected. Because of that, and because he had the gut feeling—derived from experience—that the moment was not right for them to go any further, David also knew that it would be best to close this session before much more could be said.

Still, he was hesitant about letting her go for fear she might not come back. That, he was fully aware, could be disastrous. As the admiral had pointed out so insistently, it was vitally important that every attempt be made to settle this young woman's claim, valid or not, right here on the scene.

This appointment with her had been tightly wedged into his schedule. Reluctantly, David glanced at his watch and saw it was nearly three. Even more reluctantly, he said, "I'm really sorry, but I'm going to have to cut this short. I have to go back to my office. I'm booked for three consultations in a row before I'm through for the day."

He had said something before, Kris remembered suddenly, about having Jay's records sent over from his office. She frowned slightly and asked, "Isn't this where you usually work?"

"No, it isn't," he told her, shaking his head. "I borrowed this office from a surgeon friend of mine who's operating this afternoon. I'm in the hospital quite often this time of day, so I thought it might be easier for you to meet me here. The psychiatric unit is down in the center of the base. A bit difficult to find."

"I see," Kris said stiffly.

David could feel the vibes of her hostility, and it bothered him. He said slowly, "I didn't know till the day before yesterday that you wanted to see me, Miss Sothern, or I would have allotted a longer time for our meeting. As it was, it was too late to juggle my appointments."

"It was Admiral Carrington who suggested I meet with you," Kris reminded him tautly.

"I know." David reached for the desk phone as he spoke, about to call his office and ask his secretary to book another appointment with Miss Sothern. Then he remembered that his secretary had gone home with a bad cold shortly before lunch.

Suddenly, David Jorgenson had a different idea, an idea that totally surprised him. He let it infiltrate and wondered how Kris Sothern would react. Then, without even trying to hedge, he said, "Look, to be honest, I think we'd both do better talking in a different environment, one where I didn't have to keep an eye on the clock. What I'm saying is . . . would you be able to have dinner with me? Tonight, maybe?"

CHAPTER TWO

INSTINCTIVELY, KRIS BRISTLED. Then, for a small but telltale moment, she nearly forgot why she was at the submarine base in Groton confronting this navy psychiatrist. It shocked her to discover that there was something surprisingly boyish, something very appealing about this man who was issuing perhaps the last invitation in the world she would have expected to receive.

He added hastily, "It can be an early evening, Miss Sothern...or we can talk for as long as you like. Tomorrow I'll have my secretary fine comb my schedule so we can arrange another meeting."

Kris forced herself to remember that this was the man who had killed her brother! She willed that thought to permeate her mind, but her strong sense of logic intervened. Dr. David Jorgenson had not actually killed Jay, she reminded herself. Rather, he had made a terrible blunder, which, in her opinion, was akin to murder. He had okayed Jay for further submarine duty when Jay obviously had not been psychologically fit to handle it.

Kris suddenly remembered a phone call she'd had from her brother while he'd been a student at the submarine school. That, she recalled vividly, was the first time she had heard David Jorgenson's name.

Jay had phoned early one evening. In the course of their conversation, he said, "I had a really wacky test session today. They called it a stress test. I'd call it how to induce claustrophobia in one easy lesson.''

"That bad?'' she'd rejoined.

"Uh-huh. They put you in a big tank, by yourself, give you a few tools, and you're supposed to deal with what happens. All of a sudden water starts pouring in from holes all over the place and there's no escape route. You have to plug up those holes before you drown.''

"My God!'' Kris had breathed, horrified.

"There really wasn't that much to it if you used your head,'' Jay explained, lightly passing the whole thing off. "For that matter, they'd never let you actually drown. I'll admit, though, I couldn't wait to sneak off the base and head for a place where they'd serve me a beer.'' At that point, Jay had still been underage.

She'd said quickly, "Why didn't you come over here, Jay?''

"Your apartment? You'd have been at the college, Sis.''

"Well, why don't you come over now?''

"Can't,'' he'd answered hastily. "There's someone I have to see in an hour.''

"Oh?'' She hadn't liked the way he said that. It sounded evasive—and Jay had never been evasive with her. She had tried not to sound too inquisitive as she'd asked, "Who do you have to see so urgently?''

"Well...er, he's a doctor, here on the base. A shrink.'' Jay had laughed, but Kris knew her brother. It was a forced laugh.

"You have an urgent appointment with a psychiatrist?'' she'd blurted.

"He wants me to stop by his place, that's all.''

"Why, Jay? Who is he? What's his name?''

She caught the note of hesitation before Jay said, "Dr. Jorgenson. David Jorgenson. He's a great guy. You'd like him."

Kris, though she didn't know much about the military, was aware that, generally speaking, officers and enlisted men didn't mix. Certainly a navy psychiatrist would be an officer. She would have thought that in the restricted environment of the submarine school, the line between ranks would have been kept clearly drawn.

"Just what does this doctor want to see you about?" she'd persisted. "And why at his place? Does he live on the base?"

"No. He has a house a few miles up the river in Gales Ferry."

"I see."

Jay had laughed again. "Look, Sis, you're making a big deal out of nothing," he'd told her. Then he'd gone on to say that he had the following Saturday afternoon off and suggested the two of them go out for Chinese food.

That hadn't come to pass. On Saturday, Kris had waited for a call from Jay, but evidently he'd forgotten his idea about Chinese food. Nor did she mention it the next time he called her.

Jay had referred to David Jorgenson again at the end of his first year in the submarine service. During the course of that year, he'd alternated sea and shore duty at three-month intervals. Afterward, he'd be granted a fairly lengthy leave. Soon, he'd be going to sea again.

Spring was putting its tender touches on the Connecticut countryside. Golden showers of forsythia splashed against the porch of the lovely old Victorian mansion in which Kris rented a spacious apartment. On the day Jay was due back from leave, she picked a few branches and put them in a vase on her coffee table.

She'd thought, that day, that her brother seemed tense and looked as if he hadn't been sleeping well. She'd said as much to him, but again he'd laughed in that forced manner that caught her attention. He'd told her lightly that while on leave he'd visited friends back in Pennsylvania and also spent a few days in New York City, and he'd burned the candle at both ends more than once. Then he'd mentioned that he would be having a thorough checkup, physical and psychological, before being flown to the American naval facility in Holy Loch, Scotland, where Polaris submarines—the type on which he served—were based. So, he'd concluded, she had nothing to worry about.

Later, in response to her questions about the examinations, he'd mentioned that David Jorgenson was the psychiatrist who had checked him out.

Kris remembered that vividly. She'd never forget it. Because only a few days later, while she was throwing out the wilted forsythia blossoms, they had called from the base to tell her Jay was dead.

Now, on this gray day in November, she swallowed hard. David Jorgenson was waiting for her reply to his dinner invitation. She'd been about to make it negative. But suddenly it occurred to her that regardless of how she felt about him, he was probably the only person capable of filling her in on the myriad details she needed to know about Jay.

He'd lied to her, of course, when he'd said he had never known Jay, couldn't even vaguely remember him. She wondered why, and was determined to find out. According to her brother, he and David Jorgenson had indeed known each other. They'd known each other quite well.

She said, almost abruptly, "I'll have dinner with you, Dr. Jorgenson. Shall I meet you somewhere?"

His astonishing gray eyes widened in surprise. "Why don't I pick you up?" he suggested. "If you'll tell me how to get to your place..."

He jotted down the address and directions she gave him to Granite Street, New London, and asked for her phone number as well. "Just in case I get off course and need to contact you," he said, flashing her that appealing grin of his.

KRIS WAS WAITING under the shelter of the wide front porch when David Jorgenson drove up. The rain was still pelting down. She ran for the car and opened the door on the passenger side before he had a chance to get out and assist her.

For a few awkward seconds, they faced each other across the lighted interior. She'd expected him to be in uniform. He wasn't. He was wearing a beige raincoat, the collar pulled high around his neck. She saw the edge of his slacks and noted they were dark gray, not navy blue. Saw his well-polished black loafers. Then she closed the door, plunging the car into darkness.

"Too bad it's such a rotten night," he said, breaking the ice. "But I've got a place in mind that should be cheery, despite the weather."

He took her to an old inn a few miles south of New London, right on Long Island Sound. Logs blazed in a huge open hearth, the ceilings were framed with hand-hewn timbers, the floorboards had withstood a dozen decades of use. It was a delightful setting. But as they were seated at a window table, David said apologetically, "There's not much to see through the rain and blackness, I'm afraid. In the daytime, though, the view's terrific. Sometimes I come here on Sundays for brunch."

Alone? Kris wondered. Or with a wife, perhaps? She stole a glance at his big, square left hand. No wedding ring. But that didn't necessarily mean anything.

He suggested a drink. Kris was tired. The day had been long and emotionally exhausting. But she succumbed to his further suggestion that they have Manhattans. He placed the order, then put the menu to one side without looking at it.

"I'm in no hurry," he said. "Of course, if you are..."

"No."

His dark gray suit, she saw, was well tailored. It didn't strain at his shoulders the way his white coat had. He was wearing a pale gold shirt and a tie striped in black, gold and gray. At the hospital this afternoon, she hadn't thought him handsome in the least. Now she began to revise that opinion. He was not conventionally good-looking—his features were too irregular. Still, he was an attractive man, very well put together. She liked the way he handled himself despite his size. With a certain grace, actually.

Kris had taken a while trying to decide what to wear for this strange date. She'd chosen a leaf-green wool dress, then added a few pieces of antique gold jewelry that had belonged to her mother. Aware of her pallor, she'd touched her cheeks with a blush that matched the color of her lipstick. Then she'd brushed her nut-brown hair until it shone, letting it hang loosely around her shoulders.

A candle in a cut-crystal fairy lamp glowed in the middle of the table. The candlelight made the gold earrings glint every time Kris moved her head. David Jorgenson found the effect enchanting. He'd noted, with pleasure, that she'd bothered to dress up. For him? Not necessarily, he told himself. Maybe for herself. But at least she'd bothered.

Their waiter brought the drinks, and David raised his cocktail glass in a silent toast. He'd ordered olives instead of cherries in the Manhattans, telling Kris it gave the drink an added zip. She sipped and agreed with him.

He surveyed her, wondering how to break into a conversation. He wished, fervently, that they didn't have to talk about the navy, the submarine service or her brother. If only this could be a simple dinner between two people who had met and found each other interesting. Two people who wanted to get to know each other a little better. Wanted to share some time, some thoughts.

He asked suddenly, "What do you like to do best?"

He saw her slight frown, her indecision, and wished that his training hadn't made him so conscious of every nuance of expression on a person's face. Sometimes being so observant was an asset. At other times it was a drawback. Observation led to analysis. Tonight David Jorgenson wanted to escape from his work, wanted to turn off his analytical mind.

Kris Sothern looked disconcerted yet amused, and that heartened him. She smiled as she repeated his question. "What do I like to do best? That's a funny thing to ask someone."

"I wondered, that's all."

"Well, what do *you* like to do best?"

"Hey, wait a minute," he protested, grinning. "I asked first."

"All right, you did. Well, this may sound silly to you, but one of the things I like best, especially on rainy days like this one has been, is to curl up somewhere warm and

snug with a good book and a box of chocolate candy. I
like to read and munch and maybe doze a little.''

David shook his head in disbelief. "You won't believe
this," he said, "but you've touched my Achilles' heel. I
like to do exactly the same thing."

"I can't picture you curling up with candy and a
book."

"Can't you? What can you picture me doing?"

"Something physical. Playing football, or some heavy-
duty tennis or racquetball, or maybe cross-country skiing
for miles and miles. Something like that."

He laughed. "When I was in college, everyone told me
I should try out for the football team. They said I was
built to order for it," he confessed. "I did, and I washed
out. Ran the wrong way."

She matched his laugh. "Oh, come on," she protested.

"I do play racquetball occasionally," he said, "when
there's time and a court available. Mostly, though, I like
water sports. Windsurfing, waterskiing—I'm a lot better
at that than snow skiing."

"Were you brought up near the water?"

"Yes, I was. In Maine, near Portland."

"When I was in high school," Kris said, "I played on
the girls' volleyball team, but I wasn't very good. I also
liked to ride."

"Horses, I presume?"

"Yes, horses. We had friends who had a farm with a
couple of good riding horses. I used to go there and ride.
I had wild dreams about having a horse of my own, but
then, well . . ."

He could have filled in the rest of the story for her.
Then her parents had been killed, and she'd been left with
the responsibility of keeping the house and raising her

younger brother. David thought, sadly, that it would almost be impossible to get away from the wedge of trauma that had been forced between them. But it was Kris who didn't dwell on the subject.

She said, "I try to get in some swimming whenever I can. Usually, there's pool time available at the college. There's also a health club in New London I've been thinking about joining. I tried their pool. It was great."

They were nearly through with their drinks, so David picked up the menu again. "A swimmer, eh?" he queried casually. "I've heard that swimmers have ravenous appetites. Is that true?"

Kris smiled. "Sometimes."

"Well, everything I've ever eaten here is terrific. Especially the filet mignon and the prime rib. Unless, of course, you're a vegetarian."

"No," Kris confessed. "Prime rib sounds great."

They each ordered artichoke-heart appetizers, then a filet mignon for David, prime rib for Kris. Also, baked stuffed potatoes—a specialty of the house—and fresh asparagus shipped from California.

David looked truly amazed as he watched Kris do full justice to her dinner. He'd previously concluded that she must not eat enough to keep a dove alive, she was so thin. He'd also noted that her dress, though a lovely color, seemed too big for her. The neckline accentuated shoulder bones that protruded too much, a clue that she must have suffered a significant weight loss recently.

Since her brother died, David thought grimly.

Again he became possessed of the heavy conviction that he and Kris might never get beyond that unfortunate fact. Sooner or later they would have to talk about Jay's death. He knew that, but dreaded getting into the subject with her. Regardless of what Admiral Carrington had said about trying to get through this situation with Kris Sothern by himself, he wished someone else could take over and deal with the whole issue. If it was decided that he had been at fault in any way, he'd stand ready to take the blame.

Personally, David Jorgenson was absolutely certain that Jay Sothern's suicide wasn't his fault. The one area of his life about which he was extremely self-confident, with justification, was his professional expertise. He would never, in a millenium, have passed a submariner for sea duty if he showed even the slightest sign of psychological instability. To do so would be prescribing potential disaster for every other man aboard ship.

On a submarine, the crew ceased to exist as individuals. Every member was vital to the total performance of the ship in a way not equalled by any other branch of any service. Paradoxically, for that very reason, each man became enormously valuable, with the greatest possible care taken to ensure his physical and mental well-being.

David sighed. Kris caught the sigh and instinctively knew that something between them had subtly changed within the past few seconds. She declined David's offer of dessert and accepted the suggestion that she have cappuccino. She could not repress a smile as she watched him polish off an enormous wedge of apple pie topped with two scoops of ice cream. Despite his size, there was no surplus fat on him. Although he had disclaimed being especially athletic, he obviously took steps to keep himself in shape.

A combo had started playing in an adjoining room. She sensed David's hesitation before he said, "I know we came here to talk about Jay, but...would you risk dancing with me? I'm not trying to avoid the issue, Miss Sothern. It's just that I'd like to dance with you."

Involuntarily, she froze. He was acting as if they were out on a date together. They weren't. They were here for Jay, to talk about Jay. It was he who had suggested that they might do better talking in a setting where he didn't have to clock-watch.

He said gently, "If you think my asking you to dance means I'm not taking this matter between us seriously, you're wrong. The fact is we're both tense. I know a few minutes of dancing would relax me. I'm hoping you'll agree."

A warning bell clanged at the back of Kris's mind, but she chose to ignore it. What David Jorgenson was saying didn't exactly make sense, yet what harm could come of a dance? A lot, Kris decided dismally, once they'd stepped onto the small dance floor. She scolded herself for not heeding her inner warning. This was close dancing to a leisurely tempo. Disconcertingly close.

The top of her head barely reached David Jorgenson's shoulder, and the fabric of his jacket occasionally brushed her cheek. She felt heady just breathing in his clean scent, augmented by a hint of after-shave. She was aware of an undeniable attraction in the strength of his arm around her back. And then, quite suddenly, she became aware of his pulse, close to her ear. It was pounding.

She shivered slightly, unable to deny the small waves of sensation she was feeling. Small, delightful frissons, like satin ribbons rippling up and down her spine. The dance music stopped and David felt her pull away from him. He looked down at her to find she was staring at him like a frightened bird.

"Was I that bad?" he asked.

"What? Oh, no... you're a very good dancer."

Determined to keep things light between them a little while longer, he quipped, "You fib well, too."

He was unprepared for the change in Kris's expression. Her face might as well have turned to stone. Her eyes darkened, lost their velvet softness, became crystal hard. Astonished, David had the momentary impression that she hated him. Actually hated him. He amended the verb. He had the feeling she despised him, that she was looking at him from a great distance and finding what she saw completely repugnant.

"Hey, I was only teasing," he insisted, his voice low.

"Were you?" she asked coldly. "Sometimes..."

She let the sentence dangle, and David scowled down at her from his superior height. "Finish what you were going to say," he challenged.

"I'd rather not."

"You're not being very fair, Kris."

The use of her first name came inadvertently. David wasn't aware he'd said it until it was too late and he saw the flush creep into Kris's cheeks.

The music started again, breaking the awkwardness of the moment. The combo was playing an old song from *My Fair Lady*. After a few seconds of memory scratching, David remembered the title. "I've Grown Accustomed to Her Face."

He looked down at Kris Sothern and thought it would be easy to grow accustomed to her piquant face with its rapid changes of expression. Right now, she was staring at her shoes as if they had spots on them, but the flush lingered in her cheeks.

Impulsively, he reached for her hand. "One more dance," he insisted gently.

"No, I don't think so."

But David was already leading her across the dance floor, the pressure of his hand firm. He held on to her so she couldn't pull away as he put his hand at her waist. He felt as if his hands could span her slender waist. He found himself wanting to take her someplace warm and secure, wanting to nourish her, wanting to erase the shadows of fatigue under her chocolate-colored eyes. If only he could bring a smile to her lips, put a new and honest glow into her life.

David had loved, married, divorced, had several affairs of varying degrees of importance. But these urges toward Kris were of a potency he'd never felt before.

The music ended too soon to suit him. He had to loosen his grip on Kris, had to let her go. As they returned to their table, he knew it was time to call for the check.

Outside, it was still raining. David told Kris to wait in the foyer while he went and got the car. But as he dashed through the rain, he honestly wondered if she'd be there when he pulled up in front of the entrance. Right now, she seemed as ephemeral as a will-o'-the-wisp. Quite capable of vanishing.

The road was narrow and poorly lighted. The windshield wiper scudded back and forth, making crescent patterns against the glass. Staring into the wet darkness, concentrating on driving, David asked, ''Want to stop somewhere for a nightcap?''

''No, I don't think so, thanks.''

Fighting down frustration, he went on carefully, ''I realize we need a place where we can talk, and the inn wasn't right. I'd suggest we go to my place, but I live in the BOQ on the base and privacy's rather hard to come by.''

There was a second or two of silence, then Kris queried, "What did you just say?"

Each word in her question fell like a sharp pebble onto glass. Attuned to changes in tone, David glanced across at her and tried again for the easy approach. "What did I say about what?"

"About living in the BOQ. That's the bachelor officers' quarters, isn't it?"

"That's right. But in the new navy, the BOQ is for bachelor women, too." He chuckled. "Are you questioning my marital status?"

Kris ignored that. "I thought," she said, "that you had a house a couple of miles from the base somewhere along the river."

"A house on the Thames?" he asked, perplexed. "Whatever gave you that idea?"

Too late, Kris realized that she'd revealed more than she should have. She'd intended to keep her knowledge of Lieutenant Commander David Jorgenson—especially the things Jay had told her—secret, until the right moment came to use that information. She'd gone this far, though, and there was no turning back. She would settle the question of his residence without mentioning Jay's name, then close the subject.

Calmly, she countered, "You *did* have a house by the river, didn't you? A while back, that is."

He shook his head slowly. "No, never. I've lived at the BOQ the entire time I've been at the base. I have a suite. It's comfortable and convenient and has done fine for me."

Kris couldn't imagine why he'd fabricate something like that. She tried to think of a logical explanation, because it seemed to her that his story about having always lived at the BOQ would be quite easy to check out. There could hardly be two David Jorgensons who were psychiatrists at the submarine base.

"Does a relative of yours own a house by the river?"

"I'm afraid not," David told her. "Actually, I don't have that many relatives. My father's dead and my mother lives with her sister in Clearwater, Florida. I do have an older brother back in Maine—a crusty bachelor, just as I am. Does that answer your question sufficiently?"

"I don't know."

"Well, I don't know where you could have gotten the impression I'm a homeowner," he countered. "Do we have mutual friends that you've neglected to mention to me?"

"Not to my knowledge."

"Then whoever told you..."

"I understood you had a house of your own, that's all."

"I've never had a house of my own," David replied dully. "Excuse me if I sound bitter about that, but sometimes I am. I was a late bloomer as far as medicine was concerned. Maybe that's what put me off the track. Getting my M.D. took longer than it does most people."

"Why was that?"

"Because my father," David said levelly, "was the town drunk. No one blamed him. He was a great big Swede—I'm built like him—and an expert cabinetmaker. A lot more skilled than an ordinary carpenter, that's to say. He made furniture, things of real beauty, often from his own designs. My brother has a couple of his pieces. Anyway, he lost his right arm in an accident, and that was the end of everything for him. He went straight downhill, and one day he just walked away. Walked out of town, out of our lives."

"He never came back?"

"No, he never came back. My mother didn't have the means to hire someone to find him. My brother was only fifteen at the time. I was eleven. We all went to work. Sound familiar?"

"Yes."

"So my brother and I were doing any kind of job we could find after school. My mother cleaned people's houses, sewed for them, cooked for them. When I got out of high school, I hired on as a hand on a lobster boat. In the summer, our town turned into a resort. I guess what happened next was inevitable. I began to meet some of the summer people—people from Boston, people from Canada. They'd come down to the pier to buy lobster right off the boat.

"Watching them—the way they dressed, the way they lived, the things they did—began to stir something inside me. I began to see the rut I'd be in for the rest of my life if I didn't do something drastic. Drastic, in my case, meant saving up enough money to go to college. Once I was in college, it meant studying hard, doing very well to get scholarships to help see me through. In any case, getting an education seemed the only possible way out for me."

"Was it?"

David smiled sadly. "No, not in the way I'd thought it would be," he said. "When I came back to my home-town after college, no golden opportunities were showered at my door. That summer, I went back to work on the lobster boat. A whole year passed. Then one night my brother got very sick. He damned near died. Our town doctor saved him, and pretty much saved my mother's sanity, as well. She was crazy with worry over George. My brother.

"It was like a vision, in a way. I suddenly knew that what I'd been looking for wasn't just an education, but something vitally important to do with my life. Important to me, that is. Our town doctor, whom I'd previously considered sort of a dull, shambling old man, didn't exactly become a hero to me overnight. But I began to look at him, at what he did, with new eyes. It took me two years to make it into med school. But I made it. By then I was twenty-six, four years older than most of the people in my class. Now, ten years later, that doesn't seem very important. Time levels things out."

"But you didn't really become a doctor?" Kris mused softly.

"What's that supposed to mean?"

"Well, I realize that it's necessary to have a medical degree to become a psychiatrist, but . . ."

David groaned. "Boy, is that ever a lesson in put-downs."

"That's not the way I meant it."

They had reached Granite Street. David pulled up in front of Kris's house, shut off the car motor, then leaned back, surveying her. The rain beat a staccato rhythm on the roof and windshield. The corner streetlight cast a yellow satin swath through the wetness. The beads of water on the hood glowed like pearls.

David said levelly, "Suppose you tell me exactly what you do mean, Kris. Or maybe it would be better if I told you why I chose psychiatry as my branch of medicine. Because that's exactly what it is. One of medicine's many branches."

Kris sat still. "Go on," she said.

He drew a deep breath. "I got married my first year in med school," he said. "Six months after the marriage, my wife had a complete breakdown. She miscarried and just completely fell apart. There was no way I could reach her. It took experts, real experts, to bring her back to reality.

"At that juncture of things, I began to see that healing the mind can be even more difficult than healing the body. I'm not putting down any branch of my profession. Each is of equal importance. But for me ... well, I discovered that dealing with the human mind was the challenge I was looking for.

"The mind," David continued, "is invisible. No X rays can determine what a person's thinking. No scope or scalpel can penetrate a private mental world. Sometimes, often, in fact, I still marvel at the thin line between reality and illusion, at the narrow edge between sanity and insanity. And when I've helped bring a patient back from the depths of a torment you'd have to live with and witness to understand, when I see that person clear-eyed, smiling and ready to take his place again in the so-called real world, the sense of triumph is probably the greatest ego trip anyone could ask for. Except that it's short-lived. Because for every success, there is also a failure."

At that he stopped, and Kris wondered if he was thinking of Jay. Jay, certainly, could be counted as one of David Jorgenson's failures. Very definitely, Jay was one patient with whom he had failed.

CHAPTER THREE

"MISS SOTHERN?" Cathy, the pretty blond receptionist in the admissions office at Hawthorne College, poked her head through the half-closed door of Kris's office. "There's a visitor here to see you."

"Who?" Kris asked absently. She was reviewing a pile of early applications for next year's freshman class. Hawthorne was a small school. Based on projections, nearly a thousand students were expected to apply for admission. Only three hundred fifty would be accepted.

Kris almost wished she hadn't been promoted to a position where she now had a say in who to accept and who to reject. Some of the students turned down would be kids she'd personally interview. People with good grades and ambition. But because space was so limited, a strict criterion had to be used as a measuring rod. She didn't always agree with that, but that's the way it was.

She glanced up, waiting for Cathy to answer her question, but it wasn't Cathy who filled the doorway. It was David Jorgenson. Lieutenant Commander David Jorgenson, wearing a dark blue navy winter uniform that made him look not only impressive, but dismayingly official.

Instant confusion assailed Kris. She got to her feet, not even conscious of making the movement. The papers slipped through her fingers and sailed in a dozen directions across the office floor. She rushed to retrieve them. David bent to help her. Their heads collided.

She discovered that he had an extremely solid head. Steel or cast iron—whichever was the most difficult to dent. She rubbed her forehead, then looked up to see David rubbing his.

A rueful expression crossed his interestingly aligned face. "For a small woman," he said, "your skull sure packs a wallop!"

"You're talking!" They confronted each other, scowling. Then the humor of the situation hit them both at the same time.

David's laughter rang out free and uninhibited, and Kris liked the sound of it. She wished she could laugh like that. She didn't think she'd ever laughed so freely, so fully, in her entire life. But she did manage a smile, a smile that lit up her brown velvet eyes and curved her mouth into such a kissable shape that David Jorgenson could hardly wrest his eyes away from her.

He wished he could say something, do something, to keep her face lit up like that even for a little while. But he saw the smile fade, saw the tenseness that was too constant a companion return to compress her lips into a different shape entirely. He saw the familiar bleakness creep into her eyes as she surveyed him. He wasn't surprised by that. He was chagrined at how much it hurt.

He placed the papers he'd retrieved on her desk blotter and said, "I had an appointment near here, so I thought I'd stop in with the hope you might be free to talk for a few minutes."

Kris added her collection of papers to the heap. Glancing at the stack, she said, "It's a busy afternoon."

"Yes, I can see that. But I've called a number of times and left messages. Didn't you get them?"

Kris took refuge behind her desk. David sat down in a chair facing her. It occurred to her that their roles were, in a sense, reversed. It had been just the other way around the day she'd met him at the naval hospital.

She said slowly, "Yes, I got the messages. I'm aware it was rude not to return them, but..."

"Yes?"

"I needed some time to think."

"It's been two weeks," David stated. Two weeks since he'd waited for Kris Sothern to let herself into the house on Granite Street that rainy night, then had slowly driven off into the darkness.

From the front window of her first-floor apartment, Kris had watched the taillights of his car glow red as he stopped at the end of the street, then disappear around the corner. She'd had some very strange feelings, watching him go.

When he called a couple of days later, she was still having strange feelings about him, feelings she mistrusted. It was crazy that she felt what she could only describe as a tug of attraction toward a man who'd played such a disastrous role in her brother's life. She reminded herself not to forget that, not to forget Jay.

She gave instructions to Cathy to say she was out or in conference should Commander Jorgenson happen to telephone. Messages were relayed from Cathy, subsequently, and each time she received one Kris repeated to herself, Jay, Jay, Jay. Remember, this man lied to you about knowing Jay and about the house he lived in somewhere along the Thames. Maybe he'd concocted that story about his father, too. As well as the other things he'd told her about his background. Maybe it was all a sympathy pitch.

As hard as she tried, though, it was difficult to picture David Jorgenson as a deliberate fabricator. Kris had to concede that unless he was an unusually good actor, a straightforward honesty projected from the man. There was a directness in his approach, in the way he looked at a person, in the way he spoke.

Still, Jay had told her more than once about his friendship with Dr. Jorgenson. Why had David Jorgenson denied that?

Latching on to what had to be deception—regardless of the way his character had come across to her—Kris had refrained from returning any of David's calls. She knew that sooner or later she'd have to confront him again if she wanted to learn what he knew about Jay. If she were to piece enough together to fathom why Jay had done the terrible thing he'd done. Until she could understand the reason he'd taken his life, there was no way she could hope to come to terms with her brother's suicide.

She'd decided to put off any more confrontations with David Jorgenson until she was truly ready to face him. Until she'd gotten her act totally together, and maybe done a little investigating, such as finding out about the house on the river.

Jay's psychiatrist friend—for that's the way Kris had been forcing herself to think of this man—had obviously decided to take matters in his own hands instead of waiting for her to contact him. Literally, the mountain had come to Mohammed. The problem was, Mohammed didn't know what to do with the mountain.

David said, "Since I saw you last, Kris, I've gathered together everything I could find relating to your brother. Not just his service records. I also combed through back issues of the newspapers that came out six months ago. I was on leave in Maine when he died. Up where my brother lives, it's easy to lose track of what's going on in the rest of the world. When I got back to the base, your brother's tragedy was never brought to my attention. Nor did I overhear anyone mention that a submariner had killed himself.''

"Somehow I find that hard to believe, doctor."

"Well, it's true. People in the submarine service tend not to do too much talking about things like that. There's a lot of stress involved in being a submariner even under the best conditions, so there's a calculated effort to push the positive side of things. Negative aspects are often swept under the rug.''

"Please go on."

David cleared his throat, then continued, "Well, after I got Xeroxes of the newspapers and read the stories, I decided to ask some of the men who'd been in school with Jay, or at sea with him, to stop by my office.''

Kris felt the pulse in her throat begin to throb. She leaned forward, her eyes intent on David's face. "Did they?"

"Several did, yes. We had informal conversations after I assured them there was nothing official about my summons.''

"And?"

David held Kris's gaze, and told her, "Every guy I talked to emphasized that your kid brother was probably the most levelheaded individual on the ship, even after spending three months deep under the ocean. They said he was a natural submariner.''

Kris sank back and closed her eyes wearily. David Jorgenson could not have said anything that would have made her doubt him more. Because when Jay had returned to New London after his long leave, he had seemed, to her, anything but levelheaded.

She tried to recall how he'd acted when he returned from his last tour at sea, just prior to going on leave. The impression that stuck the hardest was that for all of his boyishness, Jay had noticeably matured. She'd thought that natural enough, recognizing that a year in the submarine service would mature anyone.

He'd spoken of his ship with pride. She remembered telling him she'd always thought submarines were called "boats." He'd told her the old ones had been, but the nuclear subs, because of their much larger size and advanced capabilities, were definitely considered "ships."

Realizing that the activities of nuclear submarines were usually highly classified, Kris had not plagued Jay with questions. As it was, he liked to talk about the aspects of the submarine in which secrecy was not a factor.

Jay had managed to wangle a visitor's pass into the base and had taken her aboard an older vessel one Sunday afternoon when he was in submarine school. Down inside, she'd found everything distressingly compact. The effect, to her, had been claustrophobic.

Months later, after he'd returned from his second tour at sea, she'd told Jay that. They'd been sitting in her kitchen drinking coffee one morning, and he had laughed.

"The new ships are different," he'd said. "Because we're under for such long periods of time, everything possible has been done to make the sub a home away from home." When she'd looked at him skeptically, he'd added, "Honestly, Sis, that's the truth. For instance, each man has his own quarters."

"A room?"

"Well, no, not a room. But a large berth with built-in lockers for personal gear, curtains you can draw for privacy, and a lamp to read by. Don't look like that, Kris.

If you'll remember the sub I took you aboard, crew members slept on pipe bunks over the torpedoes.''

"I remember."

"On my ship, there are soft lights and soothing music. I'm not kidding, music is piped throughout the ship. We have plenty of fresh water for showers and laundry. There's an extremely advanced environmental control system that purifies the air and takes out odors. At the same time, temperature and relative humidity are regulated for maximum comfort. Oxygen's added constantly, extracted from the seawater. And believe me, there's a never-ending supply of that!

"We've got a well-stocked library," Jay had continued, "and the guys use it. Also, we get the latest movies, the best ones."

"And the food is strictly gourmet quality, I suppose?''

He'd chuckled. "Matter of fact, it is. Subs are noted for their excellent food. We get the best chefs in the navy. Not only that, but our meals are served at cloth-covered tables in paneled, nicely decorated dining areas." He'd grinned at her. "You don't notice that I've lost any weight, do you?"

"No," she'd admitted.

"The only thing," he added wryly, "is that it's difficult to know what time of day it is. Numbers on a clock don't mean much after a while. Your biological clock gets confused when you take away day and night. Our way of telling time is often gauged by what we have to eat."

"How so?" she'd asked curiously.

"Well, if we're served scrambled eggs and bacon, then we're reasonably sure it's morning!"

Remembering, Kris had a vision of Jay as he'd looked that morning. Smiling and fit, actually looking better than he ever had in his life. Yet there had been something about him she still couldn't put her finger on. Nothing physical, just a kind of hidden tension. A tension, she was certain, that had in some way triggered his later, terrible action.

She couldn't imagine how he'd lived in the confined quarters of a submarine for months at a time without someone becoming aware of that suppressed something that she now remembered so keenly. It didn't make sense that Jay's shipmates could have commended Jay for his levelheadedness in their conversations with David Jorgenson. Certainly, there *must* have been moments when something other than levelheadedness had shown through with Jay. Was this one of possibly many facts that David Jorgenson was keeping from her?

He was watching her with those striking gray eyes in a way that made her newly aware of his profession. He was studying her clinically, and that she resented.

Suddenly Kris realized she had this tendency to retreat into memory when she was around him. To plunge back into the past and relive scenes, remember conversations. He was letting her wander, damn it! And this made her feel like his patient, rather than someone who had sought him out because of the desire for revenge.

As if he'd read her mind, David said softly, "You can't bring him back, Kris."

Anger stirred. Then came hot tears she couldn't suppress. They stung her eyes. She brushed them aside furiously. "Don't you think I know that?" she challenged. "Don't you think I've learned it the hard way? I still dream about Jay, night after night. Do you dream about him, Dr. Jorgenson?"

The question was flung out with savage intensity, and David held back his answer.

Incensed by his silence, Kris continued, "Doesn't he, and maybe some of the other people you've dealt with in the same manner, ever come back to haunt you?"

David stiffened, but his eyes never left her face. He diagnosed that she was not far from the edge of hysteria, and he wanted to be ready to cope with her if she went over the brink. Then her anger slowly began to dissipate. He saw Kris Sothern get a grip on her emotions as if she'd been given a pair of reins and was tugging them with all her strength.

After a moment, she drew a deep breath and said, very softly, "I'm sorry. That wasn't very fair of me."

David drew his own deep breath, thought about letting her off the hook, then decided against it. "No," he said huskily, "that wasn't fair. And I think I've had about enough of that kind of thing from you, Kris. I haven't been digging into your brother's history for my sake these past couple of weeks. I've been doing it for you. I don't know you very well, but you've reached me. You've communicated all your anger and frustration and grief, perhaps better than you realize. Enough so, I've wanted to do something about it, okay? Obviously, the answers I'm getting aren't what you want to hear."

The fire in her eyes had turned to ice. "Oh?" she questioned. "What is it you think I want to hear, doctor?"

"That your brother's last tour of sea duty was psychologically too much for him," David answered, pronouncing the words as if they were a verdict. "That when he was examined before his third tour, the dodo of a shrink who checked him out failed to notice symptoms that would have told any idiot Jay Sothern wasn't fit to return to his ship. Instead, this so-called doctor okayed him. Then, before the ship left port, Jay faced up to the fact that he couldn't hack it, got hold of a revolver, went down to that amusement park on the sound, pulled over to a far corner of the parking lot and blew his brains out.''

Kris went white, deadly white. For an instant, David thought he'd pushed her too far. But then she glared at him and muttered angrily, ''You bastard.''

Chalk one up for her, David thought silently. *She's not about to fall apart.* She had the kind of guts he thought she had, but he knew she had to get straight with this or it would wreck the rest of her life. It would be a monkey on her back she would never be able to shrug off, a burden she didn't deserve. She took care of that kid brother of hers for so damned long, David realized. Now she needed someone who would love and take care of her.

He saw her shudder, and he let her deal with the vision he'd just evoked. He'd checked with the local police under whose jurisdiction Jay's suicide had come. The navy had been called first. Then someone at the base had contacted Kris and she'd gone to the New London morgue to make the identification. She'd identified Jay from a birthmark on his right thigh.

Kris reached in her desk drawer and brought out a wad of Kleenex. She sniffed into it without glancing up, and David had the sinking feeling that she probably never wanted to look at him again.

He said gently, ''I'm sorry, Kris. But that *is* what you wanted, isn't it?''

She said, still sniffing, ''What I want...is to know *why.* You must have known something. It seems to me that's why...'' She broke off, shaking her head miserably.

''I think you're wrong.''

''You *think* I'm wrong? Or you hope I'm wrong?''

''Think.''

"Do you expect me to believe that?'

Something dawned on David. There had been moments when Kris Sothern had started a sentence but hadn't finished it, as if she were afraid she'd reveal too much if she kept talking. Moments when he'd caught flashes of disbelief in her lovely brown eyes.

For some reason, a reason he couldn't imagine, she believed few if any of the things he'd been telling her. Such as the fact that he really couldn't remember her brother and that he'd never owned a house on the Thames River. This put him at a total disadvantage, something rare for him. Her lack of belief indicated that she must think he was out to save his own skin—a concept entirely foreign to his nature.

Kris's phone rang. She picked up the receiver and began talking, not looking at him. David got up and moved over to the window. The college was high on a hill. Kris's window looked out over a wide slope of green lawn, across the roofs of the Coast Guard Academy, then down to the river. Across the Thames, the sub base was clearly visible. Ironically, the distant scene was punctuated by the naval hospital.

It was a cold afternoon, no boats out on the dark pewter water, the sky a solid blur of gray. David could feel the depression seeping into him; he actually allowed it to. His mood matched the bleakness of the day, all because of this sensitive wisp of a woman sitting behind her desk, speaking in hushed tones, taking refuge in her shell.

He'd struck home with what he'd just said to Kris. His experience as a psychiatrist told him that. Personally, though, he'd flopped. She'd erected this barrier of disbelief between them he couldn't seem to get through.

David Jorgenson knew he should let his professional side take over, but his personal feelings were triumphing right now. Nor did he have the desire to summon his re-solve, nudge those feelings away and put Kris Sothern's inquiries into her brother's suicide into proper perspec-tive.

Kris was not the first woman who'd dealt him a com-pletely baffling hand of cards. Inadvertently, he thought of Jennifer, though there were no similarities between the two women. Physically, they were as different as day and night. Kris was so small, so lovely to look at, but not strikingly beautiful. Jennifer was model tall, with a head-turning figure and an astonishing face that for years had graced the covers of one fashion magazine after an-other.

Jennifer, though, when brushed by life's reality, had fallen apart. She'd been reassured time and again that the miscarriage had been nature's way of dealing with an impossible situation, that there was no reason she couldn't have a successful pregnancy—any number of successful pregnancies, her obstetrician had said after examining her. But she'd refused to risk it, refused to sleep with David again no matter what precautions were taken. Then finally she had gone into analysis.

He'd been in med school, with a punishing schedule. He knew there'd been times when Jennifer had suppos-edly "needed" him and he hadn't been able to be with her. Then, when she was at last out of those dark woods, and more vibrantly beautiful and full of life than she'd ever been, she decided it was over between them. Any love, gone. No hope of the spark coming back, no hope of their making a life together regardless of how hard he had pleaded with her to try.

The end of his relationship with Jennifer had nearly demolished David. It had taxed his emotions to the limit. But somehow he'd managed, somehow he'd done a thorough job of getting over her. There was no lingering bitterness. He'd even met her in New York for lunch a while back, and they'd had a great time together.

She'd since married an older man who pampered her the way she'd always wanted. She was beautiful, witty, delightful. As they'd parted outside a French restaurant on East Fifty-fourth Street, David had watched her walk away and wondered how in God's name he'd ever thought their marriage would work. They were poles apart. She'd been right all along. What they'd felt for each other during those turbulent months of their relationship had had very little to do with love.

After that, the women in his life had played many different roles—friends, lovers, companions. But no one had made a deep dent. Not because of what had happened with Jennifer. Just because...no one had.

He looked back over his shoulder at Kris. She'd hung up the phone and was simply sitting there. He glanced at his watch and frowned. Again, the clock was going to interrupt them.

He said, "I have to get back to the base. I have consultations lined up for the rest of the afternoon. Maybe..."

"Maybe what?"

"I don't know how to say this, Kris. That is, I don't suppose you'd have dinner with me again?"

"Not a good idea."

He moved away from the window and said, "All right. But I really do think we need to see each other."

"Then why don't you show me your house by the river?"

Kris blurted the words, stopping David in his tracks. His face was a maze of bewilderment and frustration. He drew in a quick breath, expelled it and shook his head. He managed to say, "Look, Kris," then stopped.

"Look, what?" she asked calmly.

"I don't know what the hell you are talking about!" he groaned, exasperated. "What house by the river? I've already told you, I've never owned a house by the river. Not the Thames, not any river."

She'd thought before that David Jorgenson must be either the best actor in the world or entirely honest. Right now he seemed so distraught, so totally puzzled, that it was difficult to believe he might be acting.

She surveyed the picture he made, looming larger than ever before her in his perfectly tailored uniform. The cut of the material emphasized the bulk of his physique, but also flattered him. Again, she realized that there was nothing flabby about this big man. Nothing out of control. Not in his body, not in his mind.

She wondered what David Jorgenson would be like if that control slipped, and judging by the way his jawline occasionally hardened, she imagined him capable of unleashing a thundering temper. But she also sensed his gentleness, his caring, his passion. There was a sensuality to his full mouth, a clue to his tenderness, his ability to love.

He moved to the front of her desk and rested his hands on the edge, palms down. "What is it about this house by the river, Kris?" he demanded, quietly yet firmly.

She shook her head, stalling. "Nothing, David. Just forget I ever mentioned it."

She'd called him by his first name! Was it a breakthrough? David wondered. He might have thought so with someone else. With Kris Sothern he couldn't be sure.

No, he was definitely sure about one thing. She was annoying the hell out of him. She was blurting out crazy statements and then withdrawing behind a wall before explaining them.

He snapped, "I will *not* forget it! If you're going to toss out innuendos, Kris, you'd better be prepared to back them up. If there's one thing I can't tolerate, it's stupid cat-and-mouse games. If you've got something to say to me, you should have the guts to say it!"

He was looming over her, working himself up into an honest anger. Looking up at him, Kris knew it would be easy to feel intimidated by him. Not only because of his size, but because of his integrity. Even though his professional attitude could be daunting to a layperson, there was a curious vulnerability about David Jorgenson . . . and something else. A keen sense of fair play.

Well, she could match that sense of fair play, she decided. At least, ordinarily she could. Right now, her knowledge about the house on the river and this man's friendship with her brother were the cards up her sleeve, absolutely all she had to deal with. She'd been an idiot to blurt out snatches as she had. To prevent it happening again, she closed her mouth tightly.

Above her, David thundered, "What about the goddamned house, Kris?"

She tilted her chin defiantly. "Stop shouting!" she ordered. "I'm sure they can hear you all the way across the campus."

"I don't care if they can hear me all the way across the river. You've got something to say to me and you keep skirting around the edges. So come out and say it, damn it!"

Kris had the crazy feeling that he could pick her up and break her in two with a couple of flicks of his wrists. Then she remembered dancing with him, the provocative tug of his hand at her waist, the tempo of his pulse.

Dazed, she stared into his incredible gray eyes as armies of conflicting emotions went to war inside her. She'd never in her life felt so totally mixed up. Everything within her cried out that this man standing in front of her, looking at her with that odd mixture of perplexity and rage, was deeply sincere. Everything about his manner, his expression, his voice, told her he would be true to what he believed in. Yet he was denying things her own brother had told her, things that Jay had no reason to make up.

Kris gritted her teeth, then cast her die. "Jay told me about your house," she stated defiantly. "He visited you there more than once. I got the distinct impression that you'd had a party, in fact."

David's square chin looked granite hard; his silver-gray eyes were glacial. "That's a strange kind of witch-hunt you're taking off on," he told her coldly.

"Witch-hunt?" Kris repeated, confused. "What's that supposed to mean?"

"It means that I don't trap easily, so stop trying to do exactly that. There's no need for it, Kris. I've told you the truth."

David drew in a deep breath, exhaled it slowly, forced her to meet his eyes. He said heavily, "It looks as if you're going to have to make a choice, Kris. A choice between your brother and me. I swear I'm telling you the truth... for all the good that'll probably do. Because if you accept what I'm saying, you'll also have to accept the fact that Jay lied."

CHAPTER FOUR

AS A PROFESSIONAL, David was accustomed to giving his total concentration to the matter at hand. But that afternoon, as he put in several hours at the base psychiatric clinic, he had a hard time keeping his mind from wandering. He couldn't erase the image of an angry Kris, or her staggering accusation, from his thoughts.

Why would her brother have created the story about him having a house on the Thames River in Gales Ferry? It was cruel irony, really. David had so often dreamed of having even a cabin he could call his own, but had yet to manage this given his life-style and commitment to the navy. In the eyes of Jay Sothern, though, he'd been a property owner. It just didn't make sense.

It was with tremendous effort—and only because he was so disciplined in the practice of psychiatry—that David temporarily shoved aside speculation and carefully listened to the problems of a young submariner who was having a recurring nightmare.

David was the only psychiatrist attached to the clinic at present. His two colleagues were psychologists. They were both lieutenants, senior grade, so technically he outranked them. But David Jorgenson was by nature an unmilitary type of person. He seldom paid much attention to rank. Perhaps because of that, his relationship with the personnel under his "command" was excellent. It had been ever since he'd gone on active duty with the

navy to pay back the scholarship money advanced to him
for his medical-school education.

All afternoon, thoughts of Kris continuously sabo-
taged his ability to concentrate. For once he wanted to
pull rank, wanted to order his colleagues to take over his
patient load. But that would hardly be fair, as they had
very full schedules of their own. The best he could do was
brood about Kris for a few minutes in between appointments, hoping that he'd reach a conclusion about what
to do next.

She'd stared at him coldly when he'd inferred that her
brother must have lied to her. Her unspoken anger had
been far harder to take than if she'd slapped him in the
face. Professionally, he wished Kris had simply given vent
to everything she was holding back, wished she'd managed to cry or swear or blow up in some manner. Only
then would she expunge the fury and frustration from her
system. As it was, she'd held it all in and had ended their
impromptu meeting by telling him she had an appointment with one of the faculty advisors.

David had stalked out into dreary weather that
matched his mood. He'd been late for his first patient,
but by midafternoon he'd caught up, as the consultations were relatively simple. Lucky for him, he thought
wryly, considering the way he was tending to wool-gather.

He was between patients, in one of those woolgather-
ing moments, when his phone rang. Normally, calls were
not put through to him during consultation hours. This
call must be important, he decided, or his secretary
wouldn't have bent the rules. Briefly, his pulse skipped.
Was there a chance Kris might be on the line?

He picked up the receiver. "Dr. Jorgenson," he said
steadily.

"Hello, David," a female voice said.

It was Marianne Phillips, the wife of a navy chaplain, Evan Phillips, his closest navy friend. Evan, this past year, had been one of the two chaplains attached to the sub tender at Holy Loch, Scotland. His job was ministering to the men on the Polaris subs berthed at the U.S. naval facility there. The normal tour of duty for a chaplain on this assignment was thirty months, provided he was accompanied by his family. If unaccompanied, the stay was reduced to twelve months, which meant Evan should be coming home very soon.

"I have to see you, David," Marianne blurted, before he had the chance to speak. "It's urgent," she added, her voice vibrating with tension.

This was both alarming and disconcerting. David had long considered Marianne a perfect service wife. She was a stunning brunette, coolly efficient, a dedicated wife and mother. He admired the way she ran her household—whether Evan was at home or away, she was the person at the helm. He admired the way she was bringing up her two teenage daughters, both attending a private school in New London.

Marianne was active in the Navy Wives Support Group, an organization that focused on helping the wives of submariners cope with the demands their husbands' careers placed upon them. She was also a volunteer at the Navy Relief Office in the Family Service Center on the base. A busy woman, by any standard.

Abruptly, he remembered that Marianne had invited him to the Phillips's home for supper. With Evan overseas, she often asked him to share a supper with the girls and herself, strictly for friendship and company. On these occasions when he managed to join them, he felt like a surrogate father. He'd laughingly related as much to Evan during a long-distance phone call not too long ago.

Evan had chuckled, then turned serious. "I appreciate your spending time with my family, Dave," he'd said. "The girls think the world of you, as does Marianne. Anyway, it's the girls I'm primarily concerned about. At their age . . . well, let's just say I wish I had my trio of lovely ladies over here with me in Scotland."

Deborah was fifteen, Patricia sixteen. They were both normal American teenagers. That is, a handful for their mother. Thinking that, David frowned. "Is something wrong with one of the girls?" he asked automatically.

"No, they're fine."

"Well, I'm rather busy at the moment. I'm coming over to your house for dinner, remember? Can't this wait till then?"

"I don't want you to come to the house tonight."

He didn't like the way she said that, but he chose to adopt a casual position. "That's okay," he said lightly. "If something's come up, it's fine with me. I've been sitting around too much, lately. This'll give me a chance to get in some racquetball."

"I want you to take me out to dinner," Marianne announced, in that same daunting tone.

David forced a laugh. "Aren't you afraid we might raise a few eyebrows if we're seen dining together?"

"Afraid, no," Marianne allowed. "Of course, if any of the other wives saw us, we'd probably be the subject of gossip," she added bitterly. "Anyway, we can go to some place in New London. Some hole-in-the-wall where it's doubtful we'll be recognized. Or all the way to New Haven, if you want. I really don't care. I need to see you, that's all, and it would be impossible at the house. The girls will be home tonight. They planned especially to be home because they knew you were coming to dinner."

"What are you going to tell them if I don't show up?" David asked reasonably. "Not to mention telling them that you've decided to head out by yourself?"

"I'll think of something," Marianne assured him. "Look, David, I just got off the phone with Evan. He said he'll be home a few days before Thanksgiving. That's next week!"

"Terrific! It'll be great to see him."

"Well, it was a shock to me," Marianne said, as if she hadn't even heard him. "It gives me very little time."

"Very little time for what?"

"That's what I want to discuss with you. And why the girls can't be around to hear."

Suddenly, David's heart felt like a lump of lead. "What are you saying, Marianne?" he demanded.

"Nothing, right now," she retorted. "Why don't we meet in the parking lot by the bus station over in New London? We can leave one car there and drive someplace together."

David didn't like the thought of what he might be getting himself into. Yet his friend's wife had put him on a hook. He couldn't dangle at the end of it indefinitely. "What time?" he asked tersely.

"How about eight?"

"All right, eight o'clock."

For the balance of the afternoon, the conversation with Marianne thrust Kris out of David's mind...most of the time. Occasionally, she would intrude, and he'd silently groan. Still, Marianne's needs had to take priority. He owed that much to Evan.

He'd first met Evan when they'd taken a short trip on one of the subs to get the feel of living in an artificially created atmosphere deep under the ocean's surface. This was not a military requirement—neither doctors nor chaplains were required by the navy to go to sea in a sub. Still, both Evan and David had felt they would understand the problems of submariners better if they experienced a taste of the lives those men led.

Back onshore, they'd continued with the discussions they'd started far out in the Atlantic in their silent, submerged world. David ministered to the mind, Evan to the spirit. In each case, the emotions were involved. It was interesting to theorize about mind, spirit and emotion and to discover similarities in many aspects of their work. To find a new friend was added good fortune.

David had teased Evan that he'd never personally known a man of the cloth. He'd expected Evan to be far more pious and pompous. Evan had made a few pithy observations of his own about psychiatrists. The bonds of friendship had been knit and strengthened ever since. David had sorely missed Evan this past year. Hearing that he'd be returning to Groton in just a few days was the best news to come his way in months. Except for Marianne's attitude about it.

As he pulled into the bus station parking lot that evening, David felt as if he were embarking on a clandestine meeting he didn't want any part of. He got out of his car, locked it and looked around uncertainly. Almost at once, he heard Marianne call, "Over here, David."

She'd parked in the darkest corner of the lot, which further fueled his apprehensions.

He walked reluctantly toward her car. She pushed the door open for him and he slid inside. She turned the key in the ignition and the dashboard lit up as the engine started. In its light, he could see she looked wretched. That, in itself, was a shock.

"There's a little Mexican place off the interstate over on the other side of New London," she said. "I thought we might go there."

"Fine," David murmured.

"I'd just as soon not talk about anything till we get there," she warned.

"Okay."

The restaurant she'd chosen was only slightly more charming than an ordinary greasy spoon. They sat in a dimly lighted booth and ordered beer and enchiladas. Then Marianne pulled a pack of cigarettes out of her purse—another shock, as David couldn't remember ever seeing her smoke.

She was wound up tighter than a clock spring, fiddling nervously with a book of matches. Suddenly, she raised her eyes and stared at David bleakly. "This is even harder than I thought it would be," she moaned.

David felt oddly helpless. "I'm in the dark," he said.

"I know, David, I know. And it's unfair of me to put you in the middle of this. I shouldn't have, but I couldn't help myself. There's no one else I can turn to."

"I don't intend to be put in the middle of anything, Marianne. Especially when I don't even know what it is."

She nodded grimly. "All right, then. I know I have to come out with this, so I will." She paused to draw on her cigarette, then blew out a thin stream of smoke. "I...I'm going to ask Evan for a divorce."

The shock was staggering. David recoiled against the back of the booth as if he'd been shoved by an evil force. Next, he was fidgeting terribly, searching for an escape hatch.

Marianne said ruefully, "You look like I just hit you with a sledgehammer."

"You might as well have."

"Dave...all this time, haven't you had any idea things weren't that good between Evan and me?"

"No," he said, stunned. "Never."

"Then I guess I put up a better front than I realized. I just thought that maybe you might have seen through it, that's all. I mean, you are a psychiatrist. You're trained to notice people's problems."

David reached for his beer. "Yeah," he said disgustedly. "I'm trained, all right." A hell of an observer, he berated himself silently. Totally obtuse where my best friends are concerned. But I never thought of Marianne or Evan as patients, for God's sake!

The cold beer made his throat tingle, numbed his vocal cords. He sounded hoarse as he asked, "If things have been that bad for such a long time, why have you waited till now, till Evan's coming home, to tell me about it?"

"I hadn't planned on telling you anything at all," Marianne admitted quietly. She paused to light another cigarette, then went on, "I thought it was something I could handle by myself. It's my marriage, my problem. Why involve you, I thought. I knew it would hurt you, Dave. And I didn't want to do that. But then all at once today, when I pictured Evan coming back, when I saw us sitting down to have Thanksgiving dinner together...I panicked. I had to call you. I had to let some of this spill over."

"Tell me, Marianne, were you thinking of me as a psychiatrist or as a friend?" David asked sourly.

"Does it matter?"

"Yes, it matters." Silence stretched between them. Then David said, "Friendship, real friendship like ours, is intensely personal. It clouds objective professional judgment. That's why when a doctor becomes a friend of a patient he often suggests taking the medical problems to another physician. You get to know someone too well and it's impossible to keep the necessary objectivity." He paused, then asked, "Do you think I react like this whenever a submariner confronts me with a dilemma? Do you think I get downright angry every time the order of things comes apart?"

"I'm sorry, Dave," Marianne mumbled miserably.

"I know you are," he told her, his voice low. "I know you are."

He looked out the window into the dark night. Inevitably, a picture of Kris came into his mind. Certainly he couldn't say they were friends. Not at this juncture, perhaps not ever. He'd started out with her intending to be completely objective, but that soon became a lost cause. Kris tore at his heart when she looked at him with those soft brown eyes of hers. Her silent reproach, very much in evidence when he'd left her this afternoon, was almost unbearable.

Somehow, I've got to convince her that I never knew her brother. That this house on the river is a complete mystery. Somehow, I've got to discover the truth about Jay Sothern. Things his sister obviously has no knowledge of.

The words came to David like a self-written prescription and he sighed deeply. Turning back to Marianne, he said heavily, "Since you've brought this up, I feel I have a right to ask why. Why do you want a divorce after eighteen years of marriage? You said things weren't that good between you and Evan. What things, Marianne? Are you talking about sex?"

He saw with satisfaction he'd jolted her. To his mind, that was a healthy sign—a lot healthier than the zombie-like expression she'd been wearing thus far.

"Is this the doctor or the friend asking?" she queried.

"I'm not sure," David admitted. "I think a lot of you both, you know that. But Evan is my best friend, damn it!"

Marianne closed her eyes wearily. "I know he's your best friend, Dave. I'm also beginning to realize that I never should have gotten you into this."

"Well, it's too late to backtrack now. So spill it out, okay?" He managed a grim smile. "I'll try to put on my doctor hat while I listen."

Marianne snuffed out her cigarette, stalling. Slowly, she said, "Well . . . it isn't sex. I mean, that aspect of our relationship isn't as exciting as it once was, but I suppose that's par for the course."

David didn't comment.

After a moment, she went on, "I never thought I'd admit this to anyone. All these years, since Evan joined the submarine service as a chaplain, I've prided myself on handling things well. On being a good navy wife, a good chaplain's wife. But now, all of a sudden, I can't do it anymore. I can't take it anymore. It all falls on me—the kids, the house, keeping tabs on Evan's mother, who is in a nursing home. To top things off, Patricia is becoming increasingly difficult to get along with."

"In what way?" David asked.

"She's too interested in men for someone her age, for one thing. And in herself. Sometimes I don't think anything much concerns her except the opposite sex and staying thin."

"That's a pretty common thing with girls her age, Marianne."

"I suppose so. But Deborah's so different. She's a lot easier to deal with." Marianne shook her head. "I don't even know what I'm saying," she confessed. "But one thing's for certain—the whole damned submarine service is getting to me. I don't want to be a part of it for the rest of my life. In my volunteer work, in my work with the Navy Wives Support Group, all I hear is problems, problems, problems, most of them much too familiar. The problems of women who have to handle their lives, their homes, the lives of their children, with their husbands away at least half of each year. Then, when their husbands do come home, they can be like strangers. The wives have run the household, kept things going on the home front, so to speak. All of a sudden a man you feel you don't even know anymore comes barging into the scene and tries to assert himself as lord and master. You resent it, David. You resent it tremendously.''

"That's understandable," he said levelly. At the same time, he couldn't even begin to imagine Evan in the unflattering role Marianne had just portrayed. "How often has Evan been attached to Holy Loch?" he asked curiously.

"This is the third time. The first time, I was planning to go with him. Then Patricia got very sick with the measles, so we cancelled. That was eight years ago. The next time he went was...let me think...five years ago this coming February. We nearly went with him then, too."

"Why didn't you?"

"Well, my mother was very ill at that time. I didn't want to leave her. She died a few months later, so I was glad I hadn't gone. Still, that was also when my relationship with Evan started to become strained."

"Why didn't you go with him this last time?"

Marianne frowned. "You know the tour of duty is stretched to thirty months if a man has his family with him," she pointed out. "That's a long time, the better part of three years. I felt like the girls were at entirely the wrong age to take them away for so long. It would have meant leaving a school they love, leaving the friends they've made, disrupting their social lives, all to live in a place I feel must be the end of nowhere.''

David said mildly, ''Well, I can't swear that Holy Loch isn't isolated. But what you're talking about is routine with thousands of service families. Granted, it's a test. But families that accept the challenge often emerge much stronger. Not to mention having the experience of living abroad, of traveling.''

''You think I should have gone to Holy Loch last year?''

''I'm not saying that, Marianne. I can't put myself in your shoes, so I don't know what you should have done. Anyway, what's important to me is what you're going to do now.''

''Yes, I know.''

''Well, then, I'm going to ask something of you,'' David said frankly. ''Something I know won't be easy. But if you don't do this, I think you'll regret your decision for a long time to come.''

''What?'' she asked, her eyes widening.

She sounded frightened, for which he didn't blame her. ''Let Evan and the girls have Thanksgiving,'' he said.

''What?''

''Let them have the holiday. Grit your teeth. Test your acting ability to the hilt. Play the part of a loving wife. Evan's been away for a long and lonely time. I think he deserves that much from you. You've waited this long to lower the boom. I think you can bring yourself to wait a couple of weeks longer. Meantime, maybe I can talk with Evan myself, find out what he's feeling.''

''You mean pave the way for me?'' Marianne asked bitterly.

"I don't know," David told her. "That's something I'll have to take one step at a time."

David could be very persuasive when he wanted. He reached across the table and placed his hand over Marianne's. Her skin, he immediately noticed, felt entirely different from Kris's. Kris's skin was soft and smooth, velvet to the touch. Marianne's was taut, like everything else about her.

"Please go along with me," he urged. "Trust me about this, will you? I'm deeply fond of you two. I hate the thought of the hurt this is going to involve. If a split is absolutely unavoidable, I won't attempt to stand in your way. Just wait a little longer, okay?"

Marianne looked miserable, but she said, "Okay."

"Is that a promise?"

"I suppose so."

"You suppose so?"

She managed a faint smile. "Yes, David, it's a promise."

Half an hour later, she dropped him off at the bus station. David walked wearily across the cold asphalt to his car. He sat behind the wheel, rubbed his hand across the back of his neck. The muscles were tight, achy.

His route toward the bridge that crossed the Thames over to Groton took him close to Granite Street. On an impulse, he turned a couple of corners he didn't need to turn and pulled up in front of the house where Kris lived. He shut the motor off and sat in the darkness. The time was twenty minutes past nine. Not late, but...

She'd said her apartment was on the first floor and looked out on the street. Well, the lights were on in all five first-floor windows facing the street, and in many other parts of the big house as well. It appeared as though

Kris was still up. Perhaps she was reading or watching television.

This is crazy! an inner voice blared in warning. Yet the urge to see her became overwhelming, irresistible.

As he berated himself for behaving like a fool, David quietly got out of his car, headed up the brick walkway and carefully negotiated the steps to the porch. That was all he'd need—to crash loudly down the steps and get the attention of everyone in the house!

The front door was a masterpiece of carved golden oak. David peered through its leaded panes of glass and saw the vestibule, warm and inviting. A carpeted stairway flanked the right wall. A shaded lamp cast its nighttime glow from a tiny table placed against the opposite wall. Antique oil paintings, their subjects indistinguishable in the muted light, adorned the hall that led past the stairway.

David studied the brass plate next to the front door. He found Kris's name and pushed the buzzer before he had the chance to think twice about what he was doing.

The seconds ticked away. He nearly retreated to the sanctuary of his car. He yearned to speed off into the night. Then, as if he'd been snatched from a dream, he saw a hallway door open. Kris moved toward him, staring in surprise. He watched her struggle for a few seconds with the inside locks before she pulled the heavy door open.

"David," she managed huskily. "What are you doing here?"

She was wearing a pale yellow robe knotted loosely at the waist. She'd brushed her hair into a nutmeg cloud around her shoulders. He suspected she'd not been out of the bathtub or shower very long, as there was a slight shininess to her scrubbed face. To David, she looked about sixteen years old—and utterly adorable.

He clenched his hands into fists and held them firmly at his sides to avoid reaching out and taking her into his arms. "I was in the neighborhood," he told her.

"In the neighborhood?" she echoed.

"I had dinner with a friend," he said, as if that explained everything.

"I see," Kris managed. He looked rather unsure of himself, she realized. Almost guilty, as if he knew he shouldn't have made this unscheduled stop. At the same time, he looked curiously vulnerable, not unlike a boy who wants something badly but doesn't know how to come right out and ask for it.

"Look, Kris..."

"Yes?"

"Are you going to ask me in, or are you going to keep me standing out here in the cold?"

"I think it might be best if you simply left."

"No, Kris," he persisted. "I mean...we have to talk."

"Why?" she queried dispassionately.

David expelled a deep breath, then said unsteadily, "Because I have to know where I stand." Shocked by the sound of his voice, he added, "I have to know whether or not you believe me."

Kris tilted her chin defiantly. "You gave me the alternative of believing either you or Jay, didn't you?"

"That's right, I did."

"Well, I believe my brother."

He visibly flinched from the sting of her verdict. Kris noted the flinch and saw the glazed look in his eyes. "Look, Dr. Jorgenson—"

"I thought we'd reached the point where you were calling me David," he cut in defensively.

"Sorry," she allowed.

"Sorry not to call me by my first name?"

"Sorry to have said so flatly that I can't believe you about not knowing Jay, about denying the existence of the house on the river," she told him.

"I don't know how I can go about convincing you," David said soberly. "But I certainly intend to try."

Kris considered this. "I'd feel differently," she said, "if there was even the slightest chance that Jay could have been talking about someone else. But he mentioned your name several times, David."

"You're absolutely sure of that?"

"Yes, I'm sure. I never wrote it down, of course. But when I called Admiral Carrington, all I could think of was how you and Jay had been friends."

"But that wasn't so, don't you see?" He shook his head, hating this feeling of helplessness. "I know who my friends are, Kris. Your brother, I'm sorry to say, wasn't one of them."

Suddenly, Jay Sothern seemed like a very tangible ghost standing between them, forcibly keeping them apart. Amazing, David thought, that he couldn't even *remember* someone who was having such an overwhelming effect on his life.

"Do you have a photograph of your brother?" he asked abruptly.

Kris's eyes flickered, then widened suspiciously. "Yes," she admitted. "Why?"

"Because I'd like to see what he looked like, that's why. The newspapers didn't run any pictures, nor were there any among the reports I read."

For several seconds, Kris stood rooted to the spot, lost in thought. Suddenly, the wind gusted. The cold November air snapped her to attention. "Come in," she told David softly.

A moment later, they were inside her apartment. She closed the door behind them. David glanced around the parlor, noting the soft lights, the comfortable-looking sofa, the bookcase filled to capacity. He watched as Kris moved across the room to a large bureau and reached for the silver-framed photograph on top. Without a word, she came back to him, reluctantly thrusting the cherished object toward his outstretched hands.

It was the standard military portrait—a head-and-shoulders shot of a proud young submariner in uniform, the flag next to him. The face could have been any one of hundreds that David had encountered since he'd been stationed in Groton. Except for the strong family resemblance to this lovely young woman who had moved around to stand beside him.

She was staring at the photo. "Still say you don't remember Jay?" she asked.

David caught the note of hope in her voice, knew she wanted desperately for him to say, "Yes." And he wished, all the way to the bottom of his soul, that he could gratify her. But he could not.

"I'm sorry," he said.

Kris didn't say a word. She took the photo from his hands and returned it to its place on the bureau. She was having a hard time fighting back her natural sense of hospitality. Normally, she would have offered him coffee or a drink. Just now, she was afraid she couldn't hang on to her composure much longer.

She said, "It's late, David. I really need to get some rest. I have to be up early in the morning. I'm sure you do, too."

"Of course," he said. "I'd better be going."

A step or two from the door he hesitated, then turned to face her. Kris was close behind him. Very slowly, looking her in the eyes as he did so, David bent down and touched her forehead lightly with his lips. "I'll call you in the morning," he promised.

Kris shut her eyes tightly, appalled at the feelings his simple gesture evoked. She was torn by a storm of conflicting emotions. She wanted to believe David Jorgenson. God, how she wanted to believe him!

"Good night," she murmured, her voice husky.

"Good night, Kris. I'll let myself out."

She managed the weakest of smiles as the front door closed behind him. Then, through a crack in the curtain, she watched him walk to his car...and hot tears rolled down her cheeks.

CHAPTER FIVE

THE PHONE RANG as Kris was getting ready for work the next morning. She had just slipped into a skirt and was in the middle of zipping it up. She finished the task, then answered the pealing summons.

"Kris?"

No sense in pretending she didn't recognize David's voice. His slight trace of Down East accent was something she would never forget.

"Yes?" she asked, instantly and totally confused. She wished he hadn't called her, but was glad that he had.

"Will you have lunch with me today?"

"I have to work, David."

"Me, too. So it'll have to be a relatively short lunch. Look, the reason I'm asking you to meet me is that there's something I want to tell you."

"Can't you tell me on the phone?"

"No."

"Well, when you put it that way...yes, I guess I can meet you for lunch. I have something I want to tell you, too."

"You can't tell me now?"

"No. I want to tell you in person."

This was true. For a few seocnds, Kris reflected on what she was going to do. She'd slept scarcely at all through the night as she thought over everything David had told her. And she'd been appalled at her reflection in the mirror this morning, the result of that thinking. She looked even more exhausted than she felt.

Still, it was worth it, because she'd come to a decision. She'd made up her mind to stop delving into Jay's suicide. After all was said and done, she couldn't bring him back. Letting him rest in peace suddenly seemed so logical. It was the only thing to do.

I'll just have to stand the hurt, she told herself. *Sooner or later, it will fade. Wounds always fade. Isn't that what David said, in so many words?*

She knew that Jay's death would always plague her. She would forever wonder if she'd failed him, how she'd failed him. She'd forever wonder if there was something she could have done that she hadn't done. Something she'd neglected. She'd forever feel guilty because of the uncertainty involved. But those were feelings she would have to learn to live with. Those were feelings she'd conquer.

Lost in thought, Kris suddenly realized David had said something. "I'm sorry," she said. "What did you just say?"

"I wondered where you might like to meet, that's all."

"Well, I imagine you're busier than I am," Kris conceded. "Actually, I'm pretty much caught up with my applications, so I can take as long a lunch hour as I want."

"I wish I could say the same," he told her ruefully. "As it is, I have four consultations scheduled at the clinic this afternoon between two and five."

"Would you rather I come over to Groton?"

"If you wouldn't mind, Kris. It would give us more time," David agreed. "There's a Chinese place on Route 12 not far from the bridge."

"I think I know the place you mean. Anyway, I'll find it."

"Twelve-thirty all right?"

"Twelve-thirty would be fine."

As she hung up, Kris knew that no hour would really be "fine" when it came to meeting David Jorgenson. Every time she saw him, her emotions became hopelessly roiled. There was a total dichotomy in the way she felt toward him. He was her opponent, the man she was challenging, the man she still felt was responsible, at least in part, for Jay's final action. Yet she was insidiously attracted to him. She couldn't deny that attraction, but felt it denoted a terrible weakness on her part. She hated the idea of being so weak. But almost from the beginning there'd been a current between David Jorgenson and herself, a sexual current too strong to ignore. Each time she saw him, she was more aware of that current, more afraid of it.

As she drove across the Thames, Kris told herself that no matter what David Jorgenson might say, she must make this their last meeting.

He was waiting for her inside the restaurant, wearing civilian clothes topped by a red and black checked wool jacket. She could imagine him stalking the Maine woods, naturally at ease in the vast, rugged outdoors of his native state. She couldn't keep from wondering what it would be like to explore that wilderness with him as her guide. Or trek along the rocky seacoast where he'd been raised, where he'd worked as a lobsterman.

He would have so much to show her, so many things to teach her about a part of New England she was unfamiliar with. Something about him made her sure he loved nature. His rugged physique, his outdoors look. If things had been different—if she'd not encountered him within a situation laced with trauma—she could have shared some of his knowledge. As it was...

The restaurant was crowded, and they had to wait in line for a table. Staring down at her, his silver-gray eyes intense, David asked, "Did you get any sleep last night?"

He wasn't an easy man to dissemble with. Kris started with an affirmative, saw the expression on his face and switched to the truth. "Not too much," she admitted.

"Because of me, probably," he muttered.

"Not really."

"You mean my ill-timed visit didn't stir you up? In a negative sense, that is." He shook his head, then said, "It was spur of the moment, Kris. I'm sorry."

"There's nothing for you to be sorry about."

"No?"

Kris met his eyes, then looked away. Keeping her voice down, she said, "All right, you did stir me up a little. But I also did some thinking I should have done long before now."

"Oh?"

They'd reached the head of the line. A moment later, they were led to a table. Kris was temporarily spared detailing her answer until they'd studied the menu, ordered the special egg foo yung plate and were served a pot of fragrant jasmine tea.

"Well," David said. "Now that all of that's taken care of, you were saying you'd done some thinking. Evidently, it kept you up most of the night."

Kris nodded slowly. "I began to accept the sense of something you said to me," she told him. "I can't bring Jay back. I'll have to live with what happened, difficult as that will be. Also, I realized that it's a mistake to keep on with an investigation that can't lead anywhere."

"What makes you say it can't lead anywhere?"

"That's obvious, isn't it? Almost immediately I reach an impasse."

"Let's call it a hurdle," David suggested. "Generally speaking, you can work your way over hurdles."

"Not over this one, I can't," Kris decided. "It's better to let the whole thing go. I see that now." She sipped her tea, then added, "So, you can report back to Admiral Carrington that I have no intention of making any trouble for anyone."

"For me, you mean?"

"Well . . . yes."

To Kris's surprise, David shook his head. "I'd rather have you make trouble for me than give this up," he told her. It was not something he'd anticipated saying, and he couldn't blame Kris for looking shocked. "Damn it, this place is noisy," he muttered unhappily. "I can hardly hear myself think, let alone hope to make sense to you."

Unexpectedly, Kris smiled. She was juggling egg foo yung between two wobbly chopsticks in something of a losing battle. "Funny, I've never had any trouble with this in the past," she said with an impishness she'd not revealed before.

David stared at her. Maybe it was the hot tea, maybe it was because the restaurant was overly heated, but there was a flush to her cheeks, a gleam in her eyes. Despite the shadows of fatigue on her face, she looked incredibly lovely.

Her smile faded under his scrutiny. She said, "Well, I've had my say. Now it's your turn. You had something you wanted to tell me."

David nodded. "I wanted to let you know that I've come to exactly the opposite conclusion about your brother."

Kris stopped eating and looked up. "I don't understand, David. What's that supposed to mean?"

"Well, it's my belief that there's a reason to most things happening the way they do. So when I began to think a bit more dispassionately about what you told me yesterday, I concluded that Jay had a reason for saying that he and I were friends and for making up a story about a house on the Thames. From everything I've read about your brother, and from everything you've told me, it seems highly unlikely that he deliberately lied—that he was a pathological liar, that is."

David held up a warning hand as Kris started to object. Hunching forward, he said, "Please, Kris, hear me out. I know I told you that you can't bring Jay back, and that's true. But it's not enough to say that. It isn't that simple. The fact of his death is hard enough for you to accept. The wrenching question of why he died as he did is something else." He paused, then added gently, "I don't want you going off on guilt trips for the rest of your life, Kris. You don't need that."

She bit her lip and stared down at her plate. "No one needs that," she agreed, her voice low. "But how does one avoid it? I'll always wonder if there wasn't something I could have done that I didn't do. Some clue I was completely blind to. There's no way of getting around that."

"Yes, there is."

"Please, David," she said wearily. "That's like promising a child a balloon will never burst."

He smiled slightly. "That's an odd analogy, though I like it," he told her. "However, we're not talking about balloons, Kris. We're talking about facts, about what led Jay to say and do the things he did."

"You're telling me that if I knew the *why* I could accept Jay's taking his own life?"

"Not necessarily. I'm not sure that's something you'll ever be able to accept, totally. But knowing why would relieve your personal guilt burden."

"And how do you propose I go about discovering that?"

"I don't know," David said honestly. "But I sure as hell plan to find out."

Kris set her chopsticks down on her plate. Her fingers were trembling. She looked across at him and said unsteadily, "I don't think I understand what you're getting at."

The lunch-hour crowd seemed to be peaking instead of abating. David said, "This just isn't the time or place to go into it. I have several ideas, but I need to think them out before we proceed."

"We?"

"Yes, Kris...we." He broke off, then added reluctantly, "Look, once again, I wish I didn't have to clock-watch, but I do. I've got about a half hour to get back to the base and prep myself for my first consultation. But I want to talk to you further about this, Kris. I don't want to let it go."

She had the strange feeling that he was stalling. Was he trying to make another date with her? Was what he'd been saying merely a ruse toward that end?

Don't flatter yourself, she thought wryly. *David Jorgenson has so much charisma he doesn't need to work out ploys to get dates. And why me, anyway? Why would he want a date with me? I must seem like a sour grape to him.*

He'd managed to snag the waiter and was paying the check. As he stuffed several bills back into his wallet, he said, "I'm not playing games, Kris. We need to talk. I need information from you if we're going to do this thing right."

He was speaking in a low, level voice that had a ring of authority. She'd never heard him use this tone before. Suddenly, she realized what a force he could be to deal with. He was not the type to throw his weight around, but he'd know how to use his authority when necessary. He'd know how to take command and give orders. Once he'd set out on a mission, he'd be a hard man to deflect.

Hesitantly, she said, "I don't know what information I can possibly give you."

"A lot, I'd imagine," David replied seriously. "But we'll take that a step at a time. As I said, we need to talk about this. We need to give this matter our undivided attention. Obviously," he added with a wry smile, "restaurants are not the best settings for meetings. And as much as I love the outdoors, it is a bit cold to rendezvous in some park. Which leaves us with either my place or your place. Of the two, I'd say yours is preferable."

There was an edge of humor to his tone, as well as the essence of a challenge. Kris caught the challenge and bristled. Did he really feel it necessary to dare her to invite him to her apartment? Did she seem that much of a mouse to him?

"I agree that my apartment would offer more privacy than your quarters at the submarine base," she said rather stiffly.

"True," he agreed. "However, I do have my own suite. As for my office...we'd never get a substantial amount of time to talk there. Unless, of course, I scheduled you into a slot as a patient."

Kris wanted to smile, but she couldn't. She was suddenly remembering the yeoman who had directed her to

David that first afternoon at the hospital. He'd reminded her of Jay. Looking down over the sub base from the top of the hill had reminded her of Jay. Everything about the navy, about submarines, reminded her of Jay. And it still hurt too much to tolerate—unless she was forced to. She didn't need the added emotional exposure of "conferring" with David Jorgenson in a navy setting.

"Why don't you come over to Granite Street for supper tonight? Just something simple, so we can talk."

She heard him mutter something under his breath. Saw his mouth tighten. "I can't tonight, Kris. I have a previous engagement."

She wondered why she should feel such a letdown hearing that pronouncement. She'd just been thinking that David was loaded with charisma. It stood to reason there must be women in his life. He was thirty-six, she recalled, and possessed of a physical attractiveness that grew more alluring every time they met. He'd been married, but that was back in med school. So, he'd been a bachelor for quite a number of years.

"Would you be free tomorrow night?" he asked, breaking into her thoughts.

"Tomorrow's fine," Kris told him. She was free most nights. She didn't know that many people around New London, nor had she especially wanted companionship these past few months. She just hadn't felt like socializing.

"Why don't I pick up a pizza and stop by tomorrow evening on the early side?" David offered.

"I'd rather cook us a dinner, if you don't mind. I'm no gourmet chef, but . . . well, I'd like to, that's all."

"A home-cooked meal would be terrific." David beamed. "Even if it comes out of a can."

There was a chill wind blowing as they left the restaurant and walked to their cars. Kris shivered. "It feels like snow."

David glanced skyward. "Looks like it, too. Even smells like it. You can smell snow coming, you know."

Kris smiled. "Back in Pennsylvania, when we were kids, Jay and I would sniff the cold air and make bets on how soon the snow would start falling."

"Would you believe my brother and I did that, too?"

They reached Kris's car, a nondescript, dull blue sedan. Kris had bought it on her arrival in New London because it was cheap and mechanically sound. Now it struck her as nothing less than boring, much like her personality had been getting of late.

All at once, she felt a sharp desire for change, the need for a personal renaissance. The knowledge was a very pleasant shock, the direct result, she realized, of David's presence, his companionship.

"What time do you want me to come by?" he asked.

"Any time after six."

"Well, then." He nodded. "See you tomorrow."

Kris took advantage of giving her engine some warming-up time to watch David walk over to his car, a stylish European sedan, pale metallic gold. She hadn't even noticed his car the other night. She'd been wrapped up in anger, in hostility, because of Jay.

As David turned left on Route 12 and headed toward the submarine base, Kris silently thanked him for patiently hearing her out, for understanding her anger. At the same time, she wondered what his engagement involved . . . and with whom.

DAVID'S "ENGAGEMENT" was with the Phillips family minus Evan. Marianne had again called him at the office, midmorning, first to issue an apology of sorts over the situation she'd forced him into the evening before. Then she'd pleaded with him to come for dinner, to make up for canceling out on Patricia and Deborah.

"But I didn't cancel out," David reminded her, annoyed at her for having implied this to the girls.

"I know that, Dave, but please bear with me. I told them it was an emergency, so it didn't reflect on you. Certainly, I didn't want to tell them about our meeting."

A silent moment passed. Then David queried, "Do the girls have any idea that things aren't going well between Evan and yourself?"

"No, they don't. At least, if they do they haven't told me so. Anyway, that's not what I said."

"What didn't you say?"

"That things aren't going well between Evan and myself. If I did say that, I wasn't being accurate. Things aren't going well with *me* and my marriage. I'm sure you're going to find Evan blissfully unaware of my unhappiness."

"Are you inferring that Evan doesn't pay attention to you?"

"Evan hasn't paid attention to me in years."

They'd had to conclude the conversation at that unsatisfactory point. And what Marianne had stated as fact still bothered David that night as he walked from the BOQ to the Phillips's modest home, a two-story brick colonial set in the middle of a small but nicely landscaped lot.

The cold November air still smelled of snow. It reminded him of his winters in Maine. It reminded him of Kris and her little brother.

When she'd asked him over for supper—a surprise, even though he'd prompted the suggestion—he'd felt a sharp resentment toward Marianne Phillips. Once again, Marianne had coaxed him into a dinner date that was something out of the ordinary. He understood her concern for making everything seem as "normal" as possible for the sake of her daughters. But Patricia and Deborah weren't kids anymore. They were teenagers who deserved to know that all was not well with their parents. If Marianne kept up her front until the moment she asked for a divorce, the pain might be much worse for them.

What a hell of a homecoming for Evan! David thought moodily. He wished he could give his friend some warning, but he couldn't. Marianne had confided in him as her friend, which he was. He felt morally bound to respect that.

When he knocked on the front door of the Phillips house and let himself in, he found Patricia and Deborah arguing and Marianne conspicuously absent.

"What goes with you two?" he demanded kiddingly.

"Patty wants to watch MTV while I practice the piano," Deborah complained.

Deborah was dark like her mother, of medium height with a figure that already verged on the voluptuous. Patricia was tall and blond like her father.

The piano was in the living room. So was the television set. David surveyed both, then said, "There's an obvious solution to your problem, though it can't be accomplished tonight."

"What?" Patricia asked suspiciously.

"Move the TV to the family room in the basement. What you really want to do is work out by dancing to the videos, isn't it, Patty?"

"Is that so wrong?"

"No, it's not wrong at all. But if you moved the TV set downstairs you'd have a lot more room to dance than you do in here," he said, glancing around the rather cluttered living room. "Where's your mother, anyway?"

"She went next door to borrow some Parmesan cheese from Mrs. Bailey. We're having spaghetti for dinner and she ran out of cheese."

David nodded and settled down in an armchair. The sisters perched on the couch opposite him. Deborah, her dark eyes glowing, said, "Have you heard Dad'll be home for Thanksgiving? Isn't that great?"

David felt a pang of sorrow thinking of Marianne's decision, but he managed sincerely, "Yes, it's tremendous."

The telephone rang and Deborah bolted toward the kitchen, screeching, "I'll get it!"

Left alone with Patricia, David discovered that he had no idea what to talk to her about. It came as a shock. He'd come to know both of the girls very well in the two years since he'd met Evan. He'd always empathized with them equally.

Now, as he asked her some casual questions, general questions about school and what she was doing for fun these days, he suddenly became aware that she was smiling in an oddly adult way, and when the smile became definitely provocative, he was staggered.

The kid was flirting with him!

He vividly remembered Marianne's telling him that Patricia was too interested in the opposite sex for someone her age. He'd taken that as a mother's natural, subconscious protest toward her daughter growing up. But there was no denying the definite sexuality in Patricia's smile as she continued to focus on him.

He couldn't believe it. He was old enough to be her father! He began, haltingly, "Patricia…" then broke off. He didn't know how to continue.

Patricia totally confounded him by saying, "You know, David, I wish either I was ten years older…or you were ten years younger, or maybe both."

Deborah, fortunately burst into the room at that moment and reported, "That was Captain Ellis's wife on the phone. She wanted to talk to Mom about something to do with the support group. Mom just came back. She's on the phone with her now. She'll be in in a minute."

David was still rallying from Patricia's remark as Marianne entered the room bearing a tray with two cocktail glasses and an etched-glass pitcher filled with drink.

"I made us martinis," she announced as David got to his feet. "Deb, go get the platter of cheese and crackers out on the counter, will you? Patty, why are you looking like the cat who swallowed the canary?"

Patty had the grace to blush, and David could not repress a laugh, which earned him a dagger glance from her. Marianne didn't notice this interplay. She'd launched into a discussion of her conversation with Mrs. Ellis. David let her ramble.

Marianne was an excellent cook, and the spaghetti dinner she'd prepared was delicious. She'd simmered a roast in the sauce all day long and the results were terrific. David noticed, both amused and relieved, that Patricia ate a full helping of the pasta smothered with sauce.

After dinner, the girls went up to their rooms to do their homework. Marianne brewed a pot of coffee while David helped her organize the cleanup. Then they took their coffees back to the living room.

"Thanks, Dave," she said simply, once they were seated.

"There's nothing to thank me for," he mumbled. "Incidentally, the dinner was delicious."

"I'm glad you enjoyed it." She glanced toward the staircase. Frowning slightly, she said, "There are things I'd like to say, but I'm afraid the girls might overhear."

"Well, if you really want to talk," he said, "I'll schedule an appointment for you."

"At your office?"

"Yes."

"The word would get around. That wouldn't help the situation." Again, she glanced apprehensively toward the stairs.

"You'd be consulting me about what you're running into in connection with your volunteer work," Dave decided.

Marianne smiled gratefully. "If I can't work things out, I'll call you," she promised. "You *are* planning to have Thanksgiving dinner with us, aren't you?"

It would be his third Thanksgiving with the Phillipses, if he did. Last year, Evan had left for Holy Loch the day after the holiday. David remembered how much fun he'd had—the feast, the college football games on TV, the pleasant family camaraderie. He also remembered admiring Marianne for keeping such a stiff upper lip on the eve of being separated for a year from her husband.

He'd misread that, he realized now. And again he reminded himself that these people were his friends, not his patients.

"Are you sure you want me around?" he asked carefully. "Wouldn't you rather be by yourselves?"

"Not really," Marianne admitted sadly. Then she added, "If you could make it, Dave, it just might save my sanity."

A half hour later, as he walked back to the BOQ, David was cursing the fact that once again he'd given in to Marianne. As dear as the Phillipses were to him, he had the distinct feeling that involving himself in their deteriorating marriage was a mistake. A bad mistake.

If he'd been able to say no, he would have asked Kris to spend Thanksgiving with him. But where? he wondered unhappily. And suddenly he knew the answer.

CHAPTER SIX

KRIS WAS THANKFUL she didn't have to put in a full schedule at the office the next day. She left early, headed for her favorite supermarket and spent over an hour in the aisles working out a dinner menu that would be special but not a gamble to prepare. She'd always liked to cook, but never managed to get into serious culinary explorations or be totally inventive—a cooking talent she envied. Most of the meals she'd put together had been for Jay, and Jay had always been more interested in quantity rather than quality when it came to food.

As she drove home with her purchases, Kris tried hard to forget that Jay was the last person aside from herself whom she'd cooked dinner for. No wonder she hadn't been inventive.

She'd decided to make a chicken casserole with artichoke hearts and a subtle garlic-butter sauce. She rounded out the menu with rice pilaf studded with succulent golden raisins, glazed baby carrots and a romaine salad with a special Dijon-mustard dressing. For dessert, she opted for a Grand Marnier mousse that was easy to do with the help of her blender.

With the dinner preparations completed, she showered then put on a rose velour jumpsuit that was comfortable and pretty. Without allowing herself to analyze why she was doing this, she took more care than usual with her makeup, then brushed her hair until it shone and swirled around her shoulders.

When David rang her doorbell shortly before six-thirty, Kris was ready for him every way but emotionally. She looked up at him standing on her threshold and felt her heart clicking away as if it were taking a series of pictures to be engraved in her psyche forever. If only the circumstances were different, it would be so easy to yield to impulse with David. So easy to let herself live a little, like she'd not done in a very long time.

Suddenly Kris yearned for companionship, for fun. Suddenly she wanted to cast off the oppressive yoke that had been weighing her down since Jay's death.

"Come in, won't you?" she said to David enthusiastically.

He stepped into her living room a little more assuredly than he had two nights ago. Kris had placed a yellow chrysanthemum plant on the coffee table and logs were burning in the fireplace. She knew the room was warm and inviting.

As they moved toward her kitchen, David sniffed appreciatively. "Whatever it is you're making smells great," he said.

She laughed, and warned, "Don't expect too much."

She let him make himself a bourbon and soda and poured a glass of sherry for herself. Then she led him back to the living room carrying a plate of round cheese pastries—she called them gold dollars—which she set on the coffee table.

David munched on one and reached for another. Then he took a seat on one end of the couch. He looked tired, she thought. And pensive. Like he had a number of things on his mind, all unresolved.

"Did you have a rough day?" she queried.

He grinned ruefully. "As a matter of fact, I did. I guess it shows, right?"

"A little," Kris conceded, as she settled into the other corner of the couch.

Marianne had called him at work yet again, and he'd nearly refused to take the call. As it was, he'd warned her irritably, "Look, I'm going to have to ask you not to call during clinic hours unless it's an emergency."

She'd replied tautly, "It *is* an emergency, Dave. At least to me, it is." She'd gone on to report that last night, after he'd left and Deborah was asleep, Patricia had come into her room and made a request she just couldn't handle.

"She told me she wants a prescription for the Pill," Marianne moaned. "She wants me to help her get it. My God, Dave, she's only sixteen years old!"

David said dryly, "Girls can get pregnant when they're a lot younger than sixteen. I know my saying that doesn't help, but it's true."

"All right, I just can't face up to the thought of my child having sex when she isn't even out of high school."

"Well, I'm not going to get into statistics about the present ages regarding virginity or the lack thereof," David stated. "In any event, this isn't a problem you should be bringing to me. You should be taking it to your family physician here on the base."

"You're telling me to ask Dr. Fenwick to give Patty a prescription for birth-control pills?"

"Don't sound so horrified, Marianne. I'm neither condemning nor condoning anything Patricia's done, or anything she's about to do. But one thing's certain—she's aware of her body. Also, the facts of life are the facts of life. If she's sleeping with someone, she's playing with fire where pregnancy is concerned. You know that."

He let her mull that over, then asked, "Have you ever discussed sex with her?"

"Yes, I have," Marianne said without hesitation.

"Then why don't you make a bargain with her? Why don't you tell her that if she'll exercise some—what shall we call it?—some restraint for the next few days, you'll take up her request with Evan when he gets home."

"I should think you'd know that I don't want to get into this issue with Evan. Especially now."

"Then maybe you'd better take Patty to Dr. Fenwick yourself," David had firmly advised.

It was a sticky conversation that had concluded rather dismally. He knew he'd angered Marianne and wished it were in his power to call Holy Loch and order Evan Phillips sent back to the States on the next available transport jet. The sooner the chaplain returned to Groton, the sooner he would be brought up-to-date on the problems within his own domain—problems that David could do very little about.

Marianne's call had been followed by a consultation with a young submariner whose wife had walked out on him. He was shortly due back on sea duty, and she'd frankly told him she couldn't handle the loneliness again. He'd broken down in David's office, sobbing uncontrollably. The session had left David totally wrung out, regardless of his outward professionalism.

The other consultations hadn't been quite that traumatic. Still, they had been demanding. Thinking this, he finished his bourbon and said impetuously, "You can't imagine what it's like, Kris, coming in here and feeling you're in a home again. The relaxing atmosphere of the fire, smelling whatever it is you're cooking..."

He broke off and smiled sheepishly. "Strike that," he suggested, "or next thing you know I'll be crying on your shoulder."

Kris smiled back at him, a soft, tender smile that made David catch his breath. He had no idea how vulnerable he looked to her at that moment. Big, strong, rugged...and very, very vulnerable.

"Would you like another drink?" she asked.

He shook his head. "No, thanks, I don't think I'd better. When I'm this tired, alcohol and I don't mix very well."

"Then I'll serve dinner," she decided.

Kris's "dining room" was an alcove off the living room. Two reproduction Hepplewhite chairs flanked a round table she'd covered with an ivory cloth. A silver candelabra holding four yellow tapers was her centerpiece. The place settings featured pale yellow cloth napkins and antique silver.

She gestured to David to take his seat, then filled their crystal wine goblets before sitting down herself.

When she was settled in, he raised his glass in a toast. "To wine, candlelight, delicious food and a beautiful woman to share this with."

Kris smiled shyly. She appreciated what he was saying—and the way he'd said it—but quickly reminded herself not to wander any further toward what could be considered very dangerous ground.

David steered the conversation into general channels while they ate and skillfully ferreted out a few personal things about his hostess—what she liked to do, places she liked to go, books she liked to read. Kris realized that his success as a psychiatrist depended on "interrogations" of this kind, and had a new appreciation of how seemingly innocuous answers might actually have a lot of meaning. David didn't miss very much, she realized anew.

After dinner, as they sat on the couch in front of the fireplace sipping coffee, he said, "That was the most delicious dinner I've ever eaten. Why did you play down your abilities as a gourmet chef?"

"Because I'm not one, that's why."

"Well, in my opinion the Cordon Bleu would grant you an honorary diploma in a moment."

Kris laughed. "I doubt that."

"Whatever, you should patent that chicken recipe."

"I don't think so," she protested. And realized he was making small talk because he didn't want to get to the real reason he was here any more than she wanted him to.

Jay.

She slanted a glance at David. Despite the bantering conversation, he looked very solemn. He turned toward her at that instant and their eyes locked. Simultaneously, they blurted, "I hate—"

After a second of silence, David managed an awkward smile. "I was about to say I hate to break this spell," he said. "Were you thinking along the same lines?"

Kris felt a pang of disloyalty to Jay's memory. But she said honestly, "Yes."

"Tonight has been a joy," David told her softly.

He sounded so sincere that Kris couldn't help but feel moved.

"I wish, more than I can possibly tell you, that there were no clouds between us, Kris. No dangerous waters to cross. But there are. And until we deal with them, there's no chance for any smooth sailing." Forcing a smile, he added, "Spoken like a navy man, don't you think?"

This time, she couldn't return his smile. The truth of what he was saying was too overwhelming. Until he verbalized it, she hadn't realized just how *much* she wanted the stormy sea that separated them to be smooth. How much she'd give, right now, to have David Jorgenson take her in his arms... and make love to her.

Kris sat up straight, shocked by the thought. She'd had very little experience in the ultimate union between a man and a woman, very few "encounters" with the opposite sex. In fact, her only brush with love had occurred when she was a junior in high school, just months before her parents had been killed.

The boy, Ted Anniston, lived on a big modern farm outside Lancaster. One weekend, he asked Kris to go riding with him—the family owned several good trail horses. She loved horses so much it was an invitation she couldn't resist, though she had no idea how she'd deal with Ted himself. He was simply too much—captain of the basketball team, incredibly handsome, outgoing and confident to the point of being conceited. Kris had a crush on him just like every other girl in their class, except she was the only girl who didn't show it.

Until they came back from their ride late that Saturday afternoon, she hadn't known that Ted's parents were away for the weekend. A wedding in Harrisburg, he'd said. An affair he'd been able to "sidestep" so he could be with her, he'd added triumphantly.

The tenant farmer who supervised the farm lived with his wife a half mile from the main farmhouse, which Ted's parents had converted into a lovely country home. Ted was a gracious host in his own way, and warmed Kris up to the idea of drinking her first wine that night. Later, after a considerable battle of wits and words, he had insistently claimed her virginity.

The experience had hurt, physically and emotionally. Certainly, it was not repeated, much to Ted's chagrin. Kris, lost in a lonely corner, had been terrified her parents would find out about what had happened, terrified she might be pregnant. For three weeks she lived with the agony of apprehension. Finally, to her profound relief, she got her period.

Time had passed. Then her parents had been killed. After that, she'd been so busy bringing up Jay she hadn't had any time for romance. The experience with Ted had—she supposed in retrospect—turned her off men somewhat. But she didn't blame the entire male sex for the selfish actions of one individual.

Over the years, she'd dated a number of different men. She'd carefully kept her relationships casual, stopping short of giving herself entirely, always remembering the hasty mistake she'd once made. In all fairness, though, she hadn't met anyone that captivated her enough to want involvement, either in Lancaster or New London. Not until now, she hadn't.

Into the silence that had fallen between them, David said softly, "I have the feeling I've lost you."

"I was thinking, that's all."

"Would you share your thoughts with me?"

She smiled sadly. "Not now, but maybe sometime."

David nodded his understanding. Then he said, "Well, there's something I have to know if we're going to get anywhere."

"Yes?"

"Do you still think I had, or have, anything to do with the house on the river your brother spoke of?"

Kris hadn't expected him to probe the heart of the matter quite so abruptly. She looked away and closed her eyes. Unhappily, she said, "I don't know."

When she dared glance back at David, he was staring at the fire. His face was blank, expressionless, and though it didn't make sense to suspect she'd hurt him with her answer, she knew she had.

A long moment passed. Then David managed a shade too calmly, "That's all right." And Kris knew in her heart that it wasn't all right at all.

"I can appreciate your dilemma," he went on carefully. "But whenever I've had a spare second to indulge in personal thoughts, I've thought of nothing except this whole tragedy with Jay. It finally occurred to me that just because Jay said something I find hard to believe, it doesn't mean he was lying."

Kris sat up straighter. "I'm not sure I understand what you're getting at, David," she said.

"I'm saying that Jay may have been misinformed."

"About thinking he knew you? How could he be? He told me your name, spoke of the times he'd gone to your place."

"Let's not get into that just yet," David cautioned. "Let's concentrate on one thing—the ownership of this mystery house by the river. Maybe someone *told* Jay I owned the house. It could be that simple."

"Who would have said that? And why?"

"I don't know. But please just stick to this single issue, okay? Right now it doesn't matter who told him. Let's just explore the possibility that someone *did* tell him that I owned the house in question. Will you do that for me?"

"I suppose so," she said stiffly.

"Fine. Then let's assume for the moment that someone told Jay I owned the house they were in. He believed this person. He had no reason not to believe whomever it was. So when he told you about it, he merely passed along information that he'd been given. Namely, that he was at a house owned by a base psychiatrist named David Jorgenson. Can we get that far?"

"Go on," she agreed rather dubiously.

"Fine," David repeated. "Later, we can prove out the facts. But for now, we have to start somewhere. You can see that, can't you, Kris?" Not waiting for her answer, he continued, "I'm going to once again state something that is a fact. I don't own a house by the Thames. I don't own any house anywhere. I've never owned a piece of property, and if I sound especially emphatic about that, it's because I've wanted to for years! Even a hole-in-the-wall I could truly call my own."

"What about your family home in Maine?"

"My brother inherited it. He's the oldest. He sold it and bought a fishing camp on an inland lake. That's his business now—running a fishing camp for city guys who like to rough it in the wilderness to get rid of their tensions.

"But to get back to me, I've never owned even part of a house. And insofar as my owning property along the river is concerned, we can easily disprove that. You said this particular house is in Gales Ferry?"

"Yes. I'm pretty sure that's what Jay said."

"So, we'll check out the tax records at the town hall and find out whether or not there's any property owned by David Jorgenson. If that isn't enough to convince you, we can ask around locally. That's to say, if you think I might own a place under an assumed name, I'll be happy to prove otherwise."

David spoke rationally, almost too much so, and what he was saying made Kris feel abjectly miserable. She turned to him, her soft brown eyes contrite. "You don't have to say any more," she told him, an odd little catch to her voice. "I'll accept the fact that someone else may have told Jay you owned the house. As for going to the town hall or asking around about you, I'd rather not."

David's head swerved, and Kris felt herself bathed in the silvery gleam of his astonishing eyes. "Are you saying what I think you're saying?" he demanded.

She nodded. "I believe you," she said evenly. "About not owning the house," she added, as if she were spelling out a confession.

David sat back and sighed. "For the moment, that's all I ask," he said huskily. Then, propelled by forces beyond his control, he edged closer to Kris and his arms went out to her.

She was quivering and near tears as she moved into his embrace. He enfolded her in his arms, pressing her close to his chest. He was warm and wonderful, strong yet marvelously gentle. He smoothed her hair and gently massaged her temple with one big hand while the other embraced her tiny waist. He mumbled something she couldn't quite make out. She felt him shift position, and she thought for a moment he was releasing her. Instead, he carefully, deliberately tipped her head back with a nudging finger. And then he kissed her.

The kiss, at first, was only a touching of lips. Kris sensed David testing her reaction and knew that if she stiffened he would likely draw back. She couldn't possibly have stiffened. She was kitten-weak and pliable in David's arms. And the warmth of his mouth made her feel like she'd just stumbled from a winter storm into sanctuary.

Involuntarily, she moved closer against him. Then she was returning his kiss. Giving of herself. Letting herself indulge in tender fantasies like she'd never done before. He explored. She experienced. His mouth tantalized her lips, her cheeks, her ears. And she was responding to him. Oh, God, was she responding!

She clung to him like a person starved of love as he kissed her again and again. To her astonishment, she who had never fully known what wanting was suddenly knew that she wanted David. She wanted him fully, completely. Sensed his equal desire for her. And applauded his wisdom when he moved his lips away from hers, pressed her head against his shoulder and simply held her close. For now, holding was enough. Being with him was all that mattered.

THE INTERLUDE couldn't go on forever. Finally, David gently maneuvered himself from Kris's grasp and stood up. "Mind if I throw another log on the fire?" he asked.

"Please do."

"Is there any more coffee in the pot?"

"No, but it'll only take a few minutes to make some fresh." So saying, Kris went to the kitchen. A short while later she returned, carefully carrying a cup in each hand.

David was poking the logs, scattering the glowing embers beneath them. Without turning to look at her, he asked, "Do you have any idea where the house is located? Gales Ferry is a small town, but there are still a lot of houses."

As they again took seats at opposite ends of the couch, Kris tried to accurately remember what Jay had said to her. "All I know," she finally told David, "is that he mentioned the house was along the river. I'd think that might mean it was right on the bank, or near it, wouldn't you?"

"Well, the whole town is more or less along the river," David commented.

"I should have guessed that."

A log shifted in the fireplace creating a brief shower of embers. David turned to Kris. "Do you have any other photographs of Jay? Especially photos taken since he came to Groton. Maybe when he was in the submarine school. Or with other men in his group."

"I have a shoe box full of miscellaneous snapshots stashed in my bedroom closet," Kris admitted softly. "After Jay died, I knew I wouldn't want to see those photos for quite some time."

"And you don't have to see them now," David told her. "If you'd loan the whole box to me, that is."

"Loan them to you?" Kris asked curiously. "Why?"

"Because I'd like to see if I recognize any of the guys he associated with. It would be a place to start, if I did."

Kris set her cup down on the coffee table and avoided looking him directly in the eye. "David," she said, "I meant it at lunch yesterday when I told you I've decided to give up on this."

"I know you meant it, but I hope you'll reconsider."

"I don't want to reconsider. I thought about that all day long, knowing you were coming here tonight. It won't do any good to dig up the past. I don't know why I thought it would in the first place. I guess I was motivated by the desire to get even, to have my revenge."

At that, David winced. Instinctively, Kris reached out an imploring hand. But David shook his head. "I think that proves, perhaps more than anything you might have suggested, why neither of us can drop this."

"What do you mean?"

"Consider it selfish of me if you like, but I have to find out what the truth is for my own sake," he said levelly. "I appreciate your having said I could go back to Admiral Carrington with the word you've decided not to stir things up. But that's not nearly as important to me as clearing my name with you. With *you*, understand? I'm not worried about my reputation with the navy. It's very good. But if I'm to get on with my life like I'd like to, this snag has to be confronted and untangled."

"It isn't your snag, David."

"The hell it isn't!" he blurted angrily. "You still think I'm the doctor who missed some obvious psychological problem Jay must have had. You still think I pronounced him fit for sea duty when, in your opinion, he wasn't ready to go. I dare say you still think I'm responsible for his death! Isn't that so?"

The expression on Kris's lovely face gave her away.

"Fine," David decided tersely. "You've answered the question. And until you can look me in the eye and say, 'I completely believe that you had nothing to do with anything that led to my brother's suicide,' I'm not giving up on this investigation. Is that clear?"

"Yes," Kris said. "If you'll promise to calm down."

David exhaled sharply, then managed a faint smile. "I'll try to calm down," he countered. "Which brings me back to my original request. Will you loan me the box of photographs?"

"All right," she agreed dully.

She left David and walked down the short hall to her bedroom. She got the straight-backed chair from her writing desk, positioned it in front of the closet and climbed up on the seat. The shoe box was on the top shelf stuffed somewhere back in a corner. There was a pile of odds and ends in the way—a cardboard storage box full of summer clothes, several tote bags, old purses she might as well toss out, a ratty old blanket. Kris tried to juggle things to get to the photos, but suddenly, in moving things around, she lost her balance. The chair tipped sideways and, in only an instant, she'd crashed to the floor, taking the box of clothes with her.

She hardly had time to realize what had happened when David was kneeling beside her. She started to move, but he quickly instructed her to stay still. Then he carefully and gently examined her with rather disconcerting thoroughness. Remembering the way she'd insinuated that psychiatrists were not "real" physicians, she felt her cheeks flame. David was certainly a doctor now, she knew.

Satisfied, he murmured, "You'll probably have a few bruises, but nothing more serious than that."

So saying, he lifted her up in his arms as if she were a featherweight quilt and carried her to the bed. Then he turned and surveyed the box, the scattered clothes and the tipped-over chair.

"The photos are way up in the corner of that top shelf," she said, answering his unspoken question. "I needed to move a lot of stuff to get to them."

"And you couldn't risk asking me for help?" he retorted, half serious, half teasing.

Kris watched as he gathered up the clothing and set the chair aside. Next he peered above the shelf, calmly reached in and found the correct box. Only then did he turn to look down at her, a triumphant grin on his face.

"It helps to be tall," she muttered defensively.

"It also helps to know when to ask for assistance," he advised, sitting down next to her on the bed. "And to realize that most people are more than willing to give it."

Into the silence that followed, David again sighed. Brushing back a loose strand of hair from Kris's face, he told her, "We were never meant to go each step of the way all alone, you know."

Again, Kris felt herself at the edge of tears and automatically closed her eyes. She didn't want to cry in front of David. She didn't want him to know how affected she was by his words, how deeply affected she was by him.

He was staring at her when she finally opened her eyes. Then he murmured, "Did anyone ever tell you that you're very, very lovely to look at? And like the words of that old song, you're delightful to hold? You are, Kris. Just as you're pure heaven to kiss. And if I don't get myself out of here, I'm going to forget all about my step-at-a-time resolutions and go the whole route!"

He leaned over and kissed her forehead. Then he stood up, tall and masculine and magnetic. "Call you in the morning," he promised.

A moment later Kris heard her front door shut with a gentle thud... and knew she was falling in love.

CHAPTER SEVEN

DAVID HAD NEVER BELIEVED much in Fate. But over the next few days he decided Fate was fickle, capricious, totally unreliable and definitely something to be reckoned with.

During the two and a half years he'd been stationed at Submarine Base New London, his work load had remained fairly constant. The same could be said for his leisure hours. Occasionally, he found himself with large chunks of time when he wished for something special to do, something a little different to whittle away hours that were not so much idle as they were uninteresting. Often, those extracurricular moments weighed heavily in his hands.

He knew it would be easy to make more of a social life for himself—much more of a social life! And yet he was in a transitional stage. In another few months, his service requirements would be finished and the decision about whether to enter private practice, join the staff of a hospital or become part of a community health plan would need to be made. There would be lots of changes, many adjustments. He wasn't even sure where he wanted to live and work. Maine, he suspected, but...

What about Kris?

It was ironic, really. Marianne had tried on any number of occasions to team him up with a woman. She chose her candidates well, in fact. Inevitably, the extra dinner guest—the fourth—would be attractive, intelligent and unattached. David had even dated two or three of his new acquaintances. But never for very long.

What was it about Kris Sothern? He was literally shocked at the effect she was having on him. She, of all people! A woman who'd sought him out in revenge. It was baffling, David thought, to find himself at loggerheads with the first woman in ages who truly interested him. And it was bitterly frustrating to have to prove himself blameless in the matter of her brother's death.

But that's the way it is, he decided resolutely. And it was why he yearned for more free time after his dinner date at Kris's apartment. He wanted to put out a few feelers on Kris's brother with the hope of gathering some tidbit of information that would start him on a major quest. He had to discover the truth about Jay Sothern's death. For Kris...and for himself. Otherwise, there would always be an impassable barrier between the two of them.

But, much as he wanted to plunge into an attempt to solve the mystery of Jay's suicide, David was stalled temporarily. Over the next few days, one thing after another demanded both his off-duty and on-duty attention. He only managed to glance at the contents of the box of photographs Kris had given him. Most of them, though, were solo pictures of Jay at various stages of his life and weren't of too much value.

And so it went. Each night when David finally crawled into bed, he was disgusted at how impossible setting aside time had become. He wanted desperately to see Kris. But more than that, he wanted to have something, *something*, to tell her.

Then Evan Phillips came home. The morning he was due to arrive, Marianne called the clinic despite David's firm request not to. She sounded so frantic he didn't have the heart to chastise her.

"Please," she begged, "say you'll come have drinks and dinner with us tonight!"

"Evan's first night home?" he growled.

"David, I'm praying to you!"

"Come on, Marianne. What will he think? He's been gone since last November. He'll want to be alone with you and the girls."

"But I can't be alone with him!"

"You *have* to be alone with him," David pointed out irritably. This was friendship, damn it. Time to put his professional demeanor on the shelf. "Whether or not I come to dinner," he added sarcastically, "I can't spend the night with you two."

"I'll face that when I get to it."

"Look, Marianne..."

"What?"

"You're not going to hit him over the head with your bombshell tonight, are you?"

"I have more decency than that," she retorted icily.

"All right, then. I'll make a bargain with you."

"What kind of bargain?"

"I'll come for dinner if you'll promise to wait until after Thanksgiving before you say anything to Evan about your problems."

There was total silence. Then Marianne said, "Do you realize what you're asking?"

"I realize exactly what I'm asking. For one thing, you'll have to share his bed." He paused as his irritation mounted. Then he said, his tone deliberate, "I've always had a sneaking suspicion you'd make a great actress, Marianne. And I think it's vitally important that you play this particular role well. You can tolerate being

Evan's wife a little while longer. Unless, of course, you actually hate him."

Again, there was silence. Into it, Marianne murmured sadly, "I could never hate Evan, David. That's not the problem."

"Then go along with what I'm saying."

"Well . . ."

"Oh, yes. I have one more request."

"I don't think I can take any more of your requests, David."

"This one will help ease a tense situation," he told her more gently. But suddenly his pulse was pounding.

"What is it?" she asked.

"I'd like to bring someone for Thanksgiving dinner, if I may."

"Well, well," Marianne mused.

David imagined he could hear her wheels turning and knew precisely what he would be getting himself into if she agreed to let him bring Kris to her holiday feast. Sometimes he thought Marianne should have been a professional interrogator. Yet for all her inquisitive nature, her heart was usually in the right place.

Except when it comes to her husband, he lamented.

"I'd love to have you bring a guest, David," Marianne stated, slicing into his thoughts. "Who is she?"

"Why do you say she?" He chuckled.

"One doesn't have to be a psychiatrist to make certain diagnoses from the sound of a person's voice," Marianne informed him archly.

"Touché, Mrs. Phillips."

"Well, are you going to tell me or not?"

David hesitated, wondering just how much he should say. "Her name is Kristine Sothern. She's in the admissions office at Hawthorne College."

"Fantastic!" Marianne exclaimed. "I'd love to get both Patty and Debby into Hawthorne some day. This is great." She paused to catch her breath, then demanded, "How did you meet her?"

"She came to see me about a family matter," he said carefully. "Her brother was a submariner. He died last spring."

"What did you say her name was?"

"Kristine Sothern."

There was a meaningful pause on the line. Then Marianne speculated, "Was her brother the boy who shot himself? They found him in the amusement park over on the sound."

David groaned silently. Aloud, he admitted, "Yes, that's right. Kris...well, she's still trying to come to terms with her brother's suicide. That's how she happened to contact me. But I don't think I need ask you, Marianne...if she does come to Thanksgiving dinner with me, please don't bring up any of this."

"David!"

"I know, I know. But sometimes it's easy to let things slip. So I'd rather you didn't mention anything about Kris's brother to the girls, or to Evan. Anyway, Evan was in Scotland when it happened."

More's the pity, David suddenly thought. Evan would certainly have remembered Jay's suicide if he'd been in Groton. Still, there was a chance that Evan, in his chaplain's capacity, might have counseled the boy at one time or another. Evan must have been on the base when Jay was attending submarine school, he calculated. It might be worth delving into.

Marianne said, "We'll expect you tonight, David. Is six o'clock all right?"

The change in her tone clued him to the notion that one of the girls must have come in. "Okay, I'll be there," he told her. "I just hope Evan won't think I'm horribly gauche, horning in on his first night home."

"He won't."

Marianne rang off, and David went back to work. A long while passed before he was free to dial Kris at the college. To his dismay, the receptionist in the admissions office told him that Kris had gone home with a bad sore throat.

Two hours later, minutes after finishing his last consultation, he was on his way across the Thames to the house on Granite Street. It was only when he'd arrived and was ringing her doorbell that David wondered whether he was doing the right thing by showing up unexpectedly. Chances were she was fast asleep and wouldn't welcome the intrusion.

After what seemed like forever to David, she came to the front door and let him in without so much as a smile. Then she trudged back to her apartment. Once inside, she said, "This really isn't a very good time for you to be here."

He'd half expected that kind of greeting, though it certainly was not the one he'd hoped for. He said, a shade gruffly, "It's okay, Kris. I know you left work early with a sore throat, so I'm here as a doctor."

She turned and stared into his eyes. David was shocked at how pale, haggard and totally miserable she looked. Instantly, he was concerned. Instinctively, he was worried. He cupped her cheeks gently in his hands and muttered, "What in hell have you been doing to yourself?"

"Nothing," she croaked dismally. "I've got a sore throat, that's all. It's no big deal."

"No big deal," he echoed, shaking his head.

She seemed so small, so frail, that David felt a rare wave of helplessness as he tried to decide how to proceed. She was so damned vulnerable to just about everything. He touched her forehead and found her skin burning hot. Worse, he realized it was chilly in the apartment.

He swore mildly under his breath. "Where's the thermostat?"

"On the wall over by the kitchen door," Kris rasped.

David turned up the heat, headed for her bedroom, stripped two pillows and a quilt off her bed, and in another moment, had her lying on the couch in front of the fireplace. First he tucked her in. Then he set about making a fire. When the logs had caught, he asked, "How long have you had this sore throat?"

"A day or two," Kris replied vaguely.

"What have you been doing for it?"

"I took some aspirin."

"Have you been drinking lots of fluids?"

"It hurts to swallow."

He arched an eyebrow, but said only, "I'm sure it does. Do you have any juice or soup? Things like that?"

Kris shook her head slowly, wincing from the effort. "I meant to stop at a convenience store on the way home," she told him. "But I felt too rotten."

"I can imagine."

He was heading for the kitchen as he spoke. A minute later, he'd surveyed the contents of her fridge and cupboards. Kris's food supply, he concluded, was at an especially low ebb, which made him suspect she'd been sick for longer than she was admitting.

David was again muttering to himself as he strode back into the living room. Kris had closed her eyes, but opened them as he approached the couch. She looked so weak, it daunted him. He felt a deep concern quite unlike the concern he felt for his patients. It was more a desire to cure and comfort her because...

He loved her.

After all these years, the master of resistance had fallen in love with a wisp of a young woman who still doubted his innocence in the matter of her brother's tragedy. David silently admitted his love for her, but swore aloud this time, totally frustrated. He couldn't imagine being in a worse bind. Thank God his professionalism surfaced and the physician in him began dominating the situation.

"I'm going to leave you for a short while," he said. "I could write a prescription, but it might actually be quicker to run over to the base and get what I want for you. Promise you'll stay put till I get back, okay? Where's your house key?"

"My handbag...in the bedroom," Kris managed.

He retrieved her bulging purse, handed it to her, then shook his head as she foraged through the contents. "How women ever find anything in those things is a mystery to me," he confessed.

After a second or two, Kris procured the key. He took it, then bent down to lightly kiss her forehead. "I'll be back as quickly as safe driving will permit," he promised.

David drove directly to the hospital on the sub base, got the hypodermic syringe and antibiotics he wanted and swore he would forever carry his black bag around with him in the future. Then he headed back to New London, stopping along the way at a market where he stocked up on fruit juices, bouillons, soups and sherbet.

When he let himself into Kris's apartment, she appeared to be lying exactly where he'd left her, fast asleep. She was deep asleep in fact, experiencing the lulling slumber that often accompanies a fever. She'd been dreaming—lovely dreams, though she couldn't remember what they were—and when she heard David's voice close to her ear she thought she was still dreaming.

"Dearest, I hate to do this, but I have to wake you up," he whispered. "For a little while."

Dearest. Even in her fevered state, the term of endearment registered, and Kris blinked open her eyes.

She found herself gazing into gray eyes that were like pools of clear rainwater. She saw the caring and concern etched on David's face. And suddenly she realized how beloved his face was to her. She felt emotionally choked. An inner sense of right and wrong had been constantly reminding her that her attraction for David was wrong because of Jay. Now that logic wasn't holding up.

She knew she'd be lying to herself if she denied feeling glad he was here. Glad? Much more than glad. She'd never been much for leaning on another person's shoulders. At the moment, though, what she wanted most was to have David take care of her.

She saw him reach into his black leather medical bag. Then he was taking her blood pressure, her temperature, thoroughly examining her throat and taking a culture.

"I'll get this over to the lab a little later," he said. "First, I'm going to give you a shot of antibiotic."

Kris was too weak to protest, but all she felt was a pinprick. "Not bad," she teased in a voice not more than a whisper.

David smiled. "I wanted to start you out with a real wallop," he said. "From now on, you can take the medication orally. The throat culture will verify or disprove my diagnosis, but I strongly suspect you've got a bacterial infection rather than a virus, in which case the antibiotic should work quickly."

"Don't antibiotics work with viruses?" Kris asked.

He shook his head. "No, they don't."

He was sitting on the edge of the couch as he spoke and storing his medical paraphernalia back in his black bag. Then he stood up, holding a bottle of a pinkish liquid. "This has to be kept in the fridge and taken every six hours around the clock until it's completely used up," he prescribed. "I know that's a pain, but it's important to establish a cycle and stay with it if we're going to get the infection out of your system."

"Yes, doctor," Kris murmured meekly, not repressing the slight smile that turned up the corners of her mouth.

She found herself the recipient of a highly suspicious glance. Then David returned the smile and commented wryly, "You *must* be sick! So, first time around I'll give you a choice. Would you like bouillon or sherbet?"

With a show of her usual spunk, Kris whispered hoarsely, "Look, you don't have to feed me, you know."

"Maybe I want to feed you," David replied stubbornly. "Which will it be? Bouillon or sherbet?"

"Sherbet, if you insist," Kris said with difficulty. To her dismay, her throat felt more sore than ever, and she just wasn't up to either arguing or bantering with David.

David nodded understandingly. "Something cold should feel good," he agreed. He reached down to smooth her hair off her forehead. "Don't be alarmed if you feel worse for a while instead of better," he cautioned. "It's not the treatment. It's the fact that you let this go too long. If I hadn't happened by, you might have ended up in the hospital."

He spoke matter-of-factly, and Kris knew he wasn't looking for applause or gratitude. He wasn't that kind of person. "Thank you," she said.

"There's no need to thank me, Kris."

"Well...I do thank you. Especially since I wasn't very nice when you first got here," she managed painfully.

"It doesn't matter. And stop talking, will you?" He started toward the kitchen.

When he returned with the sherbet, David propped up the pillows behind Kris's back so she could eat the frozen treat more comfortably. It was lemon-flavored, delightfully cold, and it slid down her throat with only a modicum of discomfort.

Watching her, David commented, "At least sherbet has a few calories. After this bout, we'll really have to fatten you up." David grinned, as he added, "You're beautiful in the eyes of this beholder. But you'll be even more so with a few extra pounds on that body!"

Kris glared at him and started to protest. But he merely grinned and held up a warning hand. "Spare your throat," he admonished. "Besides, it's the truth."

When she'd finished with the sherbet, he took the empty dish from her, then realigned the pillows and pulled the quilt up over her shoulders. Glancing toward the windows, he said, "It's getting dark out. Want me to draw the drapes?"

Kris nodded.

With the drapes drawn and the fire blazing in the fireplace, the room gained that special intimacy David loved. Into the quiet, he whispered, "Get some sleep, Kris."

She looked up at him. She had no right to keep him here. His time was his own, and he would have other things to do. Yet she wanted so much for him to stay.

"Are you leaving?" she croaked, swallowing away the pain.

"I'm not going until your fever breaks."

"There's a television in the kitchen..."

"I'll find something to read. Stop talking, will you?"

Kris complied. And within a few minutes, from the combination of medication and fever, she'd fallen asleep.

WHEN KRIS AWAKENED, she automatically looked for David and quickly found him sprawled in the armchair by the fire. He was fast asleep, his long legs stretched out in front of him, a magazine dropped in his lap. As she watched, his eyes blinked open. Then he yawned deeply, lifted himself to his feet and swerved his eyes in her direction.

"Been awake long?" he asked.

"Uh."

"I take it that means no?"

She nodded affirmatively as he glanced at his wristwatch. "Damn," he muttered. "I was supposed to be someplace for dinner and I forgot all about it. Mind if I use your phone?"

"It's on that end table in the corner."

She watched him cross the room, loving the way he moved. Big man that he was, David handled himself very well. She watched him switch on a lamp, reach for the phone and dial. She heard him say, "Marianne?" And she tensed, stabbed by a barb of jealousy she couldn't suppress.

"Look, I'm sorry. Something came up and I couldn't call you any sooner."

There was a pause, then he snapped irritably, "No, it was not deliberate, damn it! I hope no one overheard that remark. Good. No, don't disturb him if he and the girls are talking."

Don't disturb who? Kris wondered. And who were Marianne and the girls?

"Okay, okay...if you must," David steamed. A moment later, with an enthusiasm that certainly sounded genuine, he said, "Evan! It's great to hear your voice!"

Kris shifted her position and stared toward the fireplace, watching the logs crackle and glow. She tried very hard not to listen to any more of David's conversation. She shouldn't have listened in the first place, she told herself. It was none of her business. Yet when he hung up, she fervently wished he'd enlighten her.

"I didn't mean to eavesdrop," she began carefully, "but did you have a date tonight and stand somebody up?"

"Not exactly," David answered.

On his way back across the room, he switched on another lamp, reached for his medical bag, then sat down on the edge of the couch. He got out his thermometer again, popped it into Kris's mouth, then continued, "Evan Phillips, who is one of my closest friends, has just returned from a tour of duty in Scotland. He got back this afternoon, as a matter of fact. His wife, Marianne, invited me for a welcome-home supper tonight with Evan and their two teenage daughters. I sort of felt I'd be horning in anyway, so I appreciate your giving me a valid reason for not showing up."

He extracted the thermometer and read it. "Still up there," he observed. "By morning, however, we should see a real change."

By morning? We? Kris looked up, perplexed.

"In case you don't know it, lady," David informed her, "I'm spending the night."

IN THE MORNING, Kris's fever was gone. Still, she felt as limp as a rag. Despite all the sleep she'd had—for she'd done almost nothing but sleep since David's arrival on the scene—she had never felt so exhausted.

David assured her that actually she was doing fine. He'd slept the night in her bedroom, then showered and dressed by the time she awakened. To her rather fuzzy eyes he looked marvelous. For her breakfast, he fixed a poached egg on toast, softening the toast with hot milk. Kris couldn't recall when an egg had tasted more delicious.

It was bitter cold out and the apartment was drafty. David restarted the fire and decreed that Kris rest on the couch during the day, instead of in her bedroom. He filled a carafe with cranberry juice, admonished that she get up only to use the bathroom or replenish the carafe with juice, and told her he'd be back at lunchtime.

"But you can't," Kris croaked in protest. "I mean...you must have patients to see."

True, he did have. And would have, right through the first of the year. The holiday season was the busiest time of year at the clinic. For many patients, it was a hectic period filled with more stress than they could handle. David had learned way back as a third-year med student on his first psychiatric rotation that Christmas was not necessarily merry for people. Memories surfaced and could easily become traumatic. Problems tended to compound themselves. Frustrations about so many different things took hold, starting as small ripples but often turning into tidal waves.

He wondered how the upcoming holidays would affect Kris. This would not be her first Thanksgiving or Christmas without Jay. He'd been at sea a year ago. But he'd been *alive* then.

He said, "I'll reschedule my lunch-hour patient. And maybe Ned or Barney can take a consultation or two for me this afternoon."

"Ned or Barney?"

"The psychologists at the clinic." He was shrugging into his heavy wool parka as he spoke. "Regardless," he warned jokingly, "I'll be back to check on you at noon. So be good!"

Kris dozed during the morning, awakening every so often to dutifully drink her juice, though it hurt going down. She discovered that, as groggy as she still felt, she couldn't wait for noon to arrive and David to come back. When finally she heard the key grate in the lock, she sat bolt upright and wished she'd garnered enough strength to brush her hair and put on a daub of lipstick. For the first time in two days, she realized she looked like an absolute wreck!

Seeing David carrying another grocery bag, Kris moaned. "Don't tell me you bought more juice?"

"Yep. And more sherbet. And a couple of creamy soups that might taste pretty good." He came over to the couch and stood gazing down at her. "How are you feeling?"

"Fine."

"Liar," he teased. "You do look better than you did this morning, though. Let's check that temperature, then it'll be time for your antibiotic. After that, I'll make you some soup."

"David, I admit that a good-sized feather could probably knock me over right now. But if I take it easy, I can fix the soup and manage to take my medicine."

"Are you inferring that I'm not needed, Miss Sothern?"

"No, it's not that at all. It's just that I don't feel right about taking up your time like this."

His smile was so tender that Kris caught her breath. He said, "I can't think of anyone I'd rather give my time to. Just let it go at that, okay?"

Kris nodded and sank back against the pillows. David headed for the kitchen, got the antibiotic from the fridge and started heating some cream of asparagus soup. As she listened to him fiddle around opening drawers and cabinets, she was glad that he hadn't chosen that particular moment to take her pulse. It was behaving outrageously.

She was quiet as he returned to take her temperature, and she hoped that her heart had simmered down as he reached for her wrist. She saw him frown slightly and slant her a look of curiosity. But he didn't say a word.

The soup was delicious and Kris needed no coaxing to finish the bowl. David then went and got her a dish of raspberry sherbet. As she ate a spoonful, he casually said, "The reason I called you at your office yesterday was that I had an invitation for you."

"An invitation?"

"I know it's short notice, but I hope you haven't made plans for Thanksgiving. It's just a few days away, but you shouldn't travel anywhere. You won't be strong enough."

Kris smiled. "I haven't made any plans," she murmured.

Actually, she *had* been invited to spend Thanksgiving at the home of a distant relative who lived near Lancaster. But she'd declined. She had no desire at this point to visit the places where she and Jay had grown up.

David said, "Then I hope you'll have dinner with me at Evan and Marianne Phillips's house. I've spoken to Marianne and she says she'd love to have you."

The details of last night were a bit hazy to Kris. Her fever had been raging around in her head. She remembered listening to David talk to someone named Marianne and knew he'd made some kind of explanation to her, but his exact words were lost.

He said now, "I think I mentioned that Evan Phillips is one of my closest friends. He just returned yesterday from a year in Scotland at a place called Holy Loch. We've got a submarine group stationed there. Anyway, Evan's a great guy. I think you'd like him, Kris. He's a chaplain at the base."

Something clicked in Kris's mind and she shivered. David caught the small involuntary movement and asked quickly, "What is it, Kris?"

Unhappily, she said, "That name's familiar to me, David. Jay mentioned a chaplain named Phillips."

David's smile faded. It had happened again. A memory surfacing. A connection Kris had doubts about. Jay stepping in between them.

CHAPTER EIGHT

MARIANNE HAD SCHEDULED Thanksgiving dinner for three in the afternoon. "She says then we'll be hungry enough for cold turkey sandwiches later on," David reported to Kris.

Hearing this, Kris wondered how long Marianne Phillips expected her Thanksgiving guests to linger. Personally, she was hoping she could make a polite getaway as soon as possible after dinner. In fact, she was wishing she'd never accepted the invitation in the first place.

She'd asked David not to mention Jay's name to Evan Phillips. David had promised he wouldn't, and she knew he could be trusted to keep his word. But there was always the chance that the name Sothern might stir up a memory for the chaplain. And if Evan Phillips brought up the subject of Jay, Kris wasn't sure she could handle it.

Her illness had left her feeling weak, shaky and much too prone to tears and irritability. Between that and the terrible tug of her attraction to David, she wasn't as much in control of herself as she would have liked.

That meant she would have to watch herself very closely and think out every word she said, both with the Phillipses and with David. *But at least I realize this,* she told herself.

Despite David's sincerity and concern over the issue of Jay's suicide, Kris remained convinced that her brother should not have been okayed for further sea duty without a lot more testing. And though she realized how many submariners David saw in the course of his work—and accepted the fact that he couldn't possibly remember each and every man—there was still that thorn implanted by Jay himself.

Jay had probably been mistaken about David's ownership of the house by the river. She was willing to accept that. But why would he have maintained that David was his friend? Why would he have inferred that he and David knew each other?

David Jorgenson. Not an entirely unusual name, but by no means John Smith. Anyway, David had said he was the only psychiatrist on the base, with two psychologists under him. Whether there'd been other psychiatrists at Groton last spring, Kris didn't know. Nor was she sure she wanted to find out!

It was miserable feeling so mixed up and experiencing such inner conflict, especially when she felt weak as a kitten. But Kris began to take advantage of that weakness, something she ordinarily would have deplored. She was glad the college had insisted she take time off until she felt fully fit again. It gave her the opportunity to languish within the confines of her comfortable apartment.

David stopped by Granite Street daily to bring her surprise food packages, check her temperature and keep at her about taking her medication. But he seemed preoccupied, mostly making these trips on a quick lunch hour and without lingering.

Kris would stand at her living-room window and watch him drive away. And each time her heart would ache for his love while her reason told her it was just as well he couldn't stay. Until they discovered what really happened with Jay, it was best they cooled their feelings.

The fact that David wanted to know the truth about Jay should have proved his innocence to her. Yet her strong voice of conscience wouldn't let him off the hook so easily. "Why would Jay have lied?" it said over and over again. "Your only brother, Kris."

But suppose, just suppose, Jay had lied. Then what?

The niggling thought came that if David *had* known Jay, but couldn't place him, he would have recognized him in the photographs. Yet he'd said nothing about them, which struck Kris as very, very odd.

He was exceptionally busy, of course. He'd mentioned that the holidays tended to bring to the surface all kinds of psychological traumas people normally managed to hide. Even so, he must have glanced through the photographs. How could he not have? He had requested them, after all. But for what reason? Kris wondered.

DAVID PICKED KRIS UP at two-thirty Thanksgiving afternoon. She was watching for him at the window and slipped out the front door just as he reached the steps to the porch. The day was clear and cold, beautiful in that stark way late autumn days in New England often are. The Thames was deep blue and sparkling. The sky was cloudless. The crisp air smelled of burning wood.

David glanced at Kris and observed, "You're looking a lot better. Though I suppose the color in your cheeks comes from blush rather than nature."

"You shouldn't be so perceptive," she accused.

"It's my job," he told her seriously as they got into his car. Inside, he added casually, "So, have you been getting out of the house at all?"

"No, I haven't. I thought I'd better stay in until I finished the medication."

"I didn't say you had to do that."

"Well, you didn't say anything about going out, either."

"I guess I assumed you'd want a little fresh air and exercise," David conceded. "As long as you don't get chilled, it's the best way to get your strength back."

"My strength is back!" Kris blurted defensively.

"Really? Seems to me you were pretty wobbly getting into the car."

Kris didn't answer that, and soon they were crossing the bridge over the Thames River. Instead of turning onto Route 12, though, and heading toward the main gate of the submarine base, David swerved onto a local road that bordered the river.

He parked almost in the shadow of the bridge they'd just crossed, shut off the car motor, then sat back and gave Kris a long, level look.

"What is it?" she finally asked.

"That was going to be my question," he told her. "Did I say or do something that's bothering you? You're giving me the feeling I should put on kid gloves if I even want to talk to you."

Had he done something? The lack of an answer made Kris ache. It went to the root of their problem. She didn't know *what* he had done, back in the beginning with Jay. Not knowing was like a huge granite block that, despite a capacity to disappear for certain infrequent intervals, as when David held her in his arms, inevitably swung back into place between them.

She stirred as the ache intensified and she started to look away. But a strong finger instantly tilted her chin back to face two fantastic silver-gray eyes.

"Please, Kris...give me a chance, will you?" David implored. "At the very least, I deserve the chance to either prove myself or get caught up in some trap. That's what all this distancing I'm feeling is about, isn't it?''

She nodded miserably.

"I thought so," David said. "But according to a basic tenet of our law," he went on wryly, "a man is presumed innocent till he's found guilty. Can't I elicit so much as the benefit of the doubt from you?"

The tears Kris had been holding back for days could be restrained no longer. They spilled over. She heard David's muffled, "Oh, God!" Then felt him reach out, draw her into his arms, and hold her close while she cried. She had the crazy feeling she was like a small boat that had been floundering in rough seas, nearly capsizing, but now had miraculously managed to make its way into a safe harbor.

Gradually, the tears slowed to a trickle. When they stopped completely, David gently dabbed her cheeks with a large white handkerchief that felt wonderfully soft. Then he kissed her. He kissed her with a depth and tenderness that moved Kris clear to her soul.

When at last he released her, David touched a warning finger to her lips and said, "Please...don't say anything. For a few hours, try to leave it be, okay?"

Kris nodded mutely and glimpsed the dashboard clock. "Oh, David," she moaned. "It's after three and we're late. What are your friends going to think?"

"Nothing. Anyway, we're only a few minutes away."

"I must look like a mess!"

He surveyed her with mock seriousness. "Actually, the blush didn't even streak," he assured her.

Kris took a mirror out of her handbag, peered into it and wailed. She hastily made repairs and hoped the telltale evidence that she'd been crying would be gone by the time they reached the Phillips's house.

Evidently, it was. She was welcomed effusively by Marianne, with cordial geniality by Evan, and with a polite greeting from Deborah. But she met with a bit less enthusiasm from Patricia, which quickly made her suspect that Patricia Phillips had a crush on David, one he probably wasn't aware of.

Marianne had prepared a delicious, traditional turkey dinner with all the trimmings. Evan put some soft background music on the stereo, kept their wineglasses filled, and was a perfect host. Yet there was something not quite right. Kris caught hidden tension vibes, especially from Marianne, and wondered about them.

David hadn't spoke much about the Phillipses except to say that Evan was one of his closest friends. But then David had never said very much to her about anyone. Most of his attention, she realized now, had been centered on her.

They had coffee in the living room after dinner. The girls both had movie dates and asked to be excused. Kris offered to help Marianne with the cleanup, but Marianne said airily that she'd get to that later, adding that her dishwasher did most of the work anyway.

David suggested a game of Trivial Pursuit. Evan groaned, insisting that David always won, but he got out the board and the four of them started to play. Kris was surprised at the wide range of David's knowledge. Most of the time, he came up with the right answers on everything.

Just one more thing I like about him, she mused silently.

She gazed intently at David as she thought this, then abruptly sat up straight. Luckily, he was busy reading a question to Evan, so he hadn't caught her look. But when she glanced across at her hostess, Marianne quickly averted her eyes.

Well, Marianne got the message, Kris thought ruefully.

It was true, though. She loved him. Regardless of the circumstances that clouded their relationship, she loved him. She could see no future to that love. Neither could she wish it away nor deny it.

She and David didn't stay long enough to partake of turkey sandwiches. It was not quite eight in the evening when David stated to the audience at large that it was time he took Kris home. "She's just getting over a bad throat infection," he explained. "Matter of fact, this is her first time out."

On the bridge to New London, though, he abruptly suggested, "How about finding a quiet spot and having a drink?"

Kris looked across at him, surprised. And before she stopped to consider the wisdom of pleading understandable fatigue, she said, "All right."

David took her to a small lounge, an adjunct of a popular restaurant in a recently restored building not far from the waterfront. At this hour on Thanksgiving night, the place was not crowded.

After they settled into a corner booth, David asked, "How does a spiked eggnog sound?"

Kris laughed. "Trying to fatten me up?"

"Yes. Frankly, I am."

"Do you really think I need it that much?"

A waitress appeared, sparing David from answering. He chatted with her about the prospect of imminent snow, then ordered Kris's eggnog and bourbon on the rocks for himself. Watching him, Kris noted telltale signs of fatigue on his face—dark shadows under his eyes, lines around his mouth she didn't remember seeing before. Though he was adept at hiding it, she sensed his weariness and had a sudden urge to comfort him.

"Well," he said, after he'd tested his bourbon, "dinner at the Phillipses wasn't such an ordeal, was it?"

"Did you expect it would be?"

"No, but I had the impression you did."

Kris smiled. "Are all psychiatrists so astute?"

David flashed her one of his infectious grins, despite himself. "It didn't take any great scientific acumen to sense that you would have preferred to back out of Marianne's invitation. Gracefully, of course."

She frowned. "I hate being so transparent!"

"Your lack of poker face is one of the things I love about you."

The remark slipped out casually and David didn't follow it up. But Kris's pulse began to thump faster.

"I did rather dread being part of a gathering," she allowed, skirting the issue.

Actually, she'd been afraid that Evan might remember Jay, might bring up the subject of his death. She almost told David as much, then stopped herself. Much as she loved Jay, she was not going to let his ghost intrude between David and herself tonight. David had asked her for the chance to prove himself. Well, she would give him that chance. She owed him that much.

"You were very social, Kris. Terrific, in fact."

"Yes, well . . . I had a very pleasant time. If only . . ."

"If only what?"

She looked questioningly into David's eyes. "Are you aware that Patricia is in love with you?" she demanded, and then was horrified at herself for being so blunt.

"Good grief, she's sixteen years old!"

"Sixteen years old," Kris mused innocently.

David sipped his bourbon, then shrugged. "Okay, she has a crush on me. She'll get over it."

"Hard-hearted, aren't you?"

"Factual," he corrected. "Anything else, Miss Sothern?"

"Is there supposed to be something else?"

"Maybe not. But there is, isn't there?"

"I got some funny vibes, that's all."

"Uh-huh."

"What sort of an answer is that?"

"What sort of vibes did you get?"

Kris made a wry face. "Didn't anyone ever tell you it drives people crazy to answer a question with a question?"

"Hmm...maybe that's the problem with a lot of my patients. But seriously, what kind of vibes did you get?"

"Tension, I suppose. Something wrong between Evan and Marianne despite the pleasant surface perfection they project." She broke off considering this, then hastily added, "I'm not trying to be critical of your friends, David. I mean, I'm probably way off base, right?"

The smile faded from his face. "No," he said quietly, "you're not off base at all. So don't talk to me about my being astute! I'm surprised you picked up on that, the very first time you met them, no less. Especially since Evan himself doesn't know what it's all about."

"What what's all about?"

"Marianne wants a divorce, but she hasn't told Evan."

"Oh," Kris said softly.

"Yeah, oh," David agreed.

"Why hasn't she told him?"

"Because I asked her not to. Not until after today."

Kris sat back and pondered that. Then she said, "Why you? Do you have that much influence over her?"

Jealousy needled again, just as it had that night at her apartment when David called Marianne to explain he'd forgotten about their dinner engagement. Kris was surprised at herself. She'd thought jealousy was an emotion foreign to her nature. As it had been—until now.

David was staring moodily at his half-full glass of bourbon. He looked sharply at Kris, then a teasing smile curved his lips. "That's a leading question," he remarked coolly.

Kris knew she was blushing. Certainly, she was embarrassed. She started to stammer out an answer, but David chided, "Hey, wait a minute. I was only joking. No, I don't have that much influence over Marianne. She just needed someone to confide in and picked me probably because I'm a good friend of the family. I think she was hoping to have someone around to cushion the blow for Evan. I can't say I'm happy I was her choice, but Evan *is* going to need someone. Probably sooner than I'd hoped, the way those vibes you noted were darting around tonight."

Kris formed an image of Evan Phillips in her mind. He was a tall, slender man with sandy hair, balding slightly at the temples. His eyes were light blue and his face, while not handsome, was very pleasant to look at, attractive because of his personality. She'd liked him almost at once. When he'd said grace before dinner, she was moved by his quiet simplicity. It spoke of a deep faith. He appeared to be a calm and understanding person, someone to turn to in a time of crisis. From what David was saying, Evan would soon be needing someone to turn to himself.

"Why does Marianne want a divorce?" she asked abruptly. "Is there someone else in her life?"

"As far as I know there isn't," David told her. "In fact, I'm almost positive about that. I think it could even be said that Marianne still loves Evan."

"Why, then?"

"She can't hack the life anymore. That might sound like a stock answer, but it's a very serious problem, Kris. And not just Marianne's problem, either. Many wives of submariners have a tough time coping. True, Evan's not a submariner, but I've often thought he might as well be. When he's here on base, he's completely tied up with the men of the submarine service. Every now and then, he's assigned to duty at Holy Loch, where, if anything, he's even more involved."

"Is Holy Loch isolated?"

"Yes and no," David decided. "It's fairly close to Glasgow, but even so . . ."

"You've been there?"

"No, but Evan's shown me pictures."

"Have you ever been aboard a submarine?"

"Several times," he said soberly.

"I mean, have you ever gone to sea on a submarine?"

It was rare for Kris to voluntarily broach the subject of submarines, David noted. Aside from her mentioning Jay's involvement with the service, talking about submarines was something she tended to avoid.

"Yes, I've taken a couple of short trips. I thought I told you that."

"Maybe you did. I don't remember," Kris admitted.

David wasn't sure himself. But one thing he was sure of—the subject was still very difficult for Kris because of Jay.

"What was it like?" she queried cautiously.

"Out there?" he asked, encouraged.

"*Under* there."

David thought for a second, then said, "It was an entirely different world."

Kris was silent. Then, surprisingly, she smiled. She said, "Jay used to say the only way you could tell time was by the food. If they served bacon and eggs, you knew it was morning." She spoke easily, and this also registered with David. It was the first time she'd spoken *easily* about anything concerning Jay.

He laughed, and said, "That's true enough. Evan's also taken short trips on the subs, incidentally. It wasn't a military requirement for either of us, but we both felt it would help us in our work. Meaning, the only way to really feel what it's like to be a submariner is to go to sea on a sub yourself."

"Would you want to be a submariner, David?"

"Frankly, no," he admitted. "Maybe that's why I have the deepest admiration for the men who do that work, live that kind of life. It takes discipline and stamina, large doses of both. They're a brave and dedicated group of people."

Kris nodded slowly. "Yes, they must be." She sipped her eggnog, then observed, "Isn't it late in the day for Marianne to decide she can no longer tolerate the navy life? I mean, she and Evan have obviously been married a number of years."

"Eighteen, I believe," David concurred. "But time alone isn't an assurance that things will go smoothly. Quite the contrary, in many cases. Sometimes a person can tolerate something for years without consciously knowing that's what they're doing... *tolerating* it. Then one day reality strikes. Perhaps something specific triggers the ego to revolt. Suddenly it's the old adage of the straw that breaks the camel's back. The person comes to the end of his or her rope. There are a dozen clichés to describe the situation and its result. Sometimes the saturation point is only temporary, brought on by nerves, fatigue, undue stress or a combination thereof. Other times, it's permanent.''

David suddenly realized that all this talk about coming to the end of one's rope applied to Jay Sothern, too. He held his breath, hoping he hadn't spoiled a moment when Kris seemed to be making progress in opening up.

"Which is it with Marianne?" she asked.

"I'm not sure. Until she told me she was having serious problems, I had no idea. Evan's being away didn't help, that much is certain.''

"She could have gone to Holy Loch with him, couldn't she?''

"Yes, but she didn't want to. It would have meant spending the better part of three years in Scotland. She felt the girls were at the wrong ages for that.''

"So she put her daughters ahead of her husband?''

"Mothers often put their children ahead of their husbands, Kris," David told her. "Especially when the kids are growing up. That's when a woman's apt to consider the needs of her kids paramount and forget about the needs of her husband. Once the kids are out on their own, she tries to backtrack. Often, it's too late.''

"Yes, I can see that. I can even understand it," Kris said. "Of course, I've never had a husband or children, so I don't really know how that feels. Still, I doubt I'd lose sight of my husband in my absorption with children. I wouldn't want to.''

David heard her words and his imagination ran riot. He'd fallen in love with Kris that night she'd been at the mercy of a raging fever. He loved her doe eyes, her nutmeg hair, her compact physique, her indomitable character. He could see Kris as a wife, picture her with children, wondered what her kids would look like if he was the father...

It was a staggering thought that caught David completely off guard. For a long moment, he sat quietly opposite Kris, thinking, regrouping. Finally, he cleared his throat. "Some people," he said huskily, "can manage both. Others can't. Marianne was evidently caught in the middle and felt she had to choose. The fact that her girls loved their school and their friends here in New London definitely influenced her decision not to move to Holy Loch last year. Then, and not for first time, she was left to face everything on her own.

"In addition to her personal problems," David continued, "Marianne does a lot of volunteer work involving the wives of other submariners. So all *their* problems come into play. To make a long story short, the pressure obviously mounted until suddenly she decided she had to do something about it...or explode."

"Can't you counsel her?"

"I shouldn't and I wouldn't. With Evan between us, there's no way I could be totally objective."

"She's such a stunning woman," Kris mused. "She seems so much in control of herself."

"Inwardly, she's been coming apart at the seams for quite a while," David said. "I should have realized it, but I didn't. She covered things up extremely well. When she finally came out with everything, I was shocked. But like I told her, she and Evan are my friends, not my patients. It wasn't my business to analyze them."

"Can't you at least talk to her?"

"I can try," David admitted ruefully. "Hell, I have tried. At this stage, it isn't going to do much good. Which reminds me...will you kindly drink that eggnog? You need the calories."

Kris sipped obediently, then said softly, "All of this must be very difficult for you."

"The situation with Marianne and Evan, you mean? Yes, well . . . it's not exactly pleasant."

"I didn't mean just that. I meant your work, constantly dealing with people who have problems."

"That's what I do, Kris," David said patiently. "I already told you why I chose psychiatry. Why I decided I wanted to treat the mind rather than the body."

"Because of your wife."

"My ex-wife," he corrected. "Yes, what happened with her pointed me in the direction I've followed. At times, it *is* very difficult. The mind is invisible, Kris. A tremendous challenge. Which is why I wouldn't give up psychiatry for any other branch of medicine. Which reminds me. Tomorrow's a holiday for a lot of people, though I have several consultations scheduled. I guess we'd better get going." He managed a weary smile. "It's past your bedtime, anyway."

It was starting to snow as they left the lounge. By the time they reached his car, David's thick dark hair was sprinkled with snowflakes.

As they drove toward Granite Street, the white flakes swirled around them. Kris said, "It makes me feel like we're two figures in a paperweight."

"A paperweight?"

"You know, one of those paperweights you turn upside down and shake, then there's a snowstorm in the scene. I had a paperweight like that when I was a child. Inside, there was a miniature Christmas tree all trimmed with ornaments. When you shook it, snow fell around the tree like in a magic winter wonderland."

David sneaked a glance at Kris, wishing he'd known her when she was a child. She must have been such a lovely little girl with that soft brown hair and those huge expressive eyes. He could imagine her awe on Christmas morning when she'd go downstairs in her home back in Pennsylvania—probably with her brother Jay clutching her hand—to see the tree strung with colored lights and shiny ornaments, and stacks of presents underneath.

It was incredibly difficult to leave her at the front door of the house. David wanted terribly to go inside with her. He wanted her. He wanted to put a log on the fire in her living room, then draw her down on the couch and make love to her. Make love until he brought stars to her eyes and, like two people in a paperweight, they were swirling in the aftermath of fantasy.

Under the protection of the porch, with snow falling in the darkness, he drew Kris into his arms and kissed her. And when he'd let go of her the first time he drew her back and kissed her again.

He yearned to whisper the magic words in her ear. He yearned to say, ''I love you.'' But he couldn't. Not until he'd finished his inquiry into the truth about her brother. Until that mystery was solved—until he'd proved his innocence to her—those magic words would remain unspoken.

CHAPTER NINE

THEY SAID GOOD-NIGHT and David started down the front steps. Kris put her key in the lock, then turned around to watch him. She was so tempted to call his name that she clutched her throat to stop herself.

As he walked to his car, light from a street lamp slanted across his path, highlighting him in its soft yellow glow. Kris wished she had a camera to capture the scene forever. David's silhouette, the cone of muted yellow light, the silently falling snow.

It took all the effort she could muster to turn back to her front door and let herself into the house. But inside her apartment, she rushed to the living-room window before switching on the lights. She was just in time to see David's taillights glow red at the end of Granite Street. Then his car disappeared around the corner.

A minute later, Kris got into her favorite fleece nightgown and brewed herself a cup of herb tea. Not because she was thirsty, simply because she needed its warmth. She needed David's warmth, she thought dejectedly. She'd never felt lonelier than she felt right now. She'd never in her life wanted anyone the way she wanted David.

She switched on the television and turned to a documentary on the sea. But she might as well have stared at an empty screen. Her mind and her heart were across the

Thames in a place she'd never have thought possible—Submarine Base New London, Groton, Connecticut.

David had jotted down his private number at the BOQ for her when she'd been bedridden. "Just in case you need me for anything," he'd said. Well, she needed him now. So she ferreted the slip of paper out of her desk and dialed before she could change her mind.

He answered on the second ring. Knowing it was a foolish question, Kris asked, "I hope I didn't wake you up?"

"Kris?" He sounded dumbfounded. "No, I just got in a few minutes ago. The roads are getting pretty slippery, especially the bridge, so I took it easy. What is it? Is something wrong?"

"No, no," she assured him quickly. "I just wanted to be sure you'd gotten home safely."

There was silence. Then David managed shakily, "Thanks for your concern. I'm fine."

Kris paused uncertainly, and finally said, "There's something else, David."

"What's that?"

"Well, I know you told me back when I was really sick that I didn't need to thank you for anything. But I *want* to thank you."

"For what, Kris?" he asked, surprised.

"For being so very kind to me," she told him sincerely. "For taking care of me the way you did. For spending all those hours with me that you didn't have to spare. I'll never forget that," she finished, and whispered under her breath, "I'll never forget you."

"What is this?" David demanded. "That sounds like some kind of farewell speech."

"No, no, I didn't mean it that way. I got to thinking about you, that's all."

"And?"

"And despite everything, you've been wonderful to me," Kris said softly. "You *are* wonderful to me. I...I've seldom, if ever, told you how much I appreciate it. I've known you such a short time, David. But you really changed my life."

David's throat constricted dangerously as he struggled to choose the right words. "I hope," he said huskily, "that I've changed it for the better."

"You have," she answered. "You've taught me how to think more clearly and rationally about ... emotional issues."

"Believe me, Kris," he protested, "it wasn't my intention to teach you anything. I wouldn't be that presumptuous."

"I know you wouldn't," she agreed. "You're a very modest man. Maybe too unassuming. You downplay yourself and everything you do. Perhaps it goes back to when you had to face up to a broken marriage. You were probably rather unsure of yourself then. But now..."

"Hey, wait a minute," he broke in, his laugh unsteady. "Am I being psychoanalyzed? I thought that was my job."

"I'm only guessing," Kris said shyly.

"A lot of the time, the professionals are only guessing," David told her. "Educated guesses, maybe ... but often that's the best we can do. All in the hope of getting answers that'll open up ways to communicate and understand." Again he laughed. And the laugh was still shaky. "What are we?" he asked. "A couple of midnight philosophers?"

"It's as good a time as any."

"I suppose it is. So..."

"Yes?"

"I managed to take Evan aside before we left their house this evening. We're going to have breakfast together at a place near the base so I can talk to him privately."

"About Marianne?"

"No," David said reluctantly. "About your brother."

Kris had a sudden vision of Jay. Taller than she was, slender and with similar coloring. His hair had been a shade or two lighter. He'd been an affectionate, sensitive person. Vulnerable, in a way. Which was probably one of the reasons she'd felt so protective toward him.

She had protected him, she realized now. He'd become her responsibility after their parents were gone. When they were growing up, she'd tried to shield him from so much. Maybe that had been a mistake, though she'd only been trying to do her best for him. Still, maybe her protection had diminished his strength. Maybe it was why he hadn't been strong enough to cope with the stress of the service life he'd loved so much.

David said gently, "Kris?"

"What?" she asked nervously, so lost in thought that his voice startled her.

"There will come a time—there *has* to come a time—when it won't be like this whenever one of us mentions Jay's name. But for now," he went on, "there are going to be moments when I'll have to talk about him."

"I know," she murmured.

"And I know that doing so might be painful for you. Do you understand that hurting you is the last thing in the world I want to do?"

"Yes, I do," Kris said without hesitation.

"So...it's something we have to work our way through."

Kris clutched at the "we." She didn't want to lean on David. Yet she'd been fighting a solitary battle for so long. Now there was someone to fight the battle with . . .

"I meant it, David, when I told you I was willing to give up on this," she volunteered.

"You can't give up on it, Kris. We both know that. For your sake and for mine, the mystery of your brother's fate is something we have to unravel. Until we've gone as far as we can go, neither of us will feel truly at peace.

"But for that," David concluded, "I would never have left your house tonight."

DAVID HAD ASKED EVAN to meet him at seven-thirty at a restaurant off the base. It was on Route 12 about two miles over the town boundary that separated Groton from Gales Ferry.

He awakened early after a restless night's sleep, shaved and put on his uniform, then drove past the main gate a half hour before he had to rendezvous with Evan. The snow had stopped during the night and the roads had already been plowed. David kept on going past the restaurant, then turned off the highway toward the village of Gales Ferry. The local roads were snow-rutted and icy in patches, but navigable.

David marveled that, within a block from the main road, he'd moved from a metropolitan-suburban ambiance into a classic New England small town. Many, many years ago, a ferry operated by a man named Gales had traversed the Thames at this point. When a town grew up along the steep riverbank, the residents took his name.

White frame houses lined the quiet streets. Many of them had been meticulously restored into real show-places. The historical plaques adorning them showed dates in the 1820s through 1850s. Also, Harvard and Yale maintained boat houses here, David noticed. Come late spring, both would become beehives of activity as crews from the two Ivy League schools perpetuated their age-old rowing rivalry on the Thames. Right now, the buildings were empty and shuttered.

There were summer homes and cottages scattered among the year-round residences. One of these places, David mused, must have had significance—considerable significance—in Jay Sothern's life. Was there a chance, he wondered, that another officer in the psychiatric unit, someone who'd since been transferred, had owned a cottage here, a cottage that overlooked the Thames? Was there a chance that Jay had gotten their names mixed up?

It was possible...yet doubtful. David had been stationed in Groton for two and a half years. During that time, Jay had entered and completed submarine school, had gone to sea twice and had returned for shore duty and further study. The personnel at the clinic had undergone only minor changes—a few transfers, maybe a dozen new arrivals. David knew everyone. Most were career men who brought their families with them to Groton. It seemed unlikely that any of them would have simultaneously maintained another house along the Thames.

David felt moody and dejected as he drove back to Route 12. This spontaneous little excursion had only substantiated the difficulty of the task he faced—discovering the whereabouts of a mystery house and learning why his name had been dropped, with such disastrous results.

Evan was waiting at the restaurant. Was it his imagination, David wondered, or did Evan look considerably more strained than he had last night?

His greeting was cheery enough. Then, after they'd assured the waitress they wanted coffee before they ordered, Evan observed easily, "So...at the house yesterday, you sounded like you have something top secret on your mind."

"In a strange kind of way, it is."

"Okay, want to enlighten me?"

The waitress returned with their coffees then took their orders. The interruption nearly threw David off.

Finally, he said, "It concerns Kris Sothern."

Evan leaned back, grinning. "Somehow that doesn't surprise me, David. I suspected it might concern Kris. I couldn't help but notice the way she stole glances at you when she didn't think you were noticing. You did the same thing, you know."

"I did not."

Evan laughed. "Whatever," he said. "I like her. Of course, this will put an end to all the fun Marianne's been having trying to match you up with someone."

"Whoa! Wait a minute. It's not what you're thinking."

"Well, you *are* pretty taken with her, aren't you?"

"Right now, that's irrelevant," David stated ruefully. "We have a serious problem to work through before we can even consider a relationship."

"Oh?"

Again, the waitress arrived, this time with their breakfasts. And again, David mentally stumbled. For a minute, they ate in silence. Then Evan prompted, "Can you tell me what the problem is?"

David put down his fork and looked his friend in the eye. He said, "Kris came to see me at the base because she felt I was responsible for her brother's death."

"*What?*"

Carefully, David detailed his first meeting with Kris at the hospital and brought Evan up-to-date on everything he'd learned about the promising young submariner who had taken his own life. Evan sat back and listened without commenting. But when David reached in his pocket and drew forth a snapshot, he said, "I don't need to see that. I knew Jay Sothern, Dave, if that's what you want to know."

Dave exhaled sharply. "Whew!" he exclaimed.

"Didn't you think I'd know him?" Evan asked curiously.

"I *hoped* you'd remember him, but I wasn't sure."

"He killed himself last spring, didn't he?"

"Yes."

"Bud Lonborg wrote me about it," Evan said soberly.

"Commander Lonborg, one of the chaplains at the base?"

"Right." Evan nodded. "I'd spoken with him about Jay before I left for Holy Loch. Asked him to keep an eye on the boy from time to time. Obviously, it wasn't enough," he admitted sadly.

"Then you'd been counseling Jay?"

"He came to see me a few times," Evan said slowly. "He latched on to me only because I was assigned to the submarine school when he first arrived. As you know, there's a chaplain assigned to the school as well as to the hospital, in addition to those of us who hang our hats in the base chaplains' office.

"Anyway... Jay, as I remember, was not long out of high school when he came here. His parents died when he was quite young and he'd been brought up by an older sister." Evan paused. "That would be Kris, right?"

"Yes, that would be Kris."

"If I recall correctly, it was the first time they'd been separated. At that, the sister—Kris, that is—managed to get a job in New London and moved there so she could be closer to Jay."

"That's true, yes."

Evan frowned, then rubbed his forehead as if doing so might improve his memory. "I've seen thousands of submariners during my eight years in Groton," he recalled. "Hundreds during the past twenty-four months, both here and over at Holy Loch. Jay Sothern stands out in my mind for a number of reasons. Which doesn't mean that I'm totally clear about everything concerning him . . . especially at the beginning."

At the beginning of what? David wondered.

Evan continued, "My impression—and I hope I'm getting this straight—is that Jay was harboring some pretty heavy guilt feelings. He wanted to break away from his sister, so he joined the navy and volunteered for the submarine service. At the same time, he felt a strong sense of duty and obligation to her because she'd done so much for him. He loved her very much, I do remember him saying that. So the emotional dichotomy he was feeling made things quite tough for him. More so than he let on."

"Obviously," David concurred.

"I just hope I'm not mixing Jay up with one of the other submariners I've counseled."

"I think you're right on the money," David said quietly.

His feelings were in a turmoil. He could not possibly have analyzed himself just then and wouldn't have wanted anyone else to. Jay Sothern, until now, had been a somewhat one-dimensional figure to him despite the things Kris had said. Evan was fleshing him out, creating a portrait of someone real.

"I was concerned about Jay," Evan said abruptly.

"Concerned?" David echoed. "Why were you concerned?"

Evan was quiet for a moment, his expression pensive. Then he said, "Let's just say that Jay finally confirmed my hunch. Voluntarily...and in confidence. That confidence is something I can't break, Dave."

"Jay is *dead*, Evan."

"That doesn't alter the situation."

"Well, I'm sure you know you're about to drive me crazy," David muttered, exasperated. "This is the first lead I've had."

"Why do you call it a lead?"

"Because Jay Sothern's suicide is a mystery, and if anyone's going to solve that mystery, it's me. I'm not saying that out of conceit. I'm saying it out of duty. I want to know why Kris's brother killed himself and whether there was anything I could have done to prevent it. If you withhold information from me, Evan, you're creating a real stumbling block."

"*Withhold* information? Don't you think that's a bit strong? Keep in mind, Dave...the relationship between a chaplain and a person who comes to him with a problem is very much like the doctor-patient relationship. Things said are confidential. I wouldn't expect you to repeat the personal things your patients confide in you."

"Even if that patient had died and my knowledge could have a far-reaching effect on people who were still living, including yourself?"

"You'll have to answer that question yourself, Dave. If this was a patient of yours, would you tell me?"

"I don't know," David temporized.

"I think you do know. Anyway, let's say that I was sufficiently concerned about Jay to refer him to your office."

"You what!"

"I made an appointment for him with Cal DeMott. You remember Cal, don't you?"

"Of course I remember Cal," David snapped. "He was here when I arrived, left just a few months ago to start a private practice in San Francisco."

The idea came to him like a thunderous explosion. Perhaps Cal's files were still at the clinic! If they were, he could gain access to them. Perfectly legal, completely ethical. Still, he couldn't recall anything in Jay's records that even mentioned a session with Cal DeMott, let alone detailed what transpired.

"I knew Cal had finished his time in the service," Evan said.

"But do you know whether Jay ever kept the appointment you made for him?"

"Yes, he did. Cal phoned me about it."

David's anger was starting to steam. He knew there was no real justification for directing it at Evan. Evan was doing what he believed in, doing what he thought was right. Confidences were confidences, there was no arguing that. Chaplains, physicians, lawyers, reporters...they all followed codes of discretion, respected the privacy of their charges. Which was as it should be.

But damn it, there are exceptions! David cursed silently. *There are exceptions to every rule.*

He tried to be patient. "Evan, I think there's something here you're not seeing," he said.

"Yeah, our breakfasts are getting cold."

"Not funny, chaplain. Anyway, I've lost my appetite."

"Okay, Dave, what am I not seeing?"

"We're on the same side of the fence, that's what."

"I don't quite follow you."

David was finding it harder by the second to keep a rein on his exasperation. "I think it's pretty obvious," he said tersely. "You called Cal DeMott about Jay, instead of calling me. If you'd called me..."

"You were tied up with a patient when I dialed the clinic," Evan stated. "There was no other reason."

"All right. Cal was free, so you drew him. But it could have been me, don't you see?"

"What are you driving at, Dave?"

"If you had connected with me, I would have been the doctor whom Jay Sothern consulted."

"So?"

"So he would have been my patient, right?"

"In other words, you're asking me to reveal what Jay Sothern confided in me."

"Yes."

Evan shook his head. "I'm sorry, but I've already told you I can't do that."

"Damn it, Evan!" David thundered. He noticed two people at a nearby table glance around nervously, and lowered his voice. "If you could tell Cal what Jay told you, why can't you tell me?"

"Cal was acting in a professional capacity."

"And you think I'm not?" David glared at his friend. "You are without doubt the thickest, most stubborn individual I've ever met," he growled. "No wonder Marianne—" He halted his tongue a moment too late. Saw the glazed expression creep into Evan's light blue eyes. Felt Evan's hurt.

"She's been talking to you, hasn't she?"

David sighed heavily, not able to speak.

"Don't worry, I'm not going to ask you to breach confidence. But she *has* been talking to you, hasn't she?"

"Yes," David admitted.

Evan expelled a long deep breath and looked out the window. It was cloudy again, but peaceful and serene. Turning back to David, he said, "She wasn't asleep when I left this morning, but she pretended to be. That's the way it's been since I got home. There's not been a moment when we've really been alone together. Either it was preparations for Thanksgiving dinner, or the girls were around, or else she's headed off to bed before me and then pretended to be asleep. Well, this morning was the last time for that bit of acting. I'm going home when I leave here and have it out with her...whatever it may be."

"Look, Evan..."

"I'm not asking you anything," Evan said steadily. "Remember that, David, when I keep refusing to tell you the things Jay Sothern told me. You don't want to betray Marianne. I don't want to betray Jay. If that doesn't make sense to you, it should."

DAVID PUT IN A MISERABLE DAY, grayer than the weather. He kept thinking about Evan, wondering what was happening in the Phillips household. He and Evan had barely touched their breakfasts. Then they paid their checks and left in separate directions. It sickened David to think they might travel in separate directions for some time to come. If this morning's "discussion" had caused that much of a rift, he'd have to start repair work as quickly as possible. Evan's friendship meant too much to him to lose. Especially over such a complex issue.

On the other hand...Evan *had* infuriated him. He desperately wanted to piece together Jay's story. Evan, he was certain, could be of tremendous help. Yet he'd

Look what we've got for you:

Get 4 FREE full-length Harlequin Superromance® novels.

Plus
this handy
compact
manicure
set

Plus
a surprise
free gift

▼ **PLUS LOTS MORE! MAIL THIS CARD TODAY** ▼

Harlequin's Best-Ever "Get Acquainted" Offer

Yes, I'll try the Harlequin Reader Service under the terms outlined on the opposite page. Send me 4 free Harlequin Superromance® novels, a free compact manicure set and a free mystery gift.

134 CIH KA3F

PLACE STICKER
FOR 6 FREE GIFTS
HERE

NAME _____

ADDRESS _____ APT. _____

CITY _____

STATE _____ ZIP CODE _____

PRINTED IN U.S.A.

Don't forget...

...Return this card today to receive your 4 free books, free compact manicure set and free mystery gift.

...You will receive books before they're available in stores and at a discount off retail prices.

...No obligation. Keep only the books you want, cancel anytime.

No Postage
Necessary
If Mailed
In The
United States

BUSINESS REPLY CARD

First Class   Permit No. 717   Buffalo, NY

Postage will be paid by addressee

Harlequin Reader Service®

901 Fuhrmann Blvd.
P.O. Box 1867
Buffalo, NY 14240-9952

wrapped himself in a code of ethics that David considered hidebound, then refused to be budged.

David had consultations throughout the day and paused only for a makeshift lunch of coffee and a stale doughnut. Between appointments, his thoughts wandered from Kris to Evan to Jay to Marianne and back again. The college was closed for the holiday weekend, but Kris would be going back to work on Monday. Meantime, he wondered what she was doing with herself. A couple of times he got as far as reaching for the phone to call her, but inevitably at that moment another patient was ushered into his office.

By early afternoon, it started snowing again. It was nearly six when David left the clinic and walked across the base to the BOQ. Quite a few of the officers had taken leave over the holiday, and the building seemed empty.

It was no better in his suite. He glanced around the pleasantly furnished rooms and realized that almost nothing belonged to him. These were the navy's possessions, even to the towels and bed linens. He did have a few books scattered around, plus several stacks of magazines and medical journals. But there were no photographs, no personal bric-a-brac, nothing that gave a clue about the person—not the psychiatrist—who lived here.

He dropped ice cubes in a glass, splashed in a generous shot of bourbon and sank into an armchair. In less than six months he'd be out of the service. Afterward, wherever he went, he could buy a home to call his own. He could furnish it as he liked, indulge in whatever whimsies suited his fancy.

That rationalization didn't help much. For so many reasons, he felt overwhelmingly alone and thoroughly depressed. When the phone at his elbow rang, punctuating his morose mood, there was only one voice in the world he wanted to hear. And when Kris said, "David?" he felt flooded with relief.

KRIS HAD YEARNED to hear David's voice so badly she'd nearly called him at the clinic that afternoon. With difficulty, she managed to wait until she thought he'd be home, but the first couple of times she dialed his number there was no answer.

She wondered if maybe he'd left his office and gone out to be alone somewhere—a lounge or a movie, perhaps. She had the uncanny feeling that he'd had a rough day. Still, she kept trying to reach him while the snow fell steadily outside her windows. And it caught her off guard when he finally answered.

"I'm making corn chowder and biscuits, and I wanted to invite you over for dinner," she told him. "Now, though..."

"Well, if that isn't dangling bait under someone's nose and then snatching it away," David protested.

"It's the weather. The roads are going to be lousy again. I don't want to ask you to drive in this."

"I've driven in considerably worse. Anyway, I have new snow tires and a very sound vehicle."

"You mean... you want to come?"

"Very definitely, yes."

Kris scurried around her apartment getting ready for him. She slipped into an oversized lilac sweater and faded jeans. Then she put out a spicy dip and crackers and added two logs to the fire.

When David rang the doorbell, she counted slowly to ten to muster her composure. Even so, there were stars in her eyes when she went to open the front door. In fact, she'd never looked more beautiful.

As he gazed down at her, she knew she was making an impact. She also knew she was playing with fire, but she no longer wanted to snuff out this blaze that flared between them. Ever since last night, when she'd stood in her window and watched him drive off into the darkness, she'd known that. She'd wanted him terribly.

He stepped into her living room, moved into her heart. And for once Kris refused to let herself be led off on a guilt trip over Jay. This man standing before her was wonderful. He'd shown that to her in so many ways. He'd accepted accusations that easily could have invoked hostility instead of sympathy and compassion. He had involved himself in her problem to a most unnecessary extent. He was big in every sense of the word. Big physically, big intellectually, but so much bigger in character and understanding. In all the things that counted.

Like the capacity for love, Kris thought wondrously.

She suspected that David Jorgenson had been burned by his first marriage more than he was willing to admit. Still, his capacity for love had not diminished.

He gazed down at her longingly with those silvery eyes that had astonished her from the beginning. He held out his arms and she moved into his embrace. For a moment they held each other tenderly. Then Kris pressed herself against him and reached her hands over his shoulders. As one hand wandered through the smooth dark locks of his hair, the other nudged his face down close to hers.

She stood on her tiptoes, offering him her lips. And when he accepted her gift, the sparks that were flaring between them ignited instantly into flame.

David lifted Kris effortlessly in his arms and carried her to the couch. He lowered her onto the cushions with consummate gentleness, then bent over her and slowly undid the delicate pearl buttons that held her sweater shut. Each brought a new revelation. Though she was small, Kris was beautifully formed. Her breasts were proudly upthrust now, their creamy color a lovely contrast to the deep rose-red of her nipples.

David's hands paused only briefly in their seductive journey. Then he pushed the sweater off her shoulders and feasted his eyes on her satin-smooth body as though he'd uncovered a rare treasure. "My God, Kris, you're so beautiful!" he murmured, stunned.

He lay down next to her, still clothed. She saw the desire in his eyes. "Are you sure about this?" he asked huskily.

"Yes, David," she whispered back. "Yes, I'm sure."

He'd changed into jeans and a heavy wool shirt before he'd left the BOQ. Slowly, carefully, Kris unbuttoned his shirt, unfastened the button on his pants and urged him out of his clothes as her pulse pounded furiously.

He was incredibly attractive, she thought, incredibly masculine. Curly dark hair matted his chest. His waist tapered much more than she'd realized. His stomach was flat, his thighs muscular. And his manhood was magnificent, and fully aroused.

Acting on instinct rather than experience, Kris let her fingers trail the length of him then start back again. Here and there she paused significantly, especially when she heard him groan.

"There's a limit to temptation, you know," he warned. "And you're tempting me to the max!"

He took her roving hands and kissed each in turn. Then he nudged closer to her and started his own tactile explorations, invoking ecstasy in her such as she'd never known before. He gently removed her jeans and the lacy bikini panties she wore beneath. Then his mouth followed where his fingers had been, raining kisses upon her body. Slowly, subtly, he taught her the lessons of love she so desperately wanted to learn.

Soon they were caressing and kissing and touching together as their passions mounted. Then they surged past the point of no return and David entered her, became one with her in the ultimate of age-old ways. And as desire crested, exploded, then slowly and wonderfully ebbed, Kris knew David Jorgenson had become part of her forever... no matter what.

In the fireplace, a log sputtered. Embers showered out like molten gold. Kris gazed at them dreamily and thought they were like her love for David. Except her love for David would never die to ashes.

CHAPTER TEN

MORNING BROUGHT with it reality...sometimes the most difficult thing of all to face and accept. It was Saturday, but David had to spend a few hours at the clinic. Ned Wright, one of the psychologists on the staff, had several cases he wanted David to review, and David had agreed to meet him. The idea that he'd wake up on this particular Saturday in bed with Kris Sothern had never entered his mind.

He didn't want to move, let alone leave her apartment. It would be one thing if he could go to the clinic with the promise of returning by noon. But he knew from experience that this wouldn't happen. The "few hours" would stretch, as they always did. He'd be lucky to break away from the base by midafternoon.

He refused to let Kris get up and make breakfast for him. He kissed her tenderly, slipped out her door, and discovered that the snow had accumulated so much during the night the plows were still clearing the roads.

David's emotions were once again in a turmoil as he drove back to the base. He'd spent a fantasy night making love with Kris and sleeping with her nestled against his body. Then, frustrating as it was, he'd had to leave her.

At the BOQ, he quickly showered and donned his uniform, grabbed a cup of coffee at the deli and headed for his office. He was twenty minutes late meeting his colleague, but that didn't matter to Ned. What did matter was three of David's patients calling with problems. One man's anxiety David solved over the phone, but the other two patients he decided to see.

It was nearly four o'clock before David saw his last patient to the door. He immediately dialed Kris's number and was surprised when there was no answer. He waited fifteen minutes, then dialed again. The phone rang and rang.

The corpsman David called in to assist him stuck his head in the door. "Going to call it quits pretty soon, Commander?" he asked, obviously wanting to leave himself. He was an engaging young man, red-haired and freckle-faced. He was also quick to learn and sincerely interested in his work.

"Go ahead, Eric," Dave urged. "Don't wait for me. I have a couple of phone calls to make before I leave. Got a heavy Saturday-night date?" he added.

"I had a date this afternoon." Eric smiled. "Fortunately, she understands the fact that I don't always get out of here when I think I'm going to."

"Join the club," David kidded, and Eric laughed.

A minute later, he dialed Kris's apartment again. Still no answer. Glancing out the window, he watched the sun peek out between the clouds as it descended toward the Connecticut countryside. Soon dusk would come. The roads were surely cleared by now, but David felt Kris shouldn't be venturing out for too long in the cold weather. She was still weak, whether she knew it or not.

David thought of driving directly over to Granite Street, then decided to go back to the BOQ and change into his favorite flannel-lined chinos and a comfortable sweater. Before heading out, he'd call her one more time.

KRIS WALKED into her apartment at a quarter to five, juggling two shopping bags. The phone was ringing. She quickly set the bags on the floor and hurried to answer it, hoping it would be David.

"Where the hell have you been?" he demanded, tension making him edgy.

"Why, I went out to lunch and then did some Christmas shopping," she told him, too taken aback by his peremptory tone to be annoyed. "What's the matter?"

"I've been worried," David blurted. More calmly, he added, "With the roads icy and everything, I just wanted you to be safe at home."

"The roads weren't bad at all," Kris protested.

"Maybe not," he conceded. "But how come you decided to go shopping today? You're just getting over a serious infection. Your resistance is still low. So instead of taking it easy you go wandering around in stores that were probably overheated and filled with thousands of sniffling people."

He sounded so miffed she had to smile. It felt good having someone concerned about her. Nevertheless, she teased lightly, "Come on, David. I'm a lot stronger than you think. Where are you, anyway?"

"At the BOQ," he stated. "Look, Kris, there are a couple of things I need to talk to you about."

Things that involved Jay, she imagined, her heart sinking. More than ever, she wished Jay's tragedy didn't always come between them. Especially after last night...

Last night had been hers and David's alone. No sad memories or current distractions had intervened while they made love in front of the fire, then crawled sleepily into bed together, snuggling under her quilt. It had been a rare interlude, too good to last. To delve into the past would almost be like starting from square one, Kris lamented.

"Do you want to come over?" she asked dully.

"Well, your apartment is the best place to talk. Why don't I pick up some Chinese food on the way? We can zap it in your microwave if it gets cold."

"All right."

There was an awkward pause. Then David asked, "Did you go out to lunch by yourself?"

"Actually, no," she told him. "Marianne Phillips called me around ten this morning and said she was going Christmas shopping. She asked me to join her."

"That was nice of her."

"Yes, I thought so. She said she knew I'd been sick and imagined I might like to get out, especially if I didn't have to drive. With Christmas less than a month away, I agreed."

"I usually do my Christmas shopping on Christmas Eve," David confessed. "And get my cards out in time for Valentine Day! Anyway, how did Marianne look?"

"Tired. She was at the Navy Relief Office when she called me. I guess she'd gone in early to do some volunteer work. She said she spent all day yesterday there, too."

"Then Evan probably never got a chance to talk to her," David muttered to himself.

"Was Evan planning to talk to her, did you say?" Kris asked curiously.

"Yes, he was. After we had breakfast together, he went home specifically for that purpose. He must have missed her. She didn't say anything about it to you, did she?"

"Of course not, David. I mean, we barely know each other, so why would she confide in me?"

"Because you know me, that's why."

"Maybe," Kris admitted. "But when I asked her in for tea when she dropped me off, she said she had to get home because of the girls. She didn't mention Evan, now that I think about it. Kind of strange, don't you think?"

"Yes and no. What did she say about the girls?"

"Quite a bit, including the fact that she wants them both to go to Hawthorne."

"So I understand."

"She's a very concerned mother," Kris said. "I suppose mothers have to be concerned these days."

"Mothers have always been concerned because of the pressures that come with raising kids," David stated. "There's nothing new about the need to cope."

His tone of voice made Kris aware that David was on edge. After a moment, she ventured, "Did something go wrong for you today?"

"I don't know," David mumbled. "Oh, hell," he admitted sheepishly, "I guess I overreacted when you didn't answer your phone, that's all. Look, if I'm coming over to your place I'd better get started. I'm getting pretty hungry already, and the driving's apt to be slow. Christmas shoppers clogging the roads, you know?"

"Just get here in one piece," Kris told him.

After she hung up, Kris sat still for a while, lost in a small trance as she thought about David's concern for her. He'd sounded genuinely rattled because she hadn't been home when he called, and that baffled her. It felt... strange, being looked after and cared about. She was so accustomed to fending for herself that she couldn't quite get used to it.

As she changed into a pair of comfortable gray wool slacks and a matching oversize sweater, Kris mentally reviewed her day with Marianne Phillips. She'd been surprised when Marianne called her. Thanksgiving Day,

Marianne had certainly been cordial enough, but she'd said nothing about their getting together. Yet only two days had passed before she'd called. Probably, Kris suspected, Marianne wanted to escape not only from her house and the base, but from other navy wives!

They'd lunched in a tearoom in downtown New London. The place was crowded and noisy, not the best choice for conversation. Perhaps Marianne had selected it deliberately, Kris thought now, so she could have someone's company but not have to say very much.

They'd talked in snatches as they drove from one shopping area to the next. Marianne bought several beautiful sweaters and some exquisite lingerie for her daughters. A flannel nightgown and a lovely robe for Evan's mother, and some fashionable leisure clothes and beachwear for her own mother, who lived on the Gulf coast of Texas with her semiretired second husband. Thinking back on it, Kris realized that Marianne had not chosen a single gift for her husband.

As for herself . . . she'd picked out her first gift for David. It was a crazy gift—a handmade ceramic tableau featuring a psychiatrist in a white medical jacket sitting stoically behind a large desk surveying a patient who, to say the least, was wild-eyed and woolly-haired. The caption read, "Have you seen your shrink today?" Kris had chuckled aloud when she spotted it, and couldn't resist buying it though it was ridiculously expensive. The sculptor, the salesperson explained, was internationally famous, hence the high price tag.

She'd bought a few other things for old family friends back in Pennsylvania and tried not to dwell on how short her Christmas list was. For so many years, Jay had been the recipient of most of her gifts.

David arrived carrying a grocery bag full of the familiar little white cardboard cartons. As he set them out on the kitchen counter, he said, "I didn't stop to realize until I'd ordered this stuff that we ate Chinese food just the other day. Then it hit me. If you'd rather stash these things in your fridge for another time, I can go rustle up a couple of pizzas."

"It smells great," Kris assured him. "Would you like a drink first?"

"Sure, if you'll join me."

Kris made a strong bourbon and soda for David, a mild one for herself. Then they sat at opposite ends of the couch in front of the fireplace as if they'd made a pact not to get too close tonight.

David, watching the flames, observed, "It's started to snow again. Unusual, for this time of year. If this keeps up, we'll be in for quite a winter."

Kris had always thought that people talked about the weather when they didn't have anything else to say. But in David's case, she knew he was stalling. She was tempted to ask him straight out what it was he wanted to tell her. Something about Jay, she felt sure. Instead, she said, "You look like you had a rough day."

"I did," he admitted. "Maybe sometimes I'm not as objective as I should be. But I care about these people, damn it!"

"What happened?"

"Well, I went in to review a couple of cases with Ned Wright. Two, maybe three hours of work. Almost immediately, the phones started ringing. Normally, the corpsmen on duty would handle things, but since I was there...well, it became almost like a normal workday. Patients calling in for prescriptions, calling in to talk. This afternoon, I saw a veteran submariner, an officer who's spent his entire career in the submarine service. You'd think if any phobias were going to surface with him, they would have a long time ago. But it doesn't always work that way.''

David broke off and stared at the flames leaping up the fireplace bricks. Then he turned to Kris and said softly, "You don't know how good it is to see you, how wonderful it is to be here with you.''

"David . . .''

"I know, Kris . . . and don't worry. I'll keep my distance, if that's what you're worried about.''

"I'm not worried, David. It's just . . .''

"I know," he said again. "Last night was strictly for us. Tonight, I have a couple of things to tell you, a couple of things to ask.''

"Just as long as we understand each other," Kris said levelly, but she was trembling inside. She was reaching a point where she was afraid, terribly afraid, of finding out something she didn't want to know. If everything went full circle—if David's investigation revealed the whole story—what then? Suppose his intentions backfired and he ended up proving he really *had* been negligent in Jay's case? What would that do to them?

"Yesterday morning," he said slowly, "I told Evan that you were Jay Sothern's sister. You'd said that Jay mentioned Evan, isn't that right?''

"Yes . . . at least I think he did," Kris said hesitantly. She shook her head wearily. "Sometimes I think I'm beginning to get names mixed up.''

"I don't wonder," David told her. "And that's something we'll get back to later. Right now . . . you were right about Evan, Kris. Jay did see him, several times. He latched on to Evan because Evan had been the chaplain assigned to the submarine school when Jay first arrived."

Kris sat up straighter, conscious of a terrible feeling of dread creeping over her. It was like a cloud of impending doom darkening her personal sun, and there was nothing she could do to brush it away.

David leaned over and gently touched her cheek. "Darling," he said, "if this is too rough for you, let's wait for another time."

"No," she said firmly. "There can't be another time. You know that."

"I wish I didn't have to agree with you, but I do." He leaned back, surveying her unhappily. "Jay came to Evan after he'd done his first tour of duty aboard a sub. After talking with him, Evan felt he needed psychiatric counseling."

"Why?" Kris asked quickly. "Was he stressed out after living three months under the ocean in a submarine? Or was it something else having to do with the navy?"

"I don't know," David answered. "Evan wouldn't tell me any details. But from your brother's performance records, and from my own evaluation on him, it's clear he didn't have any problems with submarine life thus far."

Kris pondered that, then said, "What do you mean, Evan wouldn't tell you any details?"

She suddenly looked as miserable as he felt, David realized. "Well," he said, "it still irks the hell out of me, but Evan insists that your brother spoke to him in confidence . . . and he refused to tell me a thing."

"He refused to say what was bothering Jay? That confuses me, David. Why wouldn't he tell you, of all people?"

"Because in Evan's mind, it's a question of ethics. It's the relationship between a chaplain and someone who's come to him for advice, for help. Not unlike my relationship with my patients. Anyway...Evan eventually called the psychiatric unit and made an appointment for Jay."

"In your office?" Kris demanded incredulously. "When?"

"I'm not sure. Some time before he left for Holy Loch."

"And you still don't remember Jay?"

"The appointment wasn't with me, Kris. According to Evan, Jay was seen by a psychologist named Cal De-Mott. So far, I haven't found any record of the counseling on file. It certainly wasn't with the material I requisitioned before I met with you."

"Can't you ask Dr. DeMott about it?"

"I intend to," David assured her.

"Couldn't you have gotten in touch with him today?" Kris persisted.

"I tried. Cal DeMott got out of the navy a few months ago and started a private practice in San Francisco. I tried to reach him this afternoon, both at his office and at home. As luck would have it, he and his wife are vacationing in Australia and won't be back for at least another week."

"Dear God," Kris moaned helplessly. After a moment, she asked, "Do you suppose if I asked Evan Phillips, he might tell me what was bothering Jay? He's the one key we have, except for this psychologist."

"I know," David said soberly. "But I never realized until yesterday how stubborn Evan can be. I have to admit, I admire him. Obviously, he's a man you can trust with a secret...forever. In this case, I wish he'd break the rules. I practically caused a scene in the restaurant trying to get him to loosen up. Like I said, he wouldn't budge. You could try, but frankly I wish you'd wait."

"Why?"

"Well, for one thing, Evan's got his own problems right now. More important, Cal DeMott and I are on the same side of the fence, professionally speaking. I tried to tell Evan we're all in this together, but he wouldn't buy it. I'm sure when I talk to Cal, he'll tell me what went on as one colleague to another."

"You knew him, David?"

"I knew him fairly well, Kris. The clinic's not that big a place, and Cal was already stationed here when I arrived. He's a good guy."

"I suppose the only thing we can do is wait," Kris said reluctantly.

"Not entirely. The minute Cal gets back from Australia, I'll be on the phone with him. Meantime, there are other avenues I plan to explore. Before I get into that, however, there's something I want to ask you."

"Yes?"

"I realize the names of Jorgenson and DeMott don't sound at all alike. But do you think there's any chance you could have mixed up what Jay told you? Is there any chance he could have been referring to Cal, rather than me?"

Kris wished terribly that she could answer David's question affirmatively. Sadly, she could not. "No," she whispered, shaking her head.

"Well, then, let's take it a step further," David said, refusing to allow his mood to falter. "Did the name Cal DeMott ring any bells with you? Or Commander De Mott, perhaps?"

Again she shook her head and whispered, "No."

"Kris, don't take it so hard! We're only beginning, sweetheart. We're bound to turn down a few dead-end streets." He paused, then added, "Speaking of streets... Yesterday morning, before I met Evan for breakfast, I drove through Gales Ferry. It was a first for me. I hadn't realized till I checked the map that there really is a village of Gales Ferry. From the highway, you can't tell. Anyway, it's tucked away along the river, a typical little New England hamlet." David smiled wistfully. "I wish I *did* own a house there," he admitted.

"What did you expect to find?" Kris asked.

"To be honest, I didn't know. But I wonder if there's anything there that might have some meaning to you."

"How could there be? I've never been there."

"No, but maybe Jay told you something that you've forgotten. Not on purpose, Kris. Don't get me wrong. But...did he ever describe the house?"

Kris frowned, trying to remember. After a moment, she confessed, "You know something, David? I've gone blank."

"I don't wonder at that, either," David assured her. "But if you and I drove around the village together, perhaps you'd see something that would jog your memory. I know the chance of that happening is slim, but...what do you say?"

"I say I'm more than willing to try."

"Good! Now, suppose we tackle that food?"

Kris readily agreed. Not only was it time for a diversion, but suddenly she was starving. While David heated up their dinner in the microwave, she brewed a pot of jasmine tea and dug out two pairs of chopsticks she'd acquired somewhere along the way.

While they ate, David deliberately avoided talking about submarines, the navy and the Phillipses. He told

Kris about winters in Maine and about how he and his brother George had liked to go ice fishing in a secluded cave. Once he'd walked out on ice too thin, despite his brother's warning.

"It made this weird cracking noise for about fifteen seconds," he recalled. "It kind of echoed, and sounded so ominous I couldn't move. Before I knew what was happening, I was floundering around in ice water."

"My God!" Kris breathed. "How did you get out?"

"George ran for shore and got help. He had the sense to know that if he tried to rescue me by himself I'd probably pull him in. If that happened..."

Kris shivered, thinking about the consequences of what David was telling her.

"Luckily," he went on, "George spotted a couple of guys who'd just come down to do some ice fishing themselves. They had some rope in the back of their truck and tossed it out to me on the first try. By then, my hands were damned near frozen off. I didn't think I could hold on, but I did. They hauled me to safety and insisted on taking me to a hospital in the next town. I'd been in that frigid water seven or eight minutes, which is long enough to do considerable damage."

"I would think so," Kris agreed. "What happened?"

David laughed, remembering. "On the way to the hospital," he said, "George told me I'd probably have to have all my toes amputated. He had me convinced they were frozen. I was scared to death, believe me.

"Fortunately, he was wrong," David finished. "They gave me a good going over at the hospital, kept me wrapped up in an electric blanket till my body temperature was back to normal, then released me."

"You were lucky, David."

"I was at that," he nodded. "Now how about sharing that last egg roll with me?"

"No, you have it," Kris said shakily. She stared up at David, her brown eyes suspiciously moist, then turned away quickly.

"Hey, what is this?" he prodded gently.

"I...I'd like to meet your brother George, that's all," Kris managed. "I'd like to give him a huge hug and kiss for saving your life."

"Hmm," David reflected. "I think George would like that."

It only took a minute to wash their dishes and straighten up the kitchen, then David was putting another log on the fire and Kris was taking her seat on the couch. Everything in him yearned for a repeat of last night. He wanted, desperately, to make love to Kris again. Wanted to erase the haunted look that came into her eyes whenever they discussed Jay. Wanted to hold her in his arms and comfort her. But he knew this wasn't the night for those expressions of love. Maybe someday, but not tonight.

Kris knew it, too. She watched David settle into the opposite end of the couch, and she yearned to bridge the space between them. She wanted his arms around her, she wanted his mouth doing the wonderful things his mouth could do. But a little voice told her it would somehow be wrong tonight. And wouldn't be right until they knew what had happened to Jay.

If we ever do know, Kris thought abjectly.

As if he'd read her mind, David asked, "Did Jay ever mention anyone else by name? Any of his friends, or the men he served with?"

"Probably," Kris conceded. "But that's all a haze, David. I have to tell you . . . I think I deliberately tried to shut off a lot of memories after Jay died."

"Perhaps you succeeded more than you know."

"Perhaps. Still, Jay was sort of . . . shy. He really had to get to know someone well before he'd open up completely."

"When you were growing up in Lancaster, did he have any close friends?"

"We both had friends. But we ended up working so much neither of us had time for a social life."

David nodded understandably. Then he asked, "Did Jay ever have any girlfriends?"

"Well, there was a girl in high school I think he was smitten with," Kris remembered. "He took her to the movies a number of times and to the county fair in the summer. Elyse Gordon, her name was."

"Any girlfriends after he joined the navy?"

"Not really," Kris said. "He . . . he changed after submarine school."

"He grew up?" David suggested.

"Yes, but that's not what I mean. He was different, somehow. I never could put my finger on exactly how, but he was."

"Did he ever introduce you to any of his friends? Or bring anyone over here for dinner?"

"I asked him to, but he never got around to it."

"Hmm. He'd been on leave not long before he died, right?" David asked carefully.

"He went back to Pennsylvania, yes. And to New York City for a couple of days."

"To visit friends?"

"A cousin we have near Lancaster. In New York, I'm not sure."

"Forgive me for pressing you, Kris. But . . . might Jay have touched bases with any of the people he'd gone to high school with? That girl, perhaps?"

"I don't know. He never said. All I know is that once he was assigned to sea duty he was living an on-off life. Three months at sea, three months ashore, occasional leaves. There wasn't much time for developing new friendships."

"Only with the other guys in his group," David agreed.

"Whatever." Kris nodded wearily.

She'd done remarkably well, David thought. So much better than when they'd first met. If only they'd stumble upon some clue that would solve their dilemma and permit their budding love to flower.

"How about riding over to Gales Ferry tomorrow?" he asked her. And was satisfied when she nodded.

CHAPTER ELEVEN

SUNDAY WAS SUNNY and cold. David picked Kris up at eleven o'clock. He had called her half an hour earlier and warned her to bundle up, which she'd thought touching and amusing. Still, she dressed accordingly in a beige wool pantsuit and a thick cranberry-colored sweater topped with a full-length ivory parka. Better safe than sorry, she decided, heeding the old adage.

As they crossed the bridge over the river, David said, "I knew Evan was preaching the nine o'clock service at the chapel on the Thames, so I went. I was curious about what his sermon subject might be."

"Well, what was it about?" Kris asked.

"Relationships," David stated simply.

"What about relationships?"

"He discussed the way relationships—love relationships, that is—seldom if ever remain static," David told her. "They constantly change, with healthy changes leading to positive growth for each individual as well as the couple. Ideally the people involved should keep pace with each other through patience, understanding and support. Needless to say, the lines of communication must run very deep and always remain open. It's when they don't, that problems arise."

"Was he speaking about Marianne and himself?"

"I don't know. It depends on whether he prepared the sermon before or after our breakfast the other morning.

Unfortunately, he guessed that Marianne had been talking to me.''

"Was Marianne at the chapel?"

"No, she wasn't," David said. He shook his head sadly. "Damn it, I wish she'd heard Evan preach. I wish she could have forced herself to listen to him as a chaplain, not as her husband. I know that's a lot to expect, given the circumstances, but still..."

"Did you talk with him?" Kris asked.

"I tried to catch up with him after the service was over, but it was impossible. This was the first time he's preached since getting back from Holy Loch, and the chapel was crowded. He's always been popular with everyone who attends the Sunday service. Afterward, he was surrounded. I couldn't get anywhere near him."

"That's too bad."

"Yes, it is," David agreed. "Unfortunately, we didn't part on the best of terms the other morning. His obstinate attitude really got to me, and I told him so."

"Evan's friendship is very important to you, isn't it?"

"Yes, it is."

"I'd hate to think I've jeopardized it," Kris said softly.

David slanted a surprised glance in her direction. "Why should you think that?" he demanded. "You have nothing to do with what's happening between Evan and me."

"No? Well . . . Jay does."

"That's not so, Kris. It was the principle that annoyed me, not the individuals involved. I thought Evan was being unreasonably stiff-necked. No matter who we'd been talking about, I would have felt the same way."

Kris fell silent. She knew David was being honest with her, yet she couldn't help but feel that she'd been a catalyst in this disagreement with his best friend. The whole situation was getting more complicated and frustrating each day, it seemed.

As they drove past the submarine base, Kris felt that painful little twinge she always felt when she was anywhere near the place. Going to the Phillipses' for Thanksgiving dinner had been particularly tough. She'd tried to camouflage her anxiety as David drove through the main gate then headed across the very heart of the extensive naval complex. She wondered if she'd fooled him, and somehow doubted it.

"Want to stop for a cup of coffee?" he asked suddenly.

"Maybe later, unless you want to."

"I'm fine until lunch," he said.

He sounded tense, Kris realized. As if he wanted to get to Gales Ferry and get this step of their investigation over with as quickly as possible. There were certainly better ways to spend a Sunday, she thought ruefully, than chasing painful ghosts. Much better ways.

After four or five miles, David swung off Route 12 and drove down into the village. "Gales Ferry," he said.

Kris leaned forward and scanned every house and cottage they passed. Since she'd awakened this morning, she'd deliberately tried to think back to her last conversation with Jay—something she'd always avoided before. She'd tried to piece together words, tried to remember if he'd said anything specific—anything at all—about the house on the river.

The roofs of the houses were blotched with snow and ice. Blankets of clean white snow smoothed out the landscape, hid bushes and lawns, spilled into the narrow streets. Snow rimed the bare branches of the oaks, elms and maples. Snow was everywhere, sparkling in the sun.

On one buried lawn, a group of children was making a snowman, taking delight in nature's winter gift. Their excited shouts echoed in the crisp air even with the car windows closed. In front of another house, a man was stringing Christmas lights along the eaves. Here and there, wreaths with huge red bows decorated front doors. The holiday preparations were lovely, but still they saddened Kris because of Jay. Selfish, she scolded herself, but true.

She glanced at David and wondered what he planned to do for Christmas. Visit his brother in Maine, maybe? Travel to Florida and see his mother? At least he still had family to share special times with. And good friends like the Phillipses.

Stop it! Kris warned herself. *Stop feeling bitter!*

David turned down a street that ended at the river and stopped at the edge of an icy boat ramp. Turning to Kris, he asked, "Nothing rings a bell, does it?"

"So far, no," she admitted. "I've been trying, though."

"Maybe you've been trying too hard," he decided. "Straining to remember something can create quite a mental block, you know."

"Tell me about it."

David smiled encouragingly. "If you could just relax, Kris, and let impressions take over..."

"It's not that simple, David."

"I know, darling," he murmured.

For a moment they stared out across the Thames, then David carefully turned around and started back up the street toward the center of town. He drove past the Yale boat house, then turned up a steep street that ran along the riverbank.

Suddenly Kris said, "He mentioned steps, David. Steps that led down to the water." She nodded thoughtfully. "That's it, they were having a cookout...and the grill was down by the water. I remember now. Jay said they had to carry everything down the steps. I think he meant it was quite a haul."

As she spoke, Kris scanned the houses they were passing. Houses that would all have steps down to the river. "Oh, God," she moaned, "it must have been one of these places, David. They fit the description perfectly."

"It certainly sounds like this might be the place Jay was referring to," he agreed. "Though there were any number of waterfront places in the village, too."

"But they wouldn't have a long flight of steps. They were right on the water, for the most part."

"True."

Kris turned to him, her face plagued with uncertainty. "Are we whistling in the dark?" she wondered aloud.

David reflected for a moment, then said, "I don't think so, Kris. I see this as a puzzle we have to put together, and you've just discovered what could be a significant piece. It's sketchy right now, I admit. But later on this might bring the whole picture together."

The road narrowed into a dirt lane and finally ended at a private doorway. David, surveying the icy ruts and the snowbanks hemming them in on both sides, said grimly, "Let's just hope we don't get stuck."

They didn't. As he carefully turned the car around and started back in the direction of Route 12, Kris realized he handled difficult driving situations the same way he handled most everything else—patiently, competently, considering each move in advance. She suspected his training was partially responsible for that, while part of it was his nature. On the other hand, as she knew only too well, he could be surprisingly impetuous.

Once on the highway, David asked, "Would you like to have lunch at the officers club with me?"

"On the base?" Kris gasped.

"It's okay," he said quickly. "It was just an idea, that's all. I thought it might be something a little different for you. But if you'd rather not go there, we'll find someplace else."

"You mean if I'm not ready to handle it, right? That's what you're saying, isn't it?" Kris demanded.

Briefly, his eyebrows arched, but that was the only indication he gave of his surprise. Calmly, he said, "I wouldn't have put it exactly that way, but I suppose I did mean that in essence. But it's no problem, Kris. Really, it's not a problem."

Perhaps she imagined the indulgence in his tone. Perhaps he was merely being understanding and she should appreciate it. Whichever, she didn't.

"Damn it, David!" she glared. "Stop treating me like I'm one of your patients, will you? And a backward one, at that. You should know that I can't stand condescension!"

Without answering her, David pulled into a shopping plaza they were passing and parked. Kris saw the hurt in his eyes as he turned to face her, and could have kicked herself.

He said tightly, "If you're implying that I'm condescending with my patients, I resent that. I don't think I've ever in my life deliberately talked down to anyone. Regardless of that, it wasn't my intention to treat you like a patient. If I thought you needed to see a psychiatrist, I'd tell you so. But I certainly wouldn't take your case myself."

"Why not?"

"Because you're too close to me, that's why," David stated bleakly. "Because I care about you too much. I couldn't possibly be objective with you, Kris. I'd have to refer you to someone who wouldn't forget what he was doing every time he looked at you."

"You really forget what you're doing every time you look at me?" Kris murmured.

"Let's just say I have a hell of a time trying to concentrate," David told her. "I look at those soft brown eyes of yours, your tilted little nose, your cheeks, your chin, your mouth...and I want to kiss you, I want to make love to you. Fortunately, I'm capable of restraining my desires or I'd be breaking down your door every night, looking for love."

Kris stared at him, unable to speak.

"It's not just a question of sex, you know!" The words exploded from David as if they'd been kept under pressure and suddenly the pressure gauge had burst. "That first day you walked into the hospital, I took one look at you and I don't know what the hell happened. But something certainly did. I couldn't believe it. After all, I knew full well why you'd come to see me. I had no doubt you considered me first cousin to a murderer."

"David!"

"Well, it's true, isn't it?" he demanded mirthlessly. "As soon as you agreed to have dinner with me, I knew I was making a mistake. I wanted a date with you, not a dialogue about a tragedy I had nothing to do with. When I tried to talk to you, I could see you disbelieved me. But by then it was already too late. There was no way I could keep myself from seeing you again."

"David, please."

He laughed bitterly. "I asked myself a thousand times why I felt so compelled to prove my innocence to you. Especially when I wasn't guilty of a damned thing! Finally, I admitted that it had only to do with you. I knew that until I discovered what really happened to your brother, there'd never be a chance for us."

"Please," Kris murmured brokenly. "You're making me feel like an ogre. I didn't have a choice, don't you see? Jay was my only brother. He was my family. He was incredibly hard to lose."

David expelled a deep sigh, and Kris thought he'd never looked more forlorn.

"I know," he said gently. "I know. And I admit that I've tried to protect you, but from what...I have no idea. I'll tell you this, though. It's had nothing to do with my profession. I...I just truly care for you, that's all. When you were sick, I guess I acted like a frustrated nursemaid. But you looked so small, so damned fragile..."

At that, Kris sat up straight and squared her shoulders. "I am *not* fragile," she said defiantly. "Maybe I look that way, but I'm not. I'm a lot stronger than most people think. Don't you know appearances can be deceiving?"

David stared across at her, then his mouth twisted into a wry smile. "Do tell," he observed.

"I'm serious, David."

"Yes, I know you are. So from now on in, watch what you accuse me of, okay?"

"I didn't mean to accuse you of anything."

"Good. I'm glad we got that settled. Now, do you suppose we could find a nice place for brunch? This stimulating discussion we've been having has given me quite an appetite."

"The officers club would be fine," Kris managed.

David pulled out into traffic again, then said, "Sweetheart, you don't have to prove anything to me, you know."

"I wasn't trying to."

"You don't have to worry about pleasing me, either. I'm happy just to be with you. That's all the pleasure I want."

Tears stung Kris's eyes when she heard that. She said, "It pleases me just to be with you, too."

"Is that true, darling?"

"Don't you know it?"

"I hope I know it," David told her huskily. "We haven't exactly had easy sledding thus far, you and I."

"I guess not," she agreed. "But how could we have?"

David didn't answer, and Kris knew that he, too, was thinking of Jay. Determined to ward off the dark cloud of Jay's memory, she asked, "When did you say Dr. DeMott is due back from Australia?"

"Not for at least another week. But don't worry, I'm not going to wait that long to start things moving."

"What can you do?"

"Well, I can try locating some of the other young men Jay served with. Guys in his class at the submarine school. Sooner or later, someone's bound to offer us a clue."

"Sooner or later, someone has to," Kris concurred.

DAVID CHOSE THE LIGHTHOUSE INN in New London for their brunch. The old stucco and stone structure was a block from Long Island Sound and dated back to the early years of the present century. Once it had been the mansion of a wealthy industrialist. The spacious, high-ceilinged rooms with their rich wall panelings and Victorian furnishings reflected a somber but far more gracious era.

They were ushered to a window table in the dining room, where the view of the sound was spectacular. David suggested mimosas and Kris agreed. Just now, the sparkling blend of champagne and orange juice would taste perfect.

After placing their drink order with the waiter, they made their way along the buffet, easily filling their plates from an incredible assortment of foods. When they were seated again, David raised his stemmed glass in a silent toast, and Kris toasted him back with her eyes.

It was a wonderful meal in a beautiful, relaxed setting. Kris couldn't remember when she'd eaten so much, and knew that David was pleased. He'd said so often that she needed calories. Well, today she'd done something about that!

It was nearly three o'clock before they left. Inside his car, David asked, "Want to take in a movie?"

"I haven't been to the movies in ages."

"Great, neither have I."

He took her to a hilarious comedy that everyone—critics included—was raving about. He couldn't have made a better choice. Kris rocked with laughter until she thought she'd literally die laughing, all the while picking away at the enormous bucket of popcorn David insisted on buying.

It was dark and chilly when they left the theater, though it was not yet six o'clock. "Would you like to stop somewhere for supper?" David asked.

Kris stopped in her tracks and stared up at him. "We've been eating all day!" she protested.

"Not exactly."

"Well, near enough. That huge buffet, then all the popcorn. You can't actually be hungry?"

David shrugged and said, "Okay, how about stopping for a drink at the lounge we went to Thanksgiving night?"

He was stalling taking her home, Kris knew. Delaying the moment when they'd have to say good-night. She didn't want to call it an evening any more than he did. Yet she hesitated to ask him back to her apartment. The mood just wasn't right. It wasn't a question of wanting David—Kris wanted him so badly she physically ached. She just didn't feel free to make love. A little voice said no.

"Just one drink?" she asked.

"Just one," David agreed.

The lounge, such a quiet oasis on Thanksgiving night, was crowded this evening. The booths were all full, so they were placed at a tiny table. It was much too small a space for David and people kept bumping into the back of his chair.

At the house on Granite Street, he walked Kris as far as the porch steps, then stopped. "I think this is about as far as I'd better go," he said.

Inwardly, Kris groaned. Her feelings were hopelessly ambivalent. She wanted to invite him in, yet she knew it wouldn't be the wise thing to do. It would be impossible to restrain their feelings, once they were alone.

David solved her dilemma by kissing her gently on the cheek. "It's okay," he said softly. "I understand."

Those were kind words. But they didn't stop a chasm from forming in Kris's heart once he'd left.

DAVID SUMMONED ERIC BENSON to his office shortly after he arrived at the clinic the following morning. "I've asked for another corpsman to be sent down from the hospital to relieve you for the next couple of days.''

Eric looked alarmed. "Have I goofed on something, sir?'' he asked.

"Not at all, Eric. I have a special job I want you to do for me.''

David had awakened at intervals at night, longing for Kris. At three in the morning, he got out of bed and made himself a snack. While he munched, he thought out a course of action. With the arrival of dawn, it still seemed the most valid plan he could think of.

The look of relief on the redheaded corpsman's face was almost comical, and David smiled to keep from laughing. "When did you come here, Eric?'' he asked.

"Last May, sir. May fifteenth, to be exact.''

"I don't suppose you knew Jay Sothern?'' It was a shot in the dark, a target that David had no expectation of hitting.

"Jay Sothern?'' Eric mused. "Well, sir. . . the name sort of strikes a chord, but I can't place the person.''

"Jay Sothern was a young submariner who died not too long before you arrived here. He committed suicide. It made quite a stir, so perhaps that's where you heard the name.''

Eric nodded. "That's it, sir,'' he said. "When I got here the guys were still talking about it. I had a roommate, another corpsman, who knew Jay Sothern. He was really shaken up about it. I think three weeks had passed, but you would have thought it happened yesterday, the way Gary talked.''

David discovered he was holding his breath. He also discovered that hope could be like a wasp sting, quick and sharp. He asked carefully, "Do you still have the same roommate?''

"Gary? No, sir. He shipped out early in the summer."

"Where to?"

"He did a tour aboard a sub. Now he's assigned to the naval hospital at Newport."

Only a couple of hours up the road, David thought instantly. Masking his excitement, he asked, "What's his last name, Eric?"

"Blake, sir."

"Blake. Ah, I remember him. Tall, thin, dark-haired?"

"That's right."

"You've kept in touch with him?"

"Not on a regular basis, sir. I've talked with him on the phone a few times, but that's about it."

"You think he knew Jay Sothern fairly well?"

"I couldn't say, sir," Eric said. "Actually, I'm not sure he really knew him at all. Gary was working for Commander DeMott when it happened, I think."

"So he was," David recalled. Which meant that he would have filed DeMott's records, among other duties. "Okay, Eric . . . step one. I want you to search the files thoroughly and bring me anything you find that relates to Jay Sothern."

The young corpsman looked faintly puzzled by this request, but said only, "I'll get right at it, sir."

"One other thing. Can you remember anyone else ever mentioning Jay Sothern?"

"Well, there was general talk, sir. After all, it's pretty heavy stuff when something like that happens."

"But Gary was the only person you know who'd had any direct connection with Sothern?"

"Yes, Commander."

David nodded and dismissed him. A few minutes later his first patient walked into his office and after that it was consultation after consultation for the rest of the day. It was past five when the last patient left. Almost at once, Eric knocked on David's office door.

"Got a moment, sir?" he asked.

"Of course," David said quickly. "Did you find anything on Jay Sothern?"

Eric shook his head. "I've gone through every file in the place, sir. But I've drawn a complete blank on Sothern. We have nothing on him."

"Nothing?"

"Nothing."

David should have known better, but his disappointment was intense. "You're sure you didn't miss anything, Eric?"

"Yes, sir. I checked everything twice."

"Okay. Call it a day. We'll get onto something else in the morning."

Alone in his office, David stared reflectively at a large, framed color photograph of a submarine, which hung on the opposite wall. He knew from Evan Phillips that Jay had been referred to Cal DeMott and that he'd kept an appointment. Even if Cal only had one consultation with the young man, there should be a record of it. Official clinic records simply didn't vanish into thin air.

He'd been keeping the material he'd originally requisitioned on Jay in his bottom desk drawer under lock and key. He didn't know why he felt the need for security measures. Probably there was no good reason. But instinct warned him not to take chances. It was relatively easy to mislay records, misfile them, or even lose them in transport. Especially in an office where people constantly came and went.

David hadn't opened the files since that first meeting with Kris. There'd been no reason to. Before the meeting, he'd read them thoroughly. There was nothing exceptional, in the negative sense, about any aspect of Jay's performance as a submariner. Absolutely no clue indicating he was, or would become, suicidal.

Now David got the files out and went over them again, making notations as he went along. He jotted down the date of Jay's admission to the submarine school, then went back to earlier records and meticulously read over everything concerning Jay's basic training in navy boot camp.

During that time, Jay had been given a variety of tests—physical, psychological and aptitude tests—to ascertain any special skills he might possess. From day one, there had been no doubt in Jay's mind about which branch of the navy he wanted to be part of. As Kris had bitterly mentioned, her brother had always wanted to be a submariner.

Jay had done well in the testing, right across the board. In the initial psychological tests, nothing had surfaced that would indicate he was unable to handle major stress. In fact, his results proved exactly the opposite. The instructors and physicians who'd examined him noted individually and collectively that Jay was a well-coordinated young man who reacted within normal ranges to the stress tests given him. He had a natural aptitude for electronics and undoubtedly could do very well aboard a nuclear submarine.

Because so many aspects of the submarine service are highly classified, Jay's background had been carefully screened by various government agencies. There'd even been an interview with Kris and a thorough probe of the Sotherns' family history. David knew that these probes delved into everything from habits, hobbies and friends to genealogy going back as far as practicable. Even the distant cousin in Lancaster Kris had mentioned had been interviewed, as well as several people Jay had worked for during his school years.

Jay Sothern had emerged with a very clean slate.

Thinking this, David got out the box of photographs Kris had given him. He'd locked them away, too, and hadn't so much as peeked at a single shot since that brief perusal when he first got them. Somehow they'd taken on the aspect of something personal, something he wanted to respect. Now he had time to look more closely. And not surprisingly, it hurt…because he knew how much this smiling young man had meant to Kris.

There was a family resemblance, slight but there. David thought of Kris being called down to the New London morgue to identify her brother and a wave of sorrow swept over him. What an awful thing to face all alone.

Impulsively, he reached for the phone and dialed her number. When, after four rings, she answered, she sounded completely breathless.

"Did I interrupt something?" he asked.

"No, no. I was just about to jump in a bubble bath, that's all."

"Then maybe I'd better let you go. The bubbles will dissolve, won't they?" He tried not to think too much about Kris stepping into a tub full of warm water, or the fragrant bubbles cascading over her wet, pearl-toned skin.

"I'll just add more bath gel if they do," Kris quipped.

"Of course, how stupid of me."

There was a pause. Then Kris asked, "David, where are you?"

"At the clinic."

"Aren't you working kind of late?"

"I've been trying to catch up on a few things," he said evasively.

"What are you going to do now?"

"I guess I'll head over to the BOQ and grab a bite to eat. We've got a lounge and a deli in the building. The Nautilus, it's called. I can get a pizza and beer there. What about you? What are you doing tonight?"

"I'm going to heat up some soup and watch television while I hem a couple of skirts," Kris said.

"How domestic."

"Well, you have to get around to things like that sometime."

"I suppose so." Again there was a pause. Then David said, "I should do some Christmas shopping for my mother and my aunt. Do you think you could help me out?"

"Shopping, you mean?"

"Yes, shopping. I never know what to buy for women."

"I'll bet." Kris laughed.

"Seriously, why don't we go for an early dinner tomorrow night, then hit a few stores?"

"Why not?" she agreed.

"Terrific, I'll call you at noon. And Kris?"

"Yes?"

"Thank you."

"I'll see you tomorrow," she told him.

As he hung up the phone, David felt profoundly relieved knowing he'd be seeing her again. At the same time, he wondered how many more ruses he could invent to ask Kris out. Funny, though, in this case, it was true. He really did run into problems selecting gifts for his mother and his aunt.

If it was Kris he was shopping for...

David closed his eyes and dreamed. He could think of thousands of gifts he'd like to shower upon Kris.

CHAPTER TWELVE

SANTAS ON STREET CORNERS were ringing holiday bells. Stores were festooned with twinkling lights. Display windows featured dazzling assortments of gifts. There was still enough snow on the ground to create Christmas-card scenes at every turn, and the clear night sky was dotted with thousands of glittering celestial ornaments.

Kris was wearing a bright red knitted wool cloche pulled down over her ears and a matching scarf that dangled to her knees. Her cheeks were flushed from the nippy air, and also from the contagious atmosphere of the approaching holiday. She and David walked from store to store, surveying the window merchandise so he could get a few ideas before he actually began shopping.

Kris spotted some notepaper printed with coastal New England scenes and decided to buy a few packages for her co-workers at the college. She went inside the shop assuming that David was following her, but when she turned around, he was gone. David, who towered over most people, would be easy to spot. Now, he was nowhere to be seen.

She was at the sales counter making her purchases when he tapped her on the shoulder. ''Well,'' she said, ''where did you disappear to?''

''Nowhere,'' he replied innocently.

He looked guilty, Kris noted . . . and very boyish. The combination was puzzling and amusing, and she nearly teased him about it. Then she decided to hold her tongue and keep a closer eye on him.

They ended up at one of New London's newest and most attractive shopping centers. Very quickly, they came upon a woman's specialty shop that featured a large selection of cruise wear.

Surveying it, David quipped, "I always find it ironic that these boutiques are selling that stuff when it's about twenty degrees outside. Does everyone in New England except me flee south for the winter?"

"Maybe you could find something for your mother in there," Kris suggested. "Want to investigate by yourself?"

"Wait a second," he growled. "What do you think I brought you along for?"

He grabbed Kris's elbow so she wouldn't get away and steered her into the shop. Then he tried to give the salesgirl an idea of his mother's size by doing graphic hand demonstrations that had Kris laughing out loud. Finally he decided—prompted by a nudge from Kris—on two light cotton designer sweaters in luscious pastel shades, plus a colourful terry-cloth beach robe. He added a striking fabric handbag, explaining, "She has this habit of toting around half the stuff she owns."

"Doesn't everyone?" Kris queried, and smiled coyly when David shot her a suspicious glance.

"Any other ideas, Miss Sothern?" he asked.

"Well, what about perfume?"

"Maybe so." He nodded. "I might as well get a few things for my aunt, too, now that I'm in the mood."

Kris watched as he sniffed a variety of scents, analyzing each one very carefully. Finally he selected several bottles of entirely different character. "My mother and

her sister are contrasting personality types,'' he explained. ''But these should do just fine.''

''You're doing great,'' she told him encouragingly.

As David followed the salesgirl to the cash register, Kris
smiled at him with undisguised admiration. She had
never in her life known anyone like him. His caring was
underscored by the way he took his time in selecting gifts
for two older women whom he rarely saw. So many people did things out of a sense of duty, Kris mused, did
things because they thought they were required to. Not
David. He truly acted on instructions from the heart.

In another shop, he chose a handsome plaid wool
jacket and a pair of fur-lined gloves for his brother
George. ''You can never own enough warm clothing in
Maine during the winter,'' he informed Kris seriously.
''Especially where George lives.''

As his purchases were being gift wrapped, Kris asked
casually, ''Will you be going up there for Christmas?''
She'd wondered about this more and more of late, and
didn't relish the idea at all.

''No, I won't,'' he answered. ''As a matter of fact,
George is flying down to Florida to spend Christmas with
Mom.''

''Oh.'' She waited for David to tell her that he'd be
flying down to Florida, also, but he didn't. Then the
presents were finished and the moment passed.

Next, they searched the gifts for the Phillipses. David
decided that he'd better buy separate presents for Evan
and Marianne this year, as there was no telling how much
longer they'd be together. ''The past two Christmases
I've given them things for the house,'' he told Kris. ''An
ice-cream maker, an espresso maker, things like that. This
year...'' He shook his head sadly, then picked out perfume for Marianne, a magnificent book on the Himala-

yas for Evan, earrings for Patricia and a bracelet for
Deborah.

David's list of people to get presents for was not extensive, Kris realized. But the few purchases she'd made
seemed paltry in comparison. With Jay gone...

She'd always loaded Jay with gifts, but she'd never
really stopped to think why. She'd loved him dearly, of
course. But deep down inside she wondered if there were
other reasons. Reasons someone in David's profession
would recognize and be able to explain.

Had she looked out for Jay too much all those years
they lived together? The thought was incomprehensible,
and yet...why had Jay seemed so shy, so vulnerable?
Overprotection might cause that, Kris thought dismally.
Overprotection could lead to a lot of things. Was that
why Jay had been unable to face the pressures and demands of life? Could it have been something she'd done?

But he was all I had.

Kris silently expressed that thought for perhaps the
thousandth time, and something struck deep within her
conscience. Suddenly, for the first time, she saw selfish-
ness in the way she'd conducted her life. She saw the
taking outweighing the giving. Very tough to see, but
definitely there. She had made herself something of a
martyr for Jay. Willfully orchestrated their lives so that
he'd always have her to turn to, but no one else.

At the same time, she'd never seen the world in terms
of a challenge each of them had to accept individually. It
was always she and Jay...together. He'd joined the navy,
and what had she done? She'd moved to New London
within the year. Set up a new life only a few miles away.
She'd denied herself the chance to get out in the world
and live a life all her own.

All because our parents were gone? Kris wondered. *All because I had no one else to lean on?*

Maybe Jay hadn't been the weaker Sothern child. Maybe she'd taken refuge in her younger brother, hidden behind the responsibility of raising and caring for him. Kris had never before thought of herself as selfish. She was willing to admit her faults. But selfish? The idea shocked her.

Close beside her, David asked gently, "Kris, what's happened to you? All of a sudden, you've left me. There were stars in your eyes only a minute ago. What snuffed them out?"

"I was thinking, that's all," she said, evading the question.

"Then please don't think anymore tonight, okay? I want you with me. It's a beautiful night; let's enjoy it." He took her hand in his and added, "Have you had enough of shopping? Am I tiring you out? I can finish this up some other time, you know. There are plenty of other nights. As it is, I can't believe what we've accomplished. I've never been in such great shape, giftwise, with so much time to go."

Other nights? So much time to go? There was no one else Kris wanted to buy presents for... except David. So far, the only thing she'd bought for him was the ceramic shrink, a gift deliberately meant to be funny. But this time she wanted to find something very special, something that would make him remember her forever, long after they'd gone their separate ways.

It hurt to think about their going separate ways. But on that score, Kris had no illusions. David would be finished with his commitment to the navy late next spring. He'd probably be leaving Groton not long after that. She'd be leaving by then herself. She planned to tell

Hawthorne, right after Christmas vacation, that she wouldn't be staying on. There were simply too many memories that would come to haunt her, come to tear her apart. Memories were the last thing she wished to dwell on, the last thing she wanted controlling her life.

"You're doing it again," David accused. "You're drawing away from me. Hey, I've got an idea."

"What's that?"

"I happen to know a great ice-cream shop not far from here. Let's go get a banana split!"

Kris looked up at him and shook her head. But she was smiling as she said, "I don't believe you. You, a doctor, suggesting that we partake of ice cream when it's freezing out?"

"Am I missing something here?" David countered. "It is my qualified opinion that you've completely recovered from your throat infection."

"Maybe, but what about the calories?"

David looked Kris over with mock appraisal. "You are the last person in the world who needs to worry about calories," he observed.

"Even so..."

"Even so, nothing. Yes or no?"

She laughed and admitted, "I haven't had a banana split in years."

"Well, then, that settles it."

The ice-cream shop was as crowded as it might have been on a hot night in July. They had to wait a few minutes for a booth and watched in amazement as any number of customers got their orders to go, then marched outside, cones in hand, appearing completely oblivious to the chilly December air.

"New Englanders certainly are a hardy lot," Kris commented, once they'd been seated in a window booth. "Look at those people out there. My God!"

"Good for the circulation," David told her.

Kris shivered just thinking about that. "Are you really going to have a banana split?" she asked. "I don't think I could possibly work my way through a whole one." When he started to protest, she added, "I *will* have a hot-fudge sundae, though."

"With whipped cream, nuts and a cherry?"

"Uh-huh."

"Not a bad choice," he said, approving.

Kris chuckled as David tackled the enormous dessert that was placed in front of him a few minutes later.

He glanced up at her, a smudge of whipped cream making a mustache on his upper lip, and asked, "What's so funny? Haven't you ever seen a psychiatrist eat ice cream before?"

Kris shook her head and bit her lip as emotion welled inside her. "You," she managed shakily, "are wonderful."

David put his spoon down and stared across at her, his silvery gray eyes wary. "Why do you say that?" he asked.

"Because it's true." Suddenly, an attack of shyness swept over her. Kris lowered her eyes and toyed with her sundae, and wondered if David would think she was being ridiculously coy. Still, she couldn't bring herself to meet his steady gaze.

"Do you realize you're tormenting me?" he challenged.

"It's just that you're such an unusual person."

"Me?" he scoffed, genuinely astonished.

"You're such a blend of sophistication and...and youth."

At that he leaned forward and whispered, "You're not saying I'm too naive for someone my age, are you?"

"Not at all," Kris assured him quickly. "It's the way you let the little boy in you express himself that makes you so..."

"So what?" David prodded.

"So... special."

Never before in her life had Kris said such intimate things to a man. She'd nearly said "lovable," but simply couldn't mouth the word. It wasn't that little voice of conscience preventing her from saying what she felt. It was the feelings themselves.

She knew that David sensed her embarrassment, knew he was trying to let her off the hook graciously when he teased, "You're making me feel like an oversize teddy bear."

Kris wished she could be light with her reply. Wished she could say something like, "Well, you certainly are warm and cuddly." But she couldn't. She said, her voice unsteady, "You *are* wonderful, David. For so many reasons."

His grin faded. And Kris was shocked when she looked up and saw a suspicious hint of moisture in his eyes. "So are you," he said huskily.

"Me? There's nothing special about me."

She was not fishing for compliments, David knew. That wasn't her style. No, she seemed deadly serious. He wondered why. Perhaps there was a connection with the introspective mood she'd been in earlier.

"I find you *very* special," he told her. "You have much more courage, much more stalwart character, than you're giving yourself credit for. Not to mention all the love you have to give."

Kris didn't know how to answer that and was spared when a group of carolers swarmed into the shop and drowned the place in an enthusiastic rendition of "Hark, the Herald Angels Sing." A red-haired boy, who reminded David of a younger version of Eric Benson, came around with a long red stocking collecting donations. "To buy toys for kids who don't have a chimney for Santa Claus to come down," he explained.

David dropped a bill into the stocking and smiled. The boy moved on, then the carolers were on their way out the door, singing merrily.

"Hey," he said, turning back to Kris, "your sundae's melting."

"So's your banana split."

The appearance of the carolers, while a treat, had broken the mood of a moment ago. Yet something had been forged between Kris and David during that moment, a new thread of knowing and understanding, thin...but bright and shining as pure gold.

As they left the ice-cream shop, David glanced at his watch and said, "I can't believe it's not even nine o'clock. In less than three hours, I got more shopping done with your help than I would have in two days by myself. I wouldn't mind picking out a few Christmas cards, if that's all right with you?"

"Sure," Kris said quietly.

David glanced quickly at her and saw fatigue beginning to take its toll. "On the other hand," he mused, "it would be out of character for me to mail my cards any earlier than the last possible minute. Anyway, it seems a lot of stores are starting to close up." He tucked his free arm through Kris's—the other toted a large paper shopping bag full of gifts—then suggested, "How about a chorus of 'Jingle Bells'? Those carolers really gave me the urge to sing.''

"Here on the street?" Kris asked, completely taken aback.

"What better place?"

So saying, David launched into song, and Kris was further shocked by his strong baritone voice. "Come on," he said, nudging her. "Help me out."

Shyness threatened her ability to speak, let alone sing. But then David's contagious mood got the better of her, and Kris joined in. They sang all the way to his car, unaware that passersby were turning to look back at them and smile.

Back at Granite Street, David walked up the porch steps beside Kris and said, "I've had a terrific time. The most fun I've ever had Christmas shopping." He paused, then added ruefully, "I guess I'd better leave you at this point."

She didn't know what to say. She watched his breath wisp out into the chill night air and again wanted to ask him in. She yearned for his companionship, yearned for his touch, wanted him in her bed. She didn't know how much longer she could resist the overwhelming desire she had to make love to him.

He bent and kissed her lightly, then started to turn away. "Oh, I almost forgot," he said as he reached into a deep pocket of his overcoat and pulled out a brightly wrapped palm-sized package. "Here," he said, handing it to her. "This is what I was doing when I skipped out on you."

"What's this?" she asked.

David grinned, an abashed little grin that momentarily stopped Kris's heart. "It's a small token of my appreciation," he told her. "An early Christmas present. You can open it once you're inside."

"Oh, David. What am I going to do with you?"

"Nothing, tonight," he said.

Inside her apartment, Kris took off her coat and nervously sat down on the couch. Then, with shaky fingers she began unwrapping David's gift. There were layers of tissue paper through which she could feel a smooth roundish object, strangely familiar somehow... yet she couldn't be sure.

She found herself staring at a paperweight almost exactly like the one she'd described to David. The detail was lovely. A miniature decorated Christmas tree dominated a scene that looked like something out of Dickens. There was a crooked cobblestone street and a row of brownstones with smoke drifting up from their chimneys.

Kris shook it gently and watched the snowflakes swirl and drift down like memories of her childhood. Only this time she welcomed the sweet sadness, remembering the love and warmth of Christmases past.

David had touched her again in a personal way that filled her with emotion. He'd shown her how much he cared—for her, and for the things that had meaning in her life. For a long time, Kris sat on the edge of the couch and watched the snow whirl around the Christmas tree again and again. And all the while, she thought of David.

DAVID STALKED INTO THE CLINIC the next morning, his face set in exceptionally determined lines. He rather absently greeted the members of his staff, strode into his office and summoned Eric Benson.

"Good morning, Eric. Have a seat," he instructed.

The young corpsman sat down stiffly on a straight-backed chair in front of David's desk, looking so rigid David snapped, "Relax, will you?"

"Yes, sir."

He certainly couldn't knock Eric's properly military demeanor, but just now it irritated him. "Look," he said, striving for a compromise, "I've got a lot on my mind this morning, which doesn't mean I have the right to take it out on you."

"That's okay, sir."

"No, it's not okay. But please...at ease, son. We've got work to do."

After he'd left Kris last night, David had done some heavy soul-searching. He knew without conceit that he was making an increasingly emotional impact on her. He would have known that even without her halting eulogy in the ice-cream parlor.

Once, they had yielded to passion. All the other times they'd spent together, they had resisted its temptation. Most of the time he was with Kris, it was all David could do to keep from surrendering to the elemental fire that burned between them so fiercely. Fortunately—or perhaps not so fortunately, he thought bitterly—his innate discipline afforded him a great deal of restraint, especially at those moments when restraint was most necessary. Sooner or later, though, that reservoir was bound to run dry, and he would no longer be able to keep his hands off her.

He didn't want that to happen, much as he wanted her. Because of her brother, he thought wearily. Because of the unresolved issue of Jay's tragedy. Until that mystery was solved, until all the answers were known, Jay's death would always come between them. And when the truth *was* known...what then? Perhaps Kris would look back on the single night of passion they'd shared only to think how agonizing remorse can be.

Now...David's voice was tense as he handed Eric a slip of paper and said, "Here are phone numbers for Commander DeMott's home and office out in San Francisco. I want you to find out *exactly* when he's due back from Australia. All right?"

"Yes, sir." Eric nodded.

"After that," David continued, "I want you to dig up all the information you can on Jay Sothern's class here at the submarine school. How many men started, how many graduated. Where the graduates are assigned now. For those that are still based in Groton—and I'll imagine you'll find quite a few who are—I want names, addresses and phone numbers. That," he added, managing an encouraging smile, "should keep you busy till lunchtime."

"At least, sir," Eric agreed.

David had just dismissed a patient and was enjoying a much-needed cup of coffee when Eric knocked on his door. The wall clock showed it was just past eleven, a pleasant surprise. He wished he didn't have a consultation at twelve that would most likely wipe out his lunch hour. Wished that he could meet Kris somewhere, if only to talk. But more than that, he wanted to have something to tell her.

"Come in, Eric," he said, further surprised to see the corpsman holding a yellow legal pad. In fact, he was gazing at it with an irrepressible sense of satisfaction.

"I think I've got what you want, sir," he announced cheerfully. "Maybe not all of it, but at least a good start."

"Take a seat and fire away," David rejoined eagerly.

Eric did so, then began, "Okay, there were one hundred fifty-six men in Jay Sothern's class in school. One hundred twenty-three graduated, thirty-three washed out. The graduates are scattered all over the place."

"Yes, I imagined they would be," David admitted wryly.

"Still, sir...forty-eight men are stationed right here."

"On the base?"

"On the base, or very close by. Some are with Squadron Two, here right now. Others are with Group Two. They're presently finishing up a tour at sea. The rest are with Squadron Ten assigned to the State Pier in New London."

"Good work, Eric. Now...what about the thirty-three who washed out?"

"I was planning on getting their addresses and phone numbers this afternoon, sir. It might take me a while to track each guy down. I mean, it's been more than two years since some of them left the class."

David nodded thoughtfully. "Why don't you wait on that," he said. "What I'd like you to do first is contact the forty-eight men who are in and around Groton. I need to know if any of them knew Jay very well. Personally, that is. Not just as someone they worked with or attended classes with."

"Yes, sir. But don't forget, Sothern was something of a loner."

"I know that, Eric," David said patiently. "You just keep up the good work. Jay must have socialized with somebody. I want to know who."

"Yes, sir." Eric nodded doubtfully.

"Look, son. If you're worried about time, don't. This is going to take a couple of days, I realize that. So rather than knock yourself into the ground, go slowly and carefully. Go over to the State Pier, for example, and find the guys who were in Jay's class. If anyone wants to know what you're doing, tell them you're on a research project for me. Under my direct orders, in fact. I'm trying to ascertain why Jay did what he did. You've probably figured that out, but don't let on to any of the men you talk with. Follow up even the slightest lead you come up against, and don't get discouraged if a lot of what you learn seems worthless. Just write everything down and report back to me each afternoon.''

"Yes, sir," Eric said more cheerfully. "Gosh, I never thought I'd find myself playing private eye for the navy!"

"Join the club," David allowed. "Just remember, this is serious. Not a word to anyone."

THE AFTERNOON was very busy. David was forced to turn his thoughts away from Jay Sothern—and Kris—and give his patients the benefit of his undivided attention. By five o'clock he was exhausted.

Leaning back in his swivel chair and closing his eyes, he had a sudden vision of being in Kris's apartment. The drapes were drawn, a fire burned in the hearth, wonderful smells came from the kitchen. He and Kris were sitting together on the couch. Rather, she was reclining with her head in his lap. In one hand, he held a bourbon and soda. With the other, he gently stroked Kris's soft brown hair.

He shrugged away the fantasy, then reached for the phone and dialed her number.

"David," she purred. "The paperweight is absolutely beautiful. I couldn't believe it when I saw the tree."

"Is it like the one you used to have?"

"Much prettier. And there's more snow, too."

It was wonderfully heartening to hear Kris sound so happy. David hoped he wouldn't spoil this when he said, "Listen, Kris... I was going to suggest that we get together tonight, but frankly, I'm bushed. Tomorrow, though, do you think we could go out for dinner somewhere?"

There was a solemn note in his voice, a note that sounded only when David had something to say about her brother. Kris recognized this instantly and blurted, "What is it, David? Have you found out something about Jay?"

"I don't know yet," he told her honestly. "I'm hoping to have more information by tomorrow afternoon, something that might answer our questions."

Kris's pulse started thumping. The ominous cloud rushed in from the horizon. She was afraid, and she couldn't have said why. "Have you talked with Evan?" she asked levelly.

"About your brother? No, not recently. Why?"

"I just wondered, that's all. You'd said you wanted to get your friendship with Evan back on track, and I thought perhaps he might have changed his mind about talking."

"That remains to be seen, but I wouldn't count on it. You're right, though. I do have to get in touch with Evan. If I wasn't so damned tired, I'd call him now."

Admitting so readily to fatigue was highly unusual for David. Kris realized this and felt faintly alarmed. David Jorgenson had as much mental and physical energy as anyone she'd ever known. More emotional stamina, as well. Still, he was human, in every sense of the word.

What would it be like to pamper such a man, she wondered, then snuffed out the idea as quickly as it had come to her. She'd pampered a man once before. She'd pampered Jay for her own selfish reasons.

Facing up to that self-accusation, Kris swallowed hard. To David, she said, "You don't have to call Evan tonight. You don't have to call anyone, not even me. I'm prescribing that you get out of that office, go back to the BOQ, grab something from the deli, go up to your suite and get some rest."

"Is that an order, Miss Sothern?"

"Yes, it is."

"Well, in that case I'd better obey."

"One other thing, David."

"Yes?"

"Thank you again for the paperweight. I'll keep it forever and ever."

CHAPTER THIRTEEN

THE YOUNG SUBMARINER sitting across from David in a bar on the New London waterfront was avoiding something. David didn't know what it was, but the telltale signs were all too familiar. A manifest uneasiness, shifting position frequently, failure to meet his eyes, a hesitancy in speaking, intermittently looking off to the other side of the room . . . he could have written the list from memory.

He had suggested that he and the submariner—Hank O'Brien by name—get together for a beer. He'd thought O'Brien would be more relaxed in a bar than he would have been in an official setting. He'd been wrong. O'Brien was wound uptight and plainly uncomfortable.

David was sure the discomfort had nothing to do with the difference in their ranks . . . or little to do with it, anyway. They were both off duty. Neither of them—at David's request—was in uniform. But even in civilian clothes, O'Brien looked familiar. Somewhere, they'd met. David was certain of that. Perhaps when the young man was going through some of the stress tests during his training at the submarine school. He decided to ask O'Brien directly and received the affirmative he'd expected.

"That was quite a while ago, sir," he said.

About two years, David calculated. "Quite a while," he allowed, when you were barely twenty-one years old.

Eric had spoken with O'Brien during his routine checks of the men who'd been in class with Jay Sothern. He'd reported back to David that O'Brien had recently returned to New London after a tour of sea duty aboard a Polaris submarine. In fact, he'd flown in from Holy Loch with a group of other submariners only a few days earlier, and shortly would be going back to his hometown in Arizona for a Christmas leave with his family.

Eric had formed the habit of typing up succinct reports on each of his phone interviews. In his report on Hank O'Brien, he'd emphatically underlined the words, "was a friend of Sothern's."

"He said it was a real shock to him when he heard Sothern had killed himself," Eric had written.

If O'Brien had talked freely with Eric, David thought ruefully, he'd evidently decided at some point since then that he'd said all he wanted to say. At least, he wasn't talking now.

"Where did you meet Jay?" David asked casually.

"We were in class together. There were a lot of us in class together," he murmured.

"I know that," David pointed out patiently. "It was my understanding that you and Jay Sothern were friends. I'd like you to elaborate on that."

"Friends, sir?" O'Brien shook his head. "I wouldn't say we were ever *friends*."

"Did you ever go out together when you were off duty?"

"I guess Sothern tagged along with some of us a couple of times," O'Brien admitted reluctantly.

"Did you ever go to any parties with him?"

"Parties?" The voiced surprise didn't quite ring true.

"At a house up in Gales Ferry. A place along the river."

David glanced directly at O'Brien as he posed the question and noticed the very strange expression that flitted across the man's face. But he only said, stiffly, "No sir. I never went to a house in Gales Ferry with Sothern."

David stabbed in the dark, a tactic that had become all too familiar to him where anything involving Kris's brother was concerned. "You know about the house though, don't you?" he prompted.

Hank O'Brien hesitated. David saw his mouth tighten and knew there was a decided inner struggle going on. He suspected O'Brien was trying to figure out how much he knew, wondering how safe it would be to deny any knowledge of the house on the river.

David's curiosity was already stirred, and O'Brien's attitude was heightening it that much more. What was there about the Gales Ferry house that would make the young submariner want to hide his knowledge of it? That was obviously what he was doing. David would have wagered a large bet on that, even if he hadn't had years of experience analyzing the workings of the human mind.

It was nearly five o'clock. David had managed to leave his office early by rescheduling his last two patients, which meant that tomorrow would be an especially long day. He knew he should have phoned Kris at the college to firm up their dinner date. But he'd put off calling her because he first wanted to hear what O'Brien had to say.

It was coming to the point where what O'Brien *wasn't* saying was considerably more significant than anything he'd said thus far. What could Jay Sothern have gotten himself into, David wondered. And how had this young submariner sitting across from him been involved?

He knew he couldn't risk asking Hank O'Brien those questions straight out. The man was the best lead he'd come up with so far—thanks to Eric—and he didn't want to lose him. As it was, O'Brien was looking like a rabbit ready to bolt.

Stabbing in the dark again, he said, "Hank...I'd venture to say that a lot of people knew about that house. So why the secrecy?"

"It was nothing I was interested in, that's all."

David forced a smile. "Were the parties *that* wild?"

"Wild? No, sir. I don't know if you'd say they were wild, that wasn't it. I guess some of the guys had a pretty good time. That's to say, no one bothered them, if you know what I mean."

O'Brien looked hopeful as he said this, as if he'd given out a well-known clue to something equally obvious. Unfortunately, David had no idea what he was talking about. "I guess I'm not keeping up with you, Hank," he stalled.

"Oh," O'Brien said. "I kind of thought you might know."

"Might know what?"

"Nothing, sir," he said, shifting uneasily again. "It's no big deal, Commander."

"If it's no big deal, why don't you fill me in?"

"Look, Sothern's dead," the submariner stated firmly. "I told Benson I knew him, that we were in the same class. It shocked the hell out of me when I heard what he'd done, but it shocked the hell out of a lot of people. What I'm saying is, it's all over, sir. Jay is dead. So what's the point of stirring things up?"

"There are certain aspects of his death that bear further scrutiny," David said, deliberately vague.

"In the eyes of the navy, sir?"

"In a roundabout way, yes."

"I don't see why the navy should give a damn," O'Brien said bluntly.

"Jay Sothern *was* a member of the submarine service."

"Yeah, but that doesn't mean it matters why he killed himself, does it? Especially when it had nothing to do with the navy anyway."

David leaned forward, but tried not to show the impact this statement had just had on him. He didn't want to come on so intensely that O'Brien would automatically back off. But what the submariner had just said opened up whole new vistas. It was Kris, of course, who had initially put the concept into his head that her brother had killed himself because he could no longer hack life in the service. Because he couldn't take the stress.

Now...maybe the stress came from another source. Maybe Kris had been entirely wrong.

David could feel gooseflesh developing along his arms as he put his thoughts in the form of a question. "Do you think Jay Sothern killed himself for reasons that had nothing to do with the navy?" he asked, using all of his considerable willpower to force himself to sound calm.

For a moment, he thought Hank O'Brien was going to give him a direct answer. Then he saw the man's eyes shift, saw him shrug. "I wouldn't know," he said, his rugged Irish face impassive.

And that was that. O'Brien declined the offer of a second beer, saying he guessed he'd better get going if "the commander" was through with him.

David let him go.

He ordered another beer for himself simply because he wanted to keep the booth, wanted to sit there and think for a while. Sometimes it was easier to think with a lot of noise and chatter going on around you than it was within

the sanctuary of a totally quiet room. He supposed he
could have pumped O'Brien further about the house in
Gales Ferry, but doubted he would have gotten anywhere, judging from the boy's demeanor.

If he met with O'Brien again, David knew he would
start by pursuing the subject of the house where Jay had
evidently partied. Of course, O'Brien might clam up entirely. Meanwhile, he'd hopefully be meeting with other
submariners who had known Jay Sothern. Perhaps one
of them would be more forthcoming about the house on
the river.

The impression that Hank O'Brien had given him—
that Jay's suicide had had nothing to do with the submarine service—lingered, then took hold. The more David thought about it, the more it made sense. He'd fine
combed Jay's service record in preparation for his first
meeting with Kris. He'd gone over it at least three times
since. Jay had an excellent record. No black marks
against him. Nothing but favorable reports from the officers he'd served under. His dedication and enthusiasm
for the submarine service—on paper, at least—had evidently never diminished, never even briefly lagged.

Why would someone take the ultimate way out when
he was performing a job he loved, and performing it
well?

It was a circular question, going nowhere. Just around
to the beginning, then back around again. After a few
minutes, David gave up on it, paid his check and left.

On an impulse, he decided to drive straight to Granite
Street without calling Kris first. As he drove, he wondered just how much he should tell Kris at this point. Not
that he really had that much to tell. He felt he owed it to
her to say that he was checking through the list of submariners who'd been in Jay's class in school, had al-

ready spoken to one boy who'd known Jay and was planning to talk to others. What he didn't want to do was speculate with her. There was no point in starting Kris on the frustrating circular path he'd nearly gotten trapped on himself.

He pulled up in front of her house and was out of the car before he noticed that her lights weren't on. He held his wristwatch up in the yellow light from the street lamp and saw it was nearly a quarter to six. Strange, Kris was usually home by now.

He reminded himself that he wasn't her keeper. Nor was there any logical reason he should start worrying every time she wasn't exactly where he expected her to be.

On the chance that maybe she'd fallen asleep, he trudged up the front steps. He rang her doorbell, waited, rang again...and realized that she hadn't fallen asleep after all. She was still out. He supposed he could check to see if her car was parked in the small lot out back, but what would that prove?

It was ridiculous to feel so disappointed, so hurt, David told himself. He'd counted on seeing her much more than he'd realized...and that was foolish, too. He thought, grimly, that he was not at his levelheaded best where Kris was concerned and decided he'd better calm down.

Kris started up the steps just as David was turning to leave. She was carrying a shopping bag filled with packages and was wearing her red wool cloche and the matching long scarf. She looked incredibly pretty, he thought, and considerably younger than twenty-nine. He was so glad to see her that he felt his heart would burst out of his chest. But instead of conveying joy, he perversely took refuge in grumpiness.

"I thought you and I had a dinner date," he complained.

Finding him at her doorstep had set off a whole string of inner fireworks in Kris. She could feel herself glowing. But when she saw David's scowl and heard his annoyed tone of voice, her spirits started to sink.

"I'm sorry," she said. "I know you mentioned something about dinner, but I didn't realize it was definite. When you didn't call, I thought maybe you'd gotten tied up at the clinic."

"That's okay," he said, at once contrite. "I should have called. Anyway, it's still early. If you haven't eaten yet..."

"No, I haven't eaten. I went shopping after leaving work. Look, why don't I just fix us some omelets? Would that be enough for you?" She was standing beside him on the porch, but when David reached to take the bag from her, Kris said hastily, "That's okay, I've got it."

She hadn't planned on going shopping. She'd made the decision on an impulse as she was skirting a mall on her drive back from the college. She'd browsed with the thought of getting ideas for the memorable gift she wanted to buy for David. Instead, she'd picked out a variety of whimsical Christmas surprises for him, and a handsome sweater as well. The shopping bag was full of presents.

"Are you sure an omelet will be okay?" she repeated.

"More than okay."

It was cold in her apartment. As he watched her switch on the lights, David commented, "Don't you ever keep the heat on in this place?"

"I turn the thermostat down to sixty when I leave in the morning," Kris told him. "I guess I've sort of gotten

the idea of energy conservation implanted in me. Want
to make a fire while I fix some drinks?"

"Sure."

Kris got out his favorite bourbon—she kept a bottle on
hand these days in the event he might stop by—and
poured a glass of sherry for herself. Then she arranged a
plate of cheese and crackers as an appetizer. When she
walked into the living room, the fire was crackling. David was sitting on the couch, his long legs sprawled out in
front of him. The scene was especially intimate and made
Kris stop short and catch her breath.

If only he could be here all the time.

The thought started in her heart, swirled to her head
and refused to be displaced by logic. It would be wonderful to have David here all the time. To wake up by his
side in the morning, to go to bed beside him each night.
To love him...and make love to him. To share all the
little things of life with him. To share the joys, the sor-
rows, the good times and the bad.

We were never meant to go it all by ourselves.

Kris remembered David telling her that once, and it
was not the wisest thought to hold under the circumstances. Her face was alive with her emotions. Her
transparency was a weakness she'd become well ac-
quainted with since getting to know David. At the same
time, she'd become considerably more adept at camouflage. By the time David looked up at her, she'd taken her
heart off her sleeve and put it back where it belonged.

She curled up in an armchair near the fire, deliberately putting a little physical distance between David and
herself. No need to tempt fate, she reasoned. Then she
shipped her sherry, munched on a piece of cheese and
wondered why he seemed so preoccupied.

He answered her unspoken question a minute or so later after taking a hefty drink of his bourbon. Rather abruptly, he said, "I met a submariner who knew Jay, Kris. I had a beer with him just before I came over here."

Kris's eyes widened, her throat constricted and her fingers clenched the stem of her sherry glass. With difficulty, she asked, "Did he have something to tell you?"

"That depends on your definition of something," David said gruffly. "I had the feeling he could have told me more if he'd been so inclined. Not a hell of a lot more, but I'm sure he was holding something back. What, I don't know. He seemed reticent in a rather strange way I can't quite define. Anyway, he did open up a new avenue of thought."

"What are you saying?"

"He intimated that Jay's death had nothing to do with the submarine service," David reported levelly. "I'm not saying he *knows* that to be the case, but he certainly implied it. More than implied it."

Tension was making Kris's throat ache. "I don't understand," she managed hoarsely. "Who told you . . ."

"Hold it just a second," David intervened. "You confronted me in the first place because you felt I should have never okayed your brother for another tour at sea, remember? You said that further psychological tests might have revealed that he couldn't take any more stress. Submarine-related stress, that is. Correct?"

"Yes," she answered slowly.

"Well, the submariner I talked to evidently feels that Jay's action had nothing at all to do with submarines or the service."

"If it wasn't that, then what was it?" Kris demanded weakly.

"I don't know," David told her. "But if it's humanly possible, I sure as hell intend to find out!"

He took another sip of his drink, then said, "There were one hundred twenty-three men who graduated from the submarine school in Jay's class. Another thirty-three washed out. As you might imagine, they're scattered all over the place, although forty-eight are stationed at or around the base. I'm not saying that one of these young men will give us the answer we're looking for. But they're the best bet we have until Cal DeMott gets back to San Francisco. Even then, there's no guarantee Cal will know as much as I'd like to think he knows."

"That's true," Kris admitted softly.

"I've also learned of a corpsman who knew Jay. He's stationed in Newport, so I'm going to drive over there this weekend and meet with him. Meantime, in every spare moment I have, I plan to talk with the submariners from Jay's class who are presently assigned to posts in this area. I've got a corpsman helping me out. He's contacting each man to find out if they knew Jay. Anyone who did will be receiving a visit from me."

"You haven't told him why you're doing this, have you? I mean, I never wanted to stir up a lot of talk about what happened with Jay. I only wanted to find out . . ."

"If it could have been prevented," David cut in. "That's to say, if either I was responsible or somebody else was, perhaps you yourself."

Kris had always suspected that David could be extremely formidable if he wanted to be. Now he was proving it. His face was set, his voice was stern. And his last words were the coldest words he'd ever directed at her. Well, she had it coming, she admitted. She'd initiated this whole investigation to begin with, blaming David with very little tangible evidence to support her accusations. Now that they were getting closer to the truth...

"You can't do this, David," she murmured sadly.

His eyes swerved toward her, clear, gray and glistening. "What that's supposed to mean?" he challenged.

"I know what you're trying to do. And I'd say I really appreciate it, except that would sound so trite. I can't think of a word that would convey to you how much what you're trying to do means to me. I can't let you do it, that's all."

"What are you trying to tell me, Kris?"

"You don't have time for this, for one thing. Your normal work load keeps you too busy already. You don't have time to be running around interviewing dozens of submariners...no matter what you might find out." She sat up straight, her face determined. "I can't let you do this," she repeated.

David smiled wryly. "You want to know what I think, Kris...besides the fact that you're wasting your breath? I think you're afraid. Now that we're finally getting closer to the truth, you're afraid to discover what the truth is. It certainly seems apparent that you didn't know Jay quite as well as you thought you did. I don't mean that in a negative sense, Kris. I'm not putting you down. It's a fact, that's all. For more than a month now, I've been involved with this. Deeply involved. Personally, professionally, I've got to know what happened."

"I'd like to think that if I asked you to stop you'd listen to me," she replied evenly.

"Are you asking me to stop?"

Kris hesitated for a moment, then said slowly, "Yes, I am. You're the one who said nothing can bring Jay back. That's not exactly what you said, I suppose...but it's true. I even told you I realized you were right. I told you

I wanted you to inform Admiral Carrington that I wasn't going to make any more trouble. That I was content to let the matter stand."

David nodded gravely, but said, "We've gone beyond that point, Kris. Way beyond that point."

"No, we haven't, David. You tried talking with Evan Phillips about Jay, and he wouldn't tell you a thing. Now you've spoken to this one boy from Jay's class and that led nowhere. I think it's time for you to stop."

He shook his head. "First of all, the meeting this afternoon did not lead nowhere. I wasn't going to mention this, but I might as well, now."

"Mention what?"

"There was definitely a house in Gales Ferry where Jay and some of the other guys partied."

"We already knew that, David."

"We knew what Jay told you, Kris. And there were inconsistencies there, to put it mildly."

"Suppose you speak to Evan again."

David expelled a frustrated sigh. "I intended to phone Evan today, but I never got around to it."

"You would have if it hadn't been for me."

"What?" he asked, puzzled. "What do you have to do with my not finding time to call Evan?"

"Don't be obtuse, David," Kris chided. "It doesn't suit you. This quest you've gotten yourself into is going to eat up far more time than you can spare, and that isn't right."

Half to himself, David repeated, "This quest *I've* gotten myself into?" He shook his head disbelievingly. "I have the very distinct feeling that suddenly you don't want me to get to the bottom of things here. Tell me I'm wrong, Kris. You can't, can you?"

Not surprisingly, he'd hit the nail on the head. Knowing the truth about what had happened with Jay might be much worse than not knowing, Kris was beginning to realize. All along, she'd made the navy the scapegoat for Jay's tragedy. She'd needed to place the blame on something—and someone—to rid herself of a guilt burden that had threatened to swamp her. The guilt involved her conviction that she hadn't opened her eyes with Jay, hadn't seen things that should have been obvious to his sister. She should have *known* something was troubling him. She should have interceded, should have helped him work his way out of his fatal dilemma.

The submarine service and the navy had been the targets at large, huge and impersonal institutions upon which to place the blame. Then, as the terrible grief of the first few months began to abate, she'd narrowed down her focus to people...and finally was convinced that the negligence of a single individual had been responsible for Jay's tragedy. In time, she'd affixed a name to that individual and began her own safari of discovery. Even as David was doing now, in an entirely different way.

"Am I right, Kris?" he persisted. "You don't want me to get to the bottom of this, do you?"

She was sitting close to the fire, could feel its warmth. But suddenly she shivered. "I don't know," she admitted very softly. "I just don't know."

"Well, I *do* know!" David exploded angrily. "Look at me, Kris. There still remains the little matter of me clearing my name, remember?"

"What do you mean?"

"You were extremely precise, extremely definite, in your accusation. I'd venture to say you're still not completely positive in your mind about my innocence."

"I was only going on what I'd been told," she protested.

David laughed bitterly at that. "Had Admiral Carrington not always had a benevolent eye on my career, your conversation could have seriously damaged my reputation," he said. "As it was, he alerted me of the potential danger out of consideration and friendship. And because he also has a good deal of faith in me, thank God. I was fortunate. It might easily have gone the other way had you contacted another senior officer in Washington."

Kris was appalled. "I was only trying to get to the truth," she stammered.

"Then why don't you want to get to the truth now?"

"Because..." She faltered, then couldn't continue.

"Because you're afraid of it, that's why!"

His voice was cold as steel, but his eyes were on fire. Kris shivered again. Then, her voice choking, she demanded, "Why must you be so merciless?"

"Merciless? I'm merely telling it like it is. I can understand your motivations, Kris... but you should have stopped to consider the consequences of your actions before you started the ball rolling. At this point, it's too late for retractions. If you ever thought I'd sit back with an unfounded, unmerited accusation hanging over my head, you were sadly mistaken."

As frustrated and angry as he felt, David wanted desperately to tell Kris that only when they knew the truth would the path to their happiness be cleared of obstacles. Only then could they freely express their love for each other.

He opened his mouth just as Kris sprang to her feet. For a brief moment, she froze. Then she cast an anguished glance in his direction and ran out of the room.

A second later, David heard her bedroom door slam shut. Five minutes later, he knocked on the door and softly called her name. When she didn't answer, he tried turning the knob. The door was locked.

There were two ways to react to a locked door, David knew. With a heart as heavy as lead, he turned away.

CHAPTER FOURTEEN

EVAN PHILLIPS WALKED into the psychiatric clinic at noon the next day, ignored the yeoman on duty at the reception desk and burst into David's office without even pausing to knock on the door. David was with a patient who'd been through some tough times, but was responding well to counseling. The interruption was unfortunate because the man—a noncommissioned officer—had just begun to verbalize something that was deeply troubling him.

David had worked hard to build up the kind of trust and empathy that would enable his patient to let go, as he was finally doing. David looked up sharply when he heard the door open, ready to issue a stern rebuke. But the words died on his lips when he saw Evan.

"Sorry," Evan said tightly, "but I have to see you. Now."

David turned to his patient. "We'd better call it a day, Chet," he said reluctantly. He hated thinking that the mood he'd established had been shattered, for today at least. "On your way out, tell Mark to set up an appointment for you at the same time tomorrow."

The man mumbled an affirmative and left, averting his face as if he hoped Evan wouldn't recognize him.

Evan paid him no attention. He slumped into the chair that had just been vacated and closed his eyes tightly.

Then he opened them and looked around the office as if it was the last place he wanted to be.

David waited, expecting Evan to offer an apology for the interruption. After several long seconds drifted by and Evan remained silent, David asked, "Would you mind telling me what this is all about?"

The chaplain had been staring at the tips of his well-polished black shoes. Now he looked up, anger flaring in his light blue eyes. "Maybe you'd better tell me," he suggested.

David had already put in a very trying morning. He'd been so busy he hadn't even touched bases with Eric for a progress report on the other submariners who had known Jay Sothern. He'd been irritated with Evan—though he'd tried to bury it—ever since their fiasco of a breakfast conference. Remembering his friend's unyielding stand, he snapped, "Just what are you driving at? In case you don't realize it, you came in here at a very bad moment."

"Believe me," Evan said, "I wouldn't have come at all if I'd had an alternative. Marianne's left me, Dave. And you are the only person who might know why."

David had not heard a word out of Marianne since Thanksgiving. He was hoping, naively, he admitted, that no news was good news. He was praying that seeing Evan again had affected a change of heart in her.

Incredulous, he demanded, "She's *left* you?"

"She was gone when I got up this morning. Took a couple of suitcases full of clothes, from what I can determine. Left a note saying she should have had the courage to tell me to my face that she wants out of our marriage. I can only conclude that she's gone off with someone."

Evan surveyed David with eyes from which the anger had faded. They were suddenly without luster, dull as old marbles. "I thought it might be you," he said very quietly.

"Me?" David shouted the word. At the same time, he forced himself to resist the impulse to throttle Evan. He actually started to get to his feet, then sank back into his chair. "Why, in God's name, would you think I'd run off with your wife?" he demanded.

"Because even before I left for Holy Loch last year, I thought maybe Marianne had fallen in love with you," Evan said with a tired, sad smile. "You do have a way with women, Dave," he added. "Even my daughter Patricia pines for you."

"Come off it, chaplain! Your daughter Patricia is a spoiled, selfish girl who needs some sense drummed into her head. She appears to have a stupid crush on me, but that's all it is. If it weren't me, it would be someone else. Anyway, she'll outgrow it."

"Of course she will."

David sighed deeply. "I'm sorry, Evan. I guess I was blowing off some steam of my own, which you certainly don't need now. Let's take it from the beginning, okay? When did you last see Marianne?"

"Last night," Evan reported. "She went to bed early, like she's been doing every night since I got back. I don't know...she had a problem with her back a few years ago. It flares up every now and then. When that happens, she suggests one of us sleep in the guest room because she gets so restless. Thanksgiving night, right after you left, guess what?"

"Her back acted up?"

"Good guess, Dave," Evan said cynically.

David had never before heard Evan speak so bitterly. Trying to contain his shock, he asked, "What happened then?"

"I started sleeping in the guest room, and I've been sleeping there every night. But believe me, I had the sense to know that Marianne's desire for solitude wasn't entirely due to her aching back!" Evan finished.

"Probably not," David carefully agreed.

"Yes, well, I guess no one can be as stupid as a husband who doesn't see the score!" Evan took a deep breath, then went on, "When we met for breakfast and you admitted that Marianne had talked to you, I said not to worry... I wouldn't press you about what she'd said. Remember?"

"Yes, I remember."

"Well, are you willing to get into it now?"

"Put it this way, Evan, at this point, I don't feel I'm violating her confidence. What she told me in so many words was she intended to ask you for a divorce once you were back."

"She didn't even do me that courtesy," Evan stated dully.

"Yes, well... that's at least partly my fault. I persuaded her to carry on as usual until after Thanksgiving."

"Things haven't been 'as usual' for quite a while, Dave."

"I know. She told me that, too. All I can say is, I was shocked. I *am* shocked. I don't know how I could have missed it. Except... I've never looked at either of you in analytical terms."

Evan managed a smile. "Please don't apologize for that," he said.

"No, I won't. But there's one thing I have to say."

"What's that?"

"Don't go looking for another man in the picture," David advised, "because I'm at least ninety-nine percent certain there isn't one. Marianne loves you. It's the service life she can't hack anymore."

"I don't understand," Evan said, frowning. "I'm not a submariner."

"In Marianne's opinion, you might as well be. Twice you've been ordered to Scotland at what were very bad times, from her point of view."

"I'm glad you said from her point of view," Evan observed. "She should have come to Scotland with me. It would have been the best thing for all of us. I know it means thirty months, but we're a family, damn it."

"Do the girls know about this yet?"

"No. They're both in school." Evan buried his face in his hands. His voice was muffled. "How am I going to tell them, Dave? How am I going to tell *anyone*?" His laugh was shaky. "I'm a great chaplain!"

"This has nothing to do with your being a chaplain," David admonished. "In fact, it doesn't have much to do with *you*, strange though that may seem."

Evan shook his head. "You're wrong about that. I've known for a long time that Marianne wasn't happy with the service life. I didn't think she was *that* unhappy, that's all. Maybe it's part of my training—even part of my faith—but my feeling was that we're all called upon to make certain sacrifices as we go through life. I guess I thought having a husband in the service was Marianne's sacrifice, which was both pompous and stupid of me. I can see that now.

"Way back," Evan continued, raising a hand to still David as he started to speak, "Marianne asked me to resign from the navy. More than once, she has. She wanted me to find a slot in a small-town church where we could have a home that was really ours and make what she called a 'real' life for the girls and ourselves.

"I guess I should have listened to her. I probably *would* have paid more attention to her, except there were also long intervals when she seemed perfectly content. I think she got honest satisfaction out of her work with Navy Relief and the Navy Wives Support Group. I heard nothing but praise from the people who worked with her. And each time I've been at Holy Loch, she's handled everything here at home as perfectly as anyone could have."

"Maybe too perfectly," David interjected.

"Yes." Evan nodded. "I see what you mean. Maybe all that perfection was just a manifestation of her frustration."

David smiled slightly. "Continue," he said.

"Right, continue. Maybe I should lie down on the couch, huh? Maybe I could figure out where I went wrong if we did it like that."

David let a moment pass. Then he said, "I'm speaking as your friend, not your shrink, Evan. It won't do any good for you to drown yourself in a sea of guilt and doom. The important thing is for you to find Marianne and have a heart-to-heart talk with her. If you don't mind my asking, how long has it been since you two have really opened up with each other? How long since you've shared your feelings, your dreams, your fears?"

"Too long," Evan admitted sadly.

"Do you have any idea where she might have gone?"

"None whatsoever. She has relatives, but she's much too proud to take refuge with any of them. And she'd never confide her problems to any of the other wives here. I'd guarantee that. Probably she's holed up in some motel somewhere. At the very worst, she's flown some-place where she can get a quick divorce.''

There was a knock at the door. Then Mark, the corps-man filling in for Eric, poked his head in the office and said, "Commander Jorgenson? Sorry to interrupt, sir, but your twelve-thirty patient is waiting."

"I know." David nodded. "Give me a minute more."

He fished in his pocket, drew out a key and handed it to Evan. "Here," he said. "Go over to my place and try to relax for the next couple of hours. Watch TV, sleep, read, whatever...try to blank out your mind. I'll get back as soon as I can and we'll take it from there."

For a moment he thought Evan was going to refuse the key. Then Evan said, "Okay, but what about the girls?"

"What time do they usually get home?"

"Around four, I guess."

"I'll call the house a little after that. I'll tell them you and I are going to sneak out and do some Christmas shopping. It will stall things a little longer. Maybe by then we can find Marianne," he decided, with a conviction he didn't feel.

Evan was barely out the door when Mark ushered in the next patient. David immediately plunged back into his work, forcibly applying the advice he'd given Evan to blank out his mind so he could concentrate on his work.

It was ten minutes past two when Mark knocked on the door and again stuck his head in. "I know you said you weren't to be disturbed, Commander, but there's a lady on the phone who insists on talking to you. Miss Sothern, her name is. She sounds pretty frantic."

David grabbed the receiver with a muffled apology to his patient. "Kris?" he asked, his concern for her sur-mounting everything else.

"David, I'm sorry to interrupt," she began, speaking in a voice so low he had to strain to hear her.

"What is it?" he cut in.

"Marianne Phillips. She's here, David."

"What?"

"You heard me. She's here. Right now, she's taking a bath. I told her a long soak in a hot tub might be relaxing. I had to get away from her for a few minutes so I could call you."

"How long has she been at your place?"

"Since seven o'clock this morning. I woke up at the sound of someone frantically buzzing my buzzer. I thought it might be you, but it was Marianne," Kris continued. "She looked terrible. White as a sheet, and she was shaking all over. She had two big suitcases with her."

"How did she get there?"

"She took a cab. I think she lugged the suitcases as far as the main gate, then got the sentry to call her a cab. She told me, but I'm a little hazy about the exact details."

"That doesn't matter, Kris. How did she know where you lived?"

"She picked me up here the day we went Christmas shopping, remember?"

"Right. You told me that before."

"David, what has happened? All Marianne's done thus far is sit here, drink coffee and babble on about all sorts of things. I can't get her to eat even a piece of toast. Claims she's not hungry. All she does is talk...about meeting Evan when they were in college, about falling in love with him at first sight. Then about how he went on to divinity school, and she got funny feelings about marrying a minister. Told me she's never been very religious herself. But she married Evan, of course. Then he joined the navy, and they had Patty and Deborah..."

"She's been going on like that since seven o'clock this morning?" David demanded. "I take it you didn't go to work."

"No, I called and said an emergency had come up with a friend, which was true enough. I couldn't leave her, David. She's so tense, she even *looks* brittle. I wanted to call you, but she insisted that I didn't. I think she would have physically tried to stop me from using the phone, she was that determined. I keep wondering why she came to me in the first place."

"Probably because you were the one person she felt she could lean on," David said, the statement appalling him even as he made it. Vivacious, stunning Marianne, one of the most popular wives on the base, turning to someone she scarcely knew for comfort. That said a lot, he thought sadly.

"Now I suppose I've let her down, calling you," Kris said, her voice lower than ever.

"No, no, you've done exactly what you should have done, Kris. I'll be over as soon as I can get there, which may be a while," he stated ruefully.

"I'm hoping I can get her to take a nap or something," Kris confessed. "But she's so wound up."

"Just don't let her leave, that's the main thing," David cautioned. "And when I arrive, be a good actress, Kris. Pretend you didn't expect me. I want Marianne to keep that confidence she's built up in you."

"Mmm...I'm not a very good actress."

He chuckled. "I know that, darling. It's one of the many things I love about you. But this time...try."

KRIS HUNG UP THE PHONE noiselessly, then carefully began working out a plan to keep Marianne in the house. The chaplain's wife hadn't said a word about leaving or where she intended to stay the night, but given her present frame of mind, Kris knew she might decide to flee the house on Granite Street as abruptly as she'd arrived.

As a starter, she retrieved from the back of her closet the lovely emerald satin lounging robe Jay had given her for Christmas a couple of years ago. She'd worn it all during that holiday week, the last she and Jay had spent together. He'd been at sea last Christmas, and every time she saw the robe it reminded her of him—and her loneliness without him—all the more. So she'd stashed it out of sight.

The robe hung inside a zipped plastic covering. Kris removed the covering, then marched to the bathroom with the robe over her arm. She knocked, but there was silence. Not even the splashing sound of Marianne moving around in the tub.

"Marianne?" she called, momentarily struck with fear. "It's Kris. May I come in for a second?"

"Yes," came the muffled reply.

Marianne had pinned her dark hair in a rumpled heap on top of her head and was up to her neck in bubbles. Kris glanced down at her. Despite her pallor, the dark circles under her eyes and that terrible aura of tension, she looked incredibly sexy.

Wishing that Evan could see his wife now, Kris said hastily, "I brought you something to slip into when you're finished with your bath." She hung the satin robe on the door hook and in one continuous motion managed to scoop up Marianne's discarded clothes and retreat before Marianne could protest.

Marianne's overcoat and boots were still in a corner of the living room. Kris hung the coat up in her bedroom closet and stashed the boots away. Then she folded Marianne's underclothes and the pantsuit she'd been wearing and stuffed them into the bottom drawer of her dresser. They would suffer a few wrinkles, but that seemed insignificant compared to the real problems at hand.

Next, she went to the kitchen, heated a can of chicken soup and made some toast. By the time Marianne emerged from the bathroom, Kris was ready for her. Even so, she was unprepared for the impact Marianne made standing in the doorway wearing the emerald green gown.

The gorgeous color was a striking foil to her dark coloring. It made her skin look like magnolia petals, Kris thought. Also, she admitted wryly, Marianne filled out the robe a lot better than she did. The satin clung to her curves. With her dark hair in a cloud around her shoulders, and the robe voluptuously outlining her body, she could not have looked more seductive.

Kris wondered what would happen if she sneaked off, phoned Evan, and told him to get over here quick! There was no chance for anything like that, though. All she could do was stare at Marianne in admiration.

"I borrowed your hairbrush. I hope you don't mind," Marianne said.

"Not at all," Kris assured her. "I've made a fire in the living room. Why don't you have a seat in that armchair next to the fireplace. It's sort of cold in here, and I don't want you to get a chill."

As she said this, she realized that she'd turned down the thermostat out of habit early this morning, but had forgotten to turn it back up. She promptly rectified the mistake, wondering what David would say about that! Then she took Marianne's soup in to her on a tray and arranged a second tray for herself. She suspected Marianne might eat something at this point, especially if she had company. She was right.

When they'd finished the soup, Kris made a pot of decaffeinated herb tea—they'd both had enough coffee during the day to stay awake a week—and opened a box of fancy cookies she'd bought with David in mind. She was gratified when Marianne took one and slowly munched.

Only then did Marianne murmur, "Thank you, Kris."

Kris looked up, surprised. "For what?" she asked.

"For taking me in this morning. I must have looked like a lost soul seeking shelter. Which I was, come to think of it." She managed a sad smile, then went on, "Thanks for listening, too. You let me talk my heart out, talk your ears off. I've never in my life talked like that before."

"Maybe you've needed to," Kris commented softly.

"Ah, yes, I've needed to. Maybe if I *had*, a long time ago, I wouldn't have needed to come here today." She shook her head and added, "I'm still wondering what prompted me to give the cabdriver your address. It...it just seemed to well up out of my subconscious. I'd thought of going straight to the train station and catching the next train to New York. I would have been anonymous in New York, you know? I could have gotten lost there for a while, which would have given me the chance to do a little coherent thinking. But instead of that, I found myself saying to the driver, I don't know the number, but the house is on Granite Street over in New London."

"I'm glad you did that," Kris said sincerely.

"So am I." Marianne smiled wearily. "What is there about you, Kris, that makes someone know instinctively that you'll care? No wonder Dave's fallen in love with you."

Kris opened her mouth about to deny that statement. The sexual chemistry between David and herself was pretty overwhelming, there was no negating that. And her own feelings went beyond it. She loved David, felt love for him deep from the heart. It was David's feelings she wasn't sure about. She knew he cared, but David cared about a lot of people. True, caring was a necessary part of love. But the kind of love she wanted from him transcended caring. Did he feel it, as she was sure she did? Or were his feelings for her based on sympathy because of Jay? Because she had been such a lost soul herself when she first confronted him on that gray afternoon in November.

Had been. Past tense.

Kris suddenly realized that she was no longer lost. She was freshly aware of the inner strength she'd always possessed, plus a new strength, as well. She could look at Marianne wearing the green satin robe and think how great the robe looked on her without going on a sad nostalgia trip because it had been a present from Jay.

She could even think about Jay being gone without shattering inside. There would always be sorrow. As David would say, that was only human. But the sorrow was going deeper all the time, allowing room for other emotions to surface. Joy and love among them.

When she thought about how Jay had died...yes, that still hurt. Maybe David was right. Maybe it would feel like an unhealed wound until they learned the truth. Yet even if they never discovered the real reason for Jay's decision, she knew she could live with that single scar.

She could live and she could love, unburdened and free, with no shadows to mar the future.

She needed to convince David of that.

Marianne was watching her, a gentle smile on her face. "Don't try to deny it, Kris. Dave does love you. Evan and I know Dave very well. I saw his love for you at Thanksgiving, every time he looked at you. I'm sure Evan saw it, too."

Into the silence that followed, she added, "Love can be so treacherous."

"What do you mean?" Kris asked softly.

"I mean you can love someone and yet not be able to share their life any longer. Does that make sense to you?"

"To be honest, no. I would think if you truly loved someone you'd want to share their life forever."

"That's a very idealistic statement," Marianne said. "One that I might have made myself, years back. But that's not the way it's worked out for me."

Marianne Phillips had yet to spell out the precise reason she'd shown up unexpectedly on Kris's doorstep at seven in the morning, clutching two large suitcases. Kris waited, sensing that the moment had come for her to do so.

"I guess you probably realize this without my telling you," Marianne began slowly. "But . . . I've left Evan."

"Yes, I thought as much."

"I'm going to ask another favor of you. I just don't seem to have the strength to do anything right now, though that soup you just fed me helped. But will you call the railroad station for me and check the times of trains to New York? I suppose I could take a bus, but I'd rather take the train."

Kris glanced at the mantel clock. It was just past three, barely an hour since she'd talked to David. She'd gotten the distinct impression during their brief conversation that he had a heavy work load this afternoon. That it would be impossible for him to break away from the office for quite a while.

One thing was certain. She couldn't let Marianne take off before he got here. Knowing this, she clutched at a straw and asked, "What about Patricia and Deborah?"

"What about them?" Marianne countered tensely.

"Did you leave a note for them?"

"I only left one note—for Evan. I thought it would be easier if he told them than if they read something from me."

"You really think that, Marianne?" Kris challenged.

"What do you mean?"

"Do you honestly think it will be easier for your daughters to hear the news from Evan's mouth? I can't imagine that he'll be calm enough to tell them something that'll make sense."

"You don't know Evan," Marianne said simply. "Evan is a disciplined, well-trained individual. He's accustomed to putting himself on the outside of difficult situations, to rationalizing things. He'd used to subjugating his personal feelings in favor of others. I'm sure he'll handle telling the girls very well."

"I doubt it," Kris disagreed deliberately. But if she'd angered Marianne, she couldn't tell.

"What makes you say that?" Marianne asked calmly.

"Because I think Evan loves you deeply...maybe more so than you realize. I suppose after people have been married a long time, they tend to take it for granted that one spouse will automatically know how the other one feels. Maybe Evan hasn't reaffirmed his devotion to you as often as he might have. I don't know. I do know that I watched him looking at you on Thanksgiving. The love in his eyes was so radiant it made me want to cry. He looked like a man who'd discovered heaven. I assumed that stemmed from how wonderful it was for him to be home again.''

"Home again," Marianne echoed. For several seconds, she sat quietly, lost in thought. Finally, she mused sadly, "I didn't give Evan much of a homecoming, did I?''

"Maybe that hadn't dawned on him yet," Kris said.

The expression on Evan's face had been something, she recalled. True, she'd missed what must have been a corresponding lack of expression on Marianne's face. But Evan, himself, had been enough to make her conclude that the Phillipses were a deeply devoted couple.

Marianne said slowly, "I believe what you've been saying, Kris. You're a very perceptive person. If I didn't know you worked at Hawthorne, I might have thought you were a psychiatrist like David. Or a psychologist. You seem to see into people, the way David does." She gave a funny little laugh and added, "It can be rather disconcerting, you know.''

"I haven't meant to pry," Kris said quickly.

"You haven't. I know you want to help, and I truly appreciate it. But I'm afraid Evan and I are past help, sad to say. I know he loves me, loves me deeply. The crazy part of it is, I love him, too.''

She broke off, appearing to compose herself. Then she said, "Love. As wonderful as love is, it isn't always enough. In my case, it definitely isn't enough. It doesn't necessarily help you get through a twenty-four-hour day, and that's what I'd be doing if I went back. Just getting through. I'd be putting in hours, not living them. Do you know what I'm saying?''

Before Kris could answer, the doorbell rang.

Marianne immediately stood up and clutched the satin robe around her. "Are you expecting someone?" she asked nervously.

Kris hesitated for only a second. Then she said steadily, "It's David. I... asked him to come."

CHAPTER FIFTEEN

DAVID WAS NOT ALONE. Evan stood by his side.

Both men were in uniform, and they could not have looked more imposing. As she stared up at them, Kris tried to imagine what kind of reaction their austere presences would have on Marianne. The prospect worried her. But there was nothing austere about Evan when, after a brief glance at Kris, he crossed the room and grabbed his wife by the shoulders.

"Just what do you think you're doing?" he demanded.

Marianne tried to shrug him away; Evan only dug deeper. She sparked, "You're hurting me, damn it!"

"Maybe you need to have me hurt you, to prove I'm alive!" Evan snapped back.

Kris, in her lone encounter with Evan on Thanksgiving, had pegged him as a pleasantly laid-back and rather self-effacing person. Everything Marianne had said about him today had substantiated that initial impression. But this was a different Evan she was seeing now. A glance at David showed her that she was not alone in that respect. He was staring at his friend as if he were a total stranger.

"I intend to prove to you that I'm alive, Marianne," Evan told his wife, still not relinquishing his tight grip on her shoulders. "If you think for a minute that I'd let you walk out of my life, you're very much mistaken."

"I *have* walked out," Marianne managed.

"No, you haven't," he contradicted. "You walked *away*, not out. I was lucky enough to find you sooner than I thought I would, but I would have followed you to the ends of this earth if I'd had to. You belong with me, Marianne. We joined our lives together a long time ago. They're so tightly interwoven there's no way you could cast me aside this easily. Didn't that dawn on you?"

At that, he let go of her. Marianne slumped down into the armchair, her face whiter than ever, her eyes dark pools of bewilderment. She looked too shocked to speak, too stunned to move.

Realizing this, Evan shuddered. He looked down at his hands as if he couldn't believe they were his, and said softly, "You know, I never understood how a person could strangle another person."

David stepped forward quickly. "Evan," he said.

A tired smile crossed Evan's face, making him look much more like the Reverend Evan Phillips. "You don't have to worry, Dave," he said calmly. "For a fleeting second I had an inkling of what the urge to kill must be like. Overwhelming. Beyond all reason. A dark, dark side of human compulsion."

He moved to the fireplace and held his hands out toward the flames. Then he turned and met Kris's eyes. "Please forgive me," he said softly, "for bursting into your home like this."

"Evan, there's no need to apologize."

"Yes, there is," he insisted. "You knew Dave was coming, but you didn't know I was coming with him. I guess you'll have to blame that on Dave. He told me Marianne was here because he knew I was losing my mind worrying. After that, nothing would have kept me from coming over."

The room was quiet for a moment. Then Evan asked, "I don't suppose you'd have the makings for a good stiff drink?"

"I think we could all do with a drink," David answered for her. "Come on, Kris. I'll help you."

Kris followed David to the kitchen and watched him close the door behind them. "Aren't you afraid to leave those two alone?" she queried, her voice low.

"No, I'm not," David said, scanning her liquor supply. "Let's see…Evan likes Scotch, but this time around he'll have to settle for bourbon," he decided.

"I can run out and get some Scotch," Kris offered.

"Not on your life. I want you here." He set the bottle of bourbon on the counter and opened the fridge. Plunking ice cubes into glasses, he said, "You leveled with Marianne before you let us in, didn't you?"

"Yes."

"Well, you were right. I was wrong. Honesty *was* the best policy. I just thought if she knew I was coming she might duck out."

"She couldn't." Kris giggled. "I hid her clothes. It would have taken her a while to find them."

David's smile widened into a full-fledged grin. "Ingenious, aren't you?" he commented, shaking his head. "You never cease to surprise me, Kris. Would you like a sherry or bourbon?"

"Bourbon, please."

"For medicinal purposes," David agreed. "I'm going to make one for Marianne, too, on that premise."

Kris cocked an ear toward the door. "Sounds awfully quiet in there," she observed.

"Well, I doubt they'll start throwing things at each other," David said, "though it might do them some good if they did. Sometimes people vent their anger too hastily, too openly. The alternative, of course, can be more corrosive than rust. If you're ever angry at me..."

"Yes?"

"Let me know about it, okay?"

David finished placing the drinks on a tray as he spoke. Without waiting for Kris's answer, he opened the kitchen door and, balancing the tray, headed for the living room.

She followed him and was surprised to find Evan sitting cross-legged at the side of Marianne's chair, looking up at her. He was speaking to her so softly that Kris couldn't make out his words, but the intensity of his tone came across clearly.

He got to his feet, accepted a drink from David, then went and sat down on the couch. Kris took the opposite end of the couch. David, glancing toward the space in the middle, chose a straight-backed chair that looked too small for him. An awkward moment passed before David abruptly got to his feet and said, "I just remembered. I meant to call the girls."

Marianne glanced up sharply. "What are you going to tell them, Dave?"

"Not much," he said. "I'll say that Evan and I are going out to do some Christmas shopping. They'll assume you're working late at the Navy Relief Office, I imagine."

"Don't you think *you* should call them, Evan?" Marianne suggested. "If either of them happens to look in my closet they'll know something's wrong."

"Then let's hope they don't look in your closet," Evan said levelly. "Frankly, I don't want to call them right now. I doubt if I could dissemble at the moment. No, I'm sure I couldn't, especially if Patty answered the phone. She's almost impossible to fool."

"She's like you," Marianne said.

Evan had been staring at his drink. His head jerked up sharply as he heard that, but he didn't comment.

"Why not wait a while longer to call them?" David suggested. "They're used to the two of you being out when they get home from school, aren't they?"

"Well . . . yes," Marianne admitted.

"Then they'll be fine. Meanwhile, I think Kris and I *will* sneak out and do some Christmas shopping. I still need to buy cards, Kris, and time's getting short."

He didn't need to elaborate. Kris had also been trying to think up an excuse to escape this scene for a little while. As she and David started down the front steps, though, a thought occurred to her. "Do you suppose I should go back and tell Marianne where her clothes are?" she asked.

"If she wants them badly enough she'll find them," David answered dryly. "I'm hoping the two of them will just stay put and talk. Dear God, how much easier my work would be if people would just talk to each other."

Kris glanced up at him. He looked bone tired. She said compassionately, "You didn't need this."

"What didn't I need?"

"This mess between Evan and Marianne."

"Well, neither did you, Kris. You were really drawn in. It still astonishes me to think how Marianne turned to you this morning. It also shows me she's a lot more perceptive than I thought she was."

"What do you mean by that?"

"She knew pure gold when she saw it."

Kris was wearing thick wool mittens, but David still managed to take her hand in his. "Want to walk a while?" he asked. "Or shall we drive somewhere?"

"We're within walking distance of a place that sells cards," Kris said. "Or would you rather go to a mall?"

"No, thank you," David said emphatically.

Dusk had yielded to darkness. The night was cold and quiet. Most of the homes in the neighborhood were decorated with colorful Christmas lights. Tiny white lights twinkled in bushes and shrubs. The crisp air smelled of wood fires. Several homes even had their Christmas trees up already, decorated and lighted.

As she and David walked along, Kris felt something stir inside her. At first she didn't recognize what it was. Then, she identified it. Christmas spirit. She was feeling a genuine surge of Christmas spirit, all because of this big, wonderful man at her side.

The man she loved.

He was staring ahead, deep in thought, she realized. In the muted glow of a streetlight, his expression seemed bleak.

"What is it, David?" she asked anxiously.

"I don't know," he hedged. "Evan and Marianne, I guess. The fact that they've drifted so far apart, that's part of it."

"And the rest?"

"I'm not sure. The season, maybe. Joyous for many people, but so terribly difficult for others. It's easy to understand why so many people sink into deep depressions when everyone's supposed to be so damned merry."

The bitterness in his tone shocked Kris. "Do the holidays depress you?" she asked.

"To tell you the truth, yes. At least they have for a long time. Back when I was a kid, before my father had his accident, it was different. Like most kids, I couldn't wait for Christmas. George and I used to sneak downstairs in the middle of the night to see what was under the tree.

"Later...things changed. Such things do change, of course. If you're lucky, though, times get better."

"And that's never been so with you?"

David was quiet for a moment. Then he said, "Well, I spent one married Christmas. Should have been terrific, but it wasn't. After that there was more med school, then internship and residency, now life as a bachelor officer living in the BOQ. I used to have visions of finding the absolutely right person, marrying her, having a beautiful home and kids. And white Christmases with joy in the air and all the wonderful warmth and feeling..."

"But the visions stopped," Kris concluded sadly.

"Yeah, they stopped." He glanced down at her, saw her stricken face and said, "Kris, Kris, don't look like that. I was being maudlin. It's this whole business with Evan and Marianne. I'll get over it and be guzzling up Christmas cheer just like everyone else."

They reached the shop that sold cards, and Kris tried not to think about what David had just said. She forced herself to select a few Christmas cards for her own skimpy mailing list, but that lilting holiday spirit she'd been experiencing was gone.

David kept glancing at Kris, wishing he could retract the speech he'd just made. Unfortunately, it was true. More often than not, he went into a personal funk at holiday time. Ironic, considering his profession.

He would have been looking forward to this particular Christmas with all the enthusiasm he remembered having as a child. Except for Jay Sothern. In David's mind, Jay's invisible presence still stood as a barrier between him and Kris.

There had been absolutely no chance to get together with Eric this afternoon, and his frustration over that was intense. He'd gotten through his consultations as quickly as he could after Kris had called, then had bolted over to the BOQ hoping Evan had stayed put.

Evan was seated in front of the TV, obviously not absorbing the lesson in amateur oil painting being demonstrated on the screen. David had told him about Kris's call, then wished he'd kept it to himself. There was no way he could have prevented Evan from crossing the river to the house on Granite Street.

In retrospect, he didn't think he and Evan had spoken two words during the drive. They'd walked up Kris's front steps in stony silence, then Evan's sudden explosion had come as a total surprise.

Kris was heading toward the cash register to pay for her cards. David hadn't picked out nearly the number he wanted, but he followed her. Outside the store, he suggested, "How about replacing those drinks we left sitting back at your house?"

"I don't really want a drink, thank you."

David looked down into her taut face and felt all kinds of things shifting inside him, emotion clashing with emotion, one feeling supplanting another.

"Dearest," he said gently, "there's something I have to tell you, something you have to know, no matter what."

Kris was dry-eyed, but felt as if she were sobbing buckets of tears inside. "What?" she managed.

"I love you," he said simply. "I love you, Kris. No matter what . . . I love you."

A STREET CORNER in New London, especially at the height of the Christmas shopping season, wasn't the best place in the world to declare one's love, David discovered. They were jostled by passersby as they stood there staring at each other. Kris looked as if the sky had fallen in on her, and David didn't know whether that was a good sign or bad.

"We've got to find someplace where we can talk," he urged. "Let's assume your apartment is still occupied, okay?"

"I don't know what to say," Kris said. "I...I don't think I understand you."

They were standing close to the curb. David tried to nudge her back against the buildings, but it was a lost cause. "What don't you understand?" he asked.

"You just told me you no longer have the visions you used to have," she reminded him.

"Kris, I was talking off the top of my head. I wasn't even making sense. This has been a very trying day."

"It hasn't exactly been easy for me, you know. I think we'd better head back to my place, David. Either Evan or Marianne have come to some sort of truce by now, or they're tearing each other's hair out, or they've left."

"If that's what you want," he said reluctantly.

They walked in silence back to Granite Street. As they reached the porch, Kris said, "Maybe I'd better ring the bell."

David reached over and rang it for her. When there was no answer, he rang it again. "Hmm," he said.

At that, Kris got out her key and opened the front door. A moment later, they stepped into an empty apartment. In the bedroom, the green satin robe had been laid carefully across the bed. On top of it, there was a note.

"I've gone home with Evan for tonight," Marianne had written. "But I've taken the liberty of leaving my suitcases, and I'll pick them up tomorrow while the girls are at school. Meantime, Evan and I plan to do a *lot* of talking. Kris, thank you...more than I ever can say. I'll be in touch."

Evan had left his note on the coffee table in the living room. "Kris and David," it read. "We called a cab, will take it as far as the gate so as not to arouse suspicion with the girls. Without the two of you as friends, we might not have gotten even this far. Your help and concern are greatly appreciated. Thanks, Kris, for taking care of Marianne. Dave, I'll see you sometime tomorrow."

Kris was still in the bedroom when David read Evan's note. He crumpled it, and stuffed it in his pocket. It had been a totally draining day. Despite his recent declaration to her, spending the night with Kris wasn't even a consideration. Besides, her mood had also taken a turn for the worse. It was obvious she wanted to be alone.

AT SEVEN O'CLOCK the next morning, David was jostled awake by the sound of someone pounding on his door. When he found Evan standing on the threshold, he inwardly groaned. He wasn't sure he could cope with any of the Phillipses' problems this morning. His own plate was full.

"Don't worry," Evan said quickly, "I'm not here about Marianne and myself." He followed David into the suite's living room, then held out a large Styrofoam cup of coffee. "Thought this was the least I could offer for waking you up."

David accepted the coffee gratefully. He'd had a bad night's sleep and, though caffeine wasn't exactly a remedy for sleeplessness, he needed a jolt. He took a hefty swallow, then asked, "Where's Marianne?"

"Home, asleep. Somehow, we watched a couple of television shows with the kids after we got home. I think that took five years worth of self-control out of both of us. After the girls went to bed, Marianne and I talked for a while. By the time we went to bed ourselves, she was exhausted. I left a note for her, and I want to get back there before too long. But there's something I need to tell you first."

"What?"

"It's about Jay Sothern," Evan said uneasily. "I've been thinking about the way I shut you out the other day. Maybe I was wrong."

David arched an eyebrow. "Do tell," he said.

"Okay, I don't blame you for being sarcastic. But I believe in certain things."

"You don't need to convince me of that, Evan."

"No, I suppose I don't. Dave, if it had been just you involved, I wouldn't have been so reticent."

"What's that supposed to mean?"

"I watched you with Kris on Thanksgiving. I know you pretty well. I've never seen you look at a woman before the way you look at her."

"Well, the answer to that is simple enough," David said. "I love her."

"Yes, I thought so. But as happy as I am for you, it compounded my problem. My moral dilemma, I guess you could say."

"Because of what you know about Jay?"

"Yes."

"Look, Evan, if you're feeling some sense of obligation because Kris took Marianne in yesterday, and I took you to her, forget it. I'm not asking you to break your code of ethics where Jay's concerned."

"Have you contacted Cal DeMott yet?" Evan countered.

"No, not yet."

"Cal would doubtless tell you anyway, doctor to doctor," Evan said. "Maybe I hoped that's the way it would happen, if it had to happen at all. Jay is dead. The other person involved evidently isn't even around here anymore. So I saw no point in resurrecting things."

"What other person?"

"Dave . . . can I go back to the beginning?"

"If you must, Evan. God, at this rate I'm considering taking up smoking again!"

"You well might after you hear the whole story. Mind if I sit down?"

"No, of course not."

They took seats on the couch, then Evan said, "I don't know if Jay ever had any relationships back in Pennsylvania when he was a teenager. Or if this was the first time he knew what it meant to love someone aside from his sister—in a totally different way, of course."

Something in Evan's tone alerted David. He looked across at the chaplain warily, and asked, "Would you define relationships, please?"

Evan sighed heavily, then said, "There's no point in beating around the bush, Dave. Jay Sothern was gay."

It sank in slowly, but it sank all the way in. And David could only think of Kris.

Personally, he had no problems dealing with people's sexual preferences. As a psychiatrist, he knew it was usually simpler to be heterosexual, that the added pressures on many homosexuals were tremendous. The whole subject was extremely complex, even for the experts.

David had his own theories on homosexuality, but his scientific opinion was beside the point right now. He could understand, sympathize. That's what was important. In fact, Evan's pronouncement had given him a feeling of compassion toward Jay Sothern that had been lacking until now. But could Kris understand?

From everything she'd told him, Kris had been brought up in a very traditional family. David could easily imagine that certain issues were never even discussed in a family like that, let alone explained. Because of this, a certain stigma was often attached to things running counter to the mores of society. Even a sense of revulsion was planted that never should be planted at all.

David was disappointed in himself for not even considering the possibility that Jay Sothern was gay. He told himself he should start back in Psych 101, for being so obtuse. And he was virtually certain that Kris's initial reaction, should she hear this about Jay, would be disillusionment, profound disillusionment.

Kris didn't need that kind of grief.

David moistened lips suddenly gone dry, and asked, "You're sure about this, Evan?"

"Of course I'm sure. Jay came here to submarine school and fell in love. Deeply and sincerely in love."

"With someone in his class? Is that what you're saying?"

"Yes." Evan nodded. "That's exactly what I'm saying. It was the first time Jay had ever allowed himself to express his innate feelings. When they were returned...well, you could say he was staggered. Until then, Jay had spent his life in hiding, so to speak. He'd hidden his feelings from his friends and, especially, his sister. He told me he pretended to be in love with a girl in his high-school class. Did it as a ruse because he couldn't handle the way he really felt inside. Above all, he didn't want Kris to become suspicious. He adored her. He couldn't live with the idea of hurting her. I think you could even say he died so he wouldn't hurt her."

"He committed suicide over this person he fell in love with?"

"I can't swear to that," Evan said. "As you know, I wasn't even here when Jay died. But I strongly suspect that's what happened, yes."

"Do you have any ideas why?"

"Nothing concrete, no. There could have been any number of reasons. Knowing he'd have to come out in the open some day. Wondering what that would do to his career. Agonizing over how Kris would react. I don't know. Maybe the other man fell in love with someone else. That can happen, after all." He shook his head, then added, "Cal may know more about that than I do. You'll have to ask him, that's all."

"Where was this other person when Jay died?"

"I don't know," Evan admitted. "Jay told me he'd washed out of sub school. Jay, on the other hand, went on to qualify as an electronics specialist. Got high marks all the way around. I had the impression—though I could be wrong—that the other man lived nearby. That he'd settled somewhere close to Groton so he could spend time with Jay. Jay didn't come out with that. I got the feeling that he wanted very much to talk, but couldn't. He hinted that there'd been several breaks in the relationship. One time after he was graduated. And again after he was assigned to a ship and went off to sea. Whatever, the bonds between them were very strong, very deep. Whether that had anything to do with what happened, I couldn't say."

David shrugged, speechless. He took a sip of coffee and stared morosely across the room. It was cruel irony, really. Despite his training as a psychiatrist—despite the fact that he'd successfully dealt with hundreds of patients and their problems—he'd never felt more hopeless about how Kris would react.

"Jay was a terrific young man," Evan said soberly. "An excellent submariner, a credit to the submarine service. Kris should be very proud of him. What I fear, what I began to fear when you started questioning me the other day, is that if she learns the whole truth about her brother, her idol will forever after have clay feet. She'll lose sight of the real Jay, which would be a great pity. Know what I'm saying?"

"Exactly." David nodded. He didn't stop to tell Evan that he'd been thinking the same thing. Instead, he asked urgently, "Do you have even the remotest idea where this other man might be now?"

"None."

"What was his name?"

"Jay never told me," Evan said levelly. "And I never asked."

"But you still think it was something connected with him that caused Jay to kill himself?"

Evan spread his hands wide in a gesture of supplication. "Jay had everything going for him," he said. "What else could have made him want to die?"

CHAPTER SIXTEEN

DAVID WAS AT HIS OFFICE, waiting, when Eric Benson arrived.

The young corpsman looked at him quizzically. "Early, aren't you, sir?" he asked.

"I suppose so." It didn't matter, actually. He could as well have come in at dawn. Once again, he'd had a chaotic night's sleep, plagued by some very bad dreams.

"Eric," he said, hoping he didn't sound as tired as he felt, "this search of mine is narrowing down. What I need are the names of the thirty-three men who washed out of Jay Sothern's class in submarine school."

"Yes, sir," Eric replied dutifully.

"And photographs, too."

"Very well, sir."

"How long do you think it will take?"

Eric grinned. "I know my way around the files pretty good now, so...maybe by the middle of the afternoon. I'll get on it right away."

The redheaded corpsman was true to his word. Shortly past three o'clock, he arrived back at the office. David, between patients, was drinking a cup of black coffee hoping it would keep him awake. He cast an appraising eye at the bulky manila envelope Eric placed on his desk.

"You got it all?" he asked.

Eric nodded, plainly pleased with himself. "It took a while for the pictures," he allowed. "They had to make prints from negatives in some cases, but it's all there. I added all the group shots I could find, too.''

David looked up and met Eric's eyes. Managing a tired grin, he said, ''If it were in my power, I'd make you an instant admiral.''

Eric grinned back. ''I'm not sure I'd want that, sir.''

''I know what you mean.''

Once Eric had left, David stared at the envelope, curiously reluctant to open it. He had a gut feeling that the answers, which had been so elusive, were now very close at hand. Facing those answers was something else. He was actually relieved when his next patient arrived and he had to postpone that task.

He took the thick envelope back to the BOQ with him after his office hours were over. In his suite, he changed into jeans and a crewneck sweater, then got himself a cold beer. Only then did he sit down on his standard-issue sofa, pull the coffee table closer, adjust the lamp at his side to a better angle . . . and open the envelope.

A series of bright, eager faces preserved in black-and-white glossy prints looked up at him, most of them smiling. There was no stigma attached to being ''washed out'' of submarine school. The reasons for that happening were many and varied. Some were related to stress, but many were not. Academic standards in the school were high, David knew. Failures often occurred. In such cases, the trainee was given the chance to try again. If he failed his second attempt he was dismissed.

Some of these boys may have succeeded the second time around. Others might have been transferred to alternate branches of the navy. Others might have opted to return to civilian life. Generally, enrollees in the school were assigned in groups of about a dozen men. From that point on, they went through training and classes as a team. David quickly became thankful that Eric had thought to include group photos of the class. Many of these depicted teams both at work and at play.

By now, Jay Sothern's face was as familiar to David as if he'd been related to him himself. He had scanned the photos Kris had given him—mostly family shots, a few of Jay in navy uniform—over and over again. He quickly identified Jay in a group picture, then carefully scanned the other faces.

Almost immediately, a memory surfaced. One of Jay's teammates had come to him for counseling. They'd had some long, intense sessions. In the end, it was largely on his recommendation that the man had been dropped.

He remembered the man vividly, but he couldn't recall his name. Frustrated, he moved the photograph directly under the glare of the light as if that might refresh his memory. It didn't. He did notice, though, that the young man in question was standing next to Jay. Not that that necessarily meant anything, David warned himself. Still, as he went from one group photo to the next, a pattern did emerge. In every picture, Jay and this other young trainee were side by side.

David became so immersed in this that a long moment passed before he realized he'd gone offtrack. Information on this photo companion of Jay's was undoubtedly contained in the records Eric had gathered.

He rifled through a stack of reports, his heart pounding. And suddenly the name leapt out at him. Daniel Shaughnessy Kalich. How could he have forgotten?

As if it were yesterday, he saw Danny Kalich smile, heard him say, "The last name was a lot longer, sir. My grandfather shortened it to Kalich."

"Czech, isn't it?" David had asked.

"Yes, sir."

"I gather your mother was Irish?"

The boy had grinned. "As Irish as Saint Patrick's Day," he'd said.

Danny had been tall and slim, with a shock of dark hair and eloquent dark eyes. He was a sensitive kid who had frankly admitted he'd volunteered for the submarine service because he welcomed the idea of spending months out under the ocean, where he could do his job, then curl up quietly in his bunk and read.

"I guess I'm a loner," he'd confessed. "I've never been with the crowd, if you know what I mean."

He wrote poetry. At one session, when he'd come to have a great deal of confidence in David, he'd read several of his poems. They had been beautiful, David recalled—exquisite, artistic verses that told the tale of a lonely idealist with a psyche so fragile David feared it could shatter.

David had the feeling that Danny was a genius. Gentle, yet intense. Full of love, but full of fire. There was a bridled passion within him just waiting to surface. It showed itself only occasionally in his face, but always in his poems.

There was no way, David had concluded, that this man should be permitted to become a submariner. He was much too vulnerable. Though life aboard a submarine could generate its share of loneliness, homesickness and nostalgia, it was not designed for self-proclaimed "loners." Chances were ninety-nine to one, in David's estimation, that Danny Kalich would have eventually cracked under the stress of life aboard a sub. That, he couldn't allow to happen.

Had Danny Kalich been gay? Had he known he was gay?

David thought about that. Of the hundreds of young men he'd interviewed and counseled, Danny did stand out as exceptional. But gay? If Danny was gay, he'd still been deep in the closet at that time. Understandably so.

Maybe he was as good an actor as he was a poet, David thought ruefully.

Carefully, line by line, he started reading Danny's records. Certain things came back to him as he did. Danny had come from rural Vermont originally. His parents were dead. His closest living relative was a sister, Mrs. Eunice Chernowski, of Manchester, New Hampshire and Gales Ferry, Connecticut.

Gales Ferry!

David fell back against the couch cushions, then got up and walked over to his front window. The view overlooked the high-security submarine docks and the Thames itself. Small pools of gold light shimmered across the black river. The effect, David decided, was stygian.

In keeping with my mood, he thought.

Under other circumstances, he might have been elated. As it was, he'd never felt more depressed. He was very close to solving the mystery of Jay's fate, but each discovery was bringing with it a terrible blow to the knowledge that once he'd found out *everything*, he would have to tell Kris.

Slowly, he walked away from the window. Reluctantly, he found his phone book and thumbed through it. There was no listing in Gales Ferry under Chernowski or Kalich. The phone was on the corner of his desk. David picked it up, dialed information and asked for the number he sought. The answer came back in a lilting, computerized voice: "That number has been temporarily disconnected."

Probably because it's seasonal, David suspected. Still, the fact there was a phone at all indicated that Eunice Chernowski, or her brother Danny, or both of them, owned the house on the river that had figured so prominently in Jay's conversations with Kris.

David dialed information again. This time he asked for the number of Chernowski in Manchester, New Hampshire. A moment later, another lilting computerized voice spoke back to him. Time had passed, but Mrs. Eunice Chernowski hadn't moved. Of course, there was no telling where Danny Kalich might be, David warned himself, as he dialed the Manchester number.

The phone was answered on the fourth ring. David heard a child crying in the background, heard an irritated female voice say, "Be quiet! I have to talk on the telephone." Only then did the woman say, "Hello?"

"Mrs. Chernowski?" he asked, holding his breath.

"Yes?"

"My name is David Jorgenson. You don't know me. I'm assigned to the submarine base in Groton, Connecticut..."

"Did you say the submarine base?"

"That's right."

"Why are you calling me?" There was an edge to the woman's tone. She wasn't exactly hostile, but she wasn't friendly, either.

"It's about your brother, Danny Kalich," David said.

"Why are you calling me about Danny?"

Her voice had more than an edge, this time. David caught a ragged note he'd heard many times before. Often, it showed up in the voices of people bordering on hysteria.

"I'm trying to get in touch with your brother, that's all," David said, as calm and reassuring as possible.

"There's something I need to discuss with him. A personal matter."

"Danny's dead," Eunice Chernowski said. "If you knew Danny, how come you don't know *that*?" she demanded brokenly.

David could almost see the tears welling in her eyes. At the same time, he felt the bile rise in his throat. "I'm a doctor at the base, Mrs. Chernowski," he told her. "Danny was a patient of mine. Something's come up that I wanted to talk to him about and I hoped to reach him through you. I had no idea, Mrs. Chernowski. I... I'm terribly, terribly sorry."

"Excuse me a minute," she mumbled, sniffing. She went off the line and there was the muffled sound of her blowing her nose. She came back to say, "What did you want to talk to Danny about?"

"It was a personal matter. Something to do with another patient of mine. Mrs. Chernowski... when did Danny die?"

"Right at the beginning of April." She sniffed.

At the beginning of April, Jay would have been on leave. Kris had said her brother had gone back to Pennsylvania to visit friends, then had stayed a few days in New York. But had he?

"Mrs. Chernowski, this is important, or I wouldn't be bothering you," David said honestly. "Where was Danny living?"

"He'd been staying with our aunt and uncle at their place in Vermont. They have a farm just north of Rutland. He went up there when he knew how ill he was. It was his favorite place in the whole world."

"I see."

"It was cancer, doctor. It started in his spine and spread very quickly. I guess we can thank God for that.

When he got bad, they put him in the hospital in Rutland. That's where he died."

"Do you own a house in Gales Ferry, Mrs. Chernowski?"

The change of topic stopped her momentarily. Then she said, "My husband does, yes. His mother's family was from there a long time ago. He inherited the place. Sometimes we rent it out in the summer. Danny stayed there for a while after he got out of the navy. He read a lot and wrote poetry."

"Yes, I know."

"Then he got sick and moved up to Vermont."

Probably when Jay Sothern was at sea, David thought.

He decided to plunge. "By any chance did you know a man named Jay Sothern?" he asked.

"Yes," she said. And then she began to cry. "Jay and Danny... were very close," she said between sobs. "I've never really understood things like that, but they were very close. They said they were life partners. When Danny died, Jay was with him. I thought Jay was going to die, too. He looked like all the life had been drained out of him. At the funeral, my aunt and uncle kept telling him he was always welcome at the farm, but he didn't say much. I felt so bad for him, but I didn't know where to get hold of him. I thought he'd call us or something. He never did."

Eunice Chernowski sighed. "Maybe," she said, her voice steadier, "it was just as well."

KRIS TELEPHONED DAVID at nine that evening. She'd thought he would call her if only to give her some further word about Marianne and Evan, so she hadn't strayed far from the phone. Now... his phone rang and rang. She let it ring ten times, then hung up, discouraged.

Last night, things simply hadn't gone well between them. Then David had left suddenly, with hardly a word. All day long in her office, Kris had stared out the window toward the sub base across the river. All day long she wondered what he was doing.

At nine-twenty, her phone rang. She grabbed the receiver on the first ring, sure it would be David.

"Kris?" It was Marianne Phillips.

"Oh, hello," she said, fighting down disappointment.

"I meant to call you earlier. Is David there with you?"

"No."

"Hmm, I was hoping to catch him. Evan tried the BOQ a number of times, no answer. Guess he's off Christmas shopping again."

Kris hadn't thought about that possibility. Somehow, though, she doubted that's what he was doing.

"Kris, are you still there?"

"Yes, I'm here."

"I want to thank you again for yesterday," Marianne told her. "Maybe you didn't save my life, but I think you saved my marriage."

Before Kris could protest, she continued, "Evan went to see David early this morning. Then he took the day off and spent it with me, just talking. I don't think I could have handled it, Kris, if I hadn't talked to you yesterday. You let me go on and on, something I'm not used to doing. It helped me tremendously in opening up with Evan, in telling him my real feelings."

"I'm so glad, Marianne."

"So am I," she said softly. "We haven't worked it all out, yet. But at least we're listening to each other and re-

specting each other's viewpoints. And . . . we're going to
stay together.''

"Oh, Marianne . . . that's wonderful.''

"I'm the happiest I've been in months," Marianne
agreed. "So Evan and I would like to take you and David out to dinner. Someplace special where we can cele-
brate Thanksgiving all over again. Our own personal
thanksgiving, which we want to share with you and Dave.
Would Saturday night be okay?''

"I think it would be fine," Kris said hesitantly. "For
me, it is, but I'm not sure about David."

"Evan will be talking to David," Marianne promised.
"So I'll just say good-night."

Kris heard a click, but sat holding the phone until the
dial tone came on again. Then she slowly put the receiver down and looked up at the mantel clock. It was a
few minutes past nine-thirty. She picked up her copy of
the *New London Day*, scanned the front page, but not
even the headlines really registered.

Shortly after ten, she phoned the BOQ again. This
time, the line was busy. She waited, then dialed again.
There was no good reason she should feel incredible relief when she heard David's voice, but she did.

"Where *were* you?" she demanded, then wished she
could take the question back. He had a right to go where
he pleased, after all.

"I was out walking," he said, his voice sounding curiously muffled.

"Have you got a cold?" she asked, then wished she
could take that question back, too. She sounded like a
worried mother.

"I take it you've been trying to get me."

"A few times, yes."

"Any special reason?"

"You left your Christmas cards here last night," Kris temporized.

"Oh, right. Well, I didn't have time to send them out, anyway."

"David, there's something I have to say."

"You sound displeased," he observed.

"Well, I guess I am. The way you left last night...it wasn't very nice."

"What do you mean?"

"Well, you just left. You barely said good-night."

"I got the distinct impression you wanted to be alone. So, I headed back to the base."

"The base, right."

"You say that rather sarcastically, Kris. I'd almost forgotten how much you hate the place."

"What?" she asked, confused.

"I said, I'd almost forgotten how much you hate the sub base. Imagine that. Maybe I'll strike the word from my vocabulary whenever I'm around you. I certainly have no desire to stir up bad memories."

He sounded incredibly bitter, and he wasn't making any sense at all.

"I don't know how we got on this," Kris retorted, "but you don't give me credit for much, do you?"

"What's that supposed to mean?"

"I'm not a weakling, David. I don't need to be protected or mollycoddled. It was very difficult for me the first time I went back to the sub base, I admit that. That's the day I had my appointment with you. But things have changed since then."

"Perhaps. But nothing's actually happened to make you like the sub base, right?"

You have. Kris wanted to speak the words aloud, yet she held them back. Her sense of timing warned her that this was not a good moment to pour out how she felt about either David or the place where he lived and worked.

One thing was true, though. In the past few weeks, she'd come to associate the sub base far more with David than she did with Jay. Where Submarine Base New London was concerned, she had a distinctly defined sense of the present and the past. Jay was past, David was present. It was vital, she'd learned, to differentiate between the two.

David was a psychiatrist in the navy working in the submarine service right now. At the same time, he occupied a very large portion of Kris's heart.

She asked, "Did something go wrong today?"

There was dead silence. Then, "Why do you ask that?"

"Because you seem out of sorts."

He sighed. "I'm sorry I'm so obvious. A few things just got to me, that's all. I thought maybe a brisk walk in the cold fresh air would help. So I walked all over the base, up one hill, down the next." He laughed dryly. "I guess it didn't do as much good as I hoped it would."

"Did Evan reach you?"

"About having dinner Saturday? Yes, I was speaking to him just before you called. He said Marianne had already talked to you."

"Yes."

"Evan says they're going to pick out someplace really special to take us."

"You do want to go, then?"

"Why wouldn't I?"

"I don't know."

David heard the unhappiness in her voice and wished he was a better actor. He wanted so desperately to keep

Kris from ever being unhappy again. That was why he'd put on a heavy navy-issue wool coat and walked through the cold darkness for almost two hours, contemplating all the things he now knew about Jay.

He couldn't tell Kris. It was as simple as that. He couldn't tell her.

"Look, it's been a long day," he told her. "I for one need some sleep." He paused, then said, "I'll call you at the college in the morning, okay? Maybe we can get together tomorrow after work. How does that sound?"

"Sounds good," Kris murmured.

"And Kris…I love you," David said. And gently hung up.

CHAPTER SEVENTEEN

THE ANCIENT MARINER was a magnificent old inn on the shores of Long Island South, a few miles south of New London. It was so popular that usually there was a long waiting list for reservations. Evan frankly admitted that he'd lucked out in booking a table for four on such relatively short notice.

"Maybe because it's the Saturday before Christmas and a lot of people are at parties," he surmised, as he swung off Interstate 95 onto a local road that headed toward the sound.

"Maybe rank has its privileges," David observed lazily.

"My rank?" Evan asked.

"Well, you have to admit commander sounds impressive. Or did you say lieutenant commander?"

"I took full advantage," Evan said urbanely.

"And you, a man of the cloth!"

Ever since they'd picked Kris up at her apartment, the two men had been chiding each other good-naturedly as only two close friends can do. They'd decided to take Evan's comfortable, roomy sedan. Thinking about that, Kris realized it meant they'd all be returning together. The others would drop her off at Granite Street, and it would be awkward at the least to suggest that just David come in for a while. She wanted so much to be alone with him, to talk to him. She had the uneasy feeling that he'd deliberately been avoiding her these past few days.

She tried to tell herself it was probably all her imagination. Certainly, David was being affectionate enough tonight. They were sitting close together in the back seat. David had his arm around her shoulder. Suddenly she felt him lift the edge of her white wool cape and run exploratory fingers over the curve of her breast. It was all she needed to start a sensual whirlpool spinning wildly.

Evan drove up to the front door of the inn to let Marianne and Kris out. "I'm not always this chivalrous," he warned, "but you two look so incredibly gorgeous tonight, I'd hate for the wind to wreck those hairdos."

The two women discovered there was a ladies' cloakroom with a powder room beyond it. They primped, admiring both the surroundings—the Christmas decorations were exquisite, many of them dating back to Victorian times—and each other's raiments.

Marianne was wearing vivid red, the perfect foil for her dark coloring. Kris was wearing winter white. Sparkling crystal earrings shaped like miniature Christmas trees dangled from her lobes. A crystal pendant fashioned in the form of a snowflake hugged the hollow of her throat. The jewelry was another early Christmas present from David. It had been delivered to her apartment by a young submariner who'd identified himself as Eric Benson and said he worked in David's office.

"The commander knew I was coming over to New London this evening, so he asked if I'd drop this off with you," Eric had informed her. "He said to open it. He thought you might want to use it."

Kris had opened the small package and knew its treasures would be perfect to wear on Saturday night. Yet she couldn't help but wonder why David hadn't driven over with the lovely gift himself. It wasn't that far from Groton to New London. Or was it?

Even while he gently caressed her during the ride to the Ancient Mariner, even as he was evoking wonderful sensations in her, Kris sensed an uncertainty in his feelings, a peculiar restraint. It was as if David were going through the motions of being with her while his mind was far away.

He and Evan, both wearing handsome suits tonight, were waiting in the vestibule when Kris and Marianne emerged from the powder room. A headwaiter led them through the dining room to a corner window table. Outside, the trees, bushes and trelliswork were festooned with tiny white Christmas lights. It had snowed again that morning, so the ground was smooth, sparkling white.

Kris breathed, "I've never seen anything so lovely."

"I have," David murmured, close to her ear. "You."

She turned to face him and saw a trace of moisture in his beautiful silvery eyes. He said, so softly she barely caught the phrase, "I love you so much."

Her doubts should have dissolved at that, yet strangely they didn't. He was speaking as if his was a forbidden love, and that didn't make sense. She loved him at least as much as he loved her. She was anxious to put the past behind them and soar into the future. She couldn't entirely forget, she was honest about that. Little feelings of guilt would nudge her from time to time, she knew. But she would learn to live with that, because it had nothing to do with David.

She would never understand why Jay had dissembled about knowing him. Why he'd said that David owned a house on the Thames. It must have been a mistake on

Jay's part. Anyone could make a mistake. The important thing was she'd come full circle. She believed the truth of everything David had ever said to her.

Didn't he realize that?

This special dinner was neither the time nor place to get into that. Evan was exuberantly pouring champagne. Kris realized that she owed it to the Phillipses—it was their night, after all—to stick strictly to the present. To enjoy this moment with David at her side and two new-found friends sitting across from her, their faces glowing with happiness.

She held her glass high. "To both of you," she toasted Evan and Marianne. "And," she dared, turning to David, "to us."

They clicked glasses, but the look of sorrow that filled David's eyes nearly stopped Kris cold. Her fingers seemed to freeze, and it was all she could do to sip her champagne.

Fortunately, Evan and Marianne were so engrossed in each other that the incident passed without their noticing. Evan proposed another toast, then it was Marianne's turn, and then David's. In another room, a combo was playing dance music. Setting his glass down, David turned to Kris and suggested, "Shall we?"

She hadn't danced with him since the first night he'd taken her out to dinner. She remembered feeling incredibly guilty then, as if she were consorting with the enemy. Tonight she moved into his arms feeling she truly belonged there. David pressed a hand against her waist, but instead of merging on the first step, they collided. Kris was thrown off balance. Fortunately, David kept a grip on her.

"I'm sorry," he apologized. "I seem to remember telling you I'm a lousy dancer."

"No, you're not," she protested. Impulsively, she touched his shoulder, reached a hand behind his neck. His muscles were terribly tight. "You're so tense, David," she said, looking up to meet his eyes. "What is it?"

"Let's dance," he answered tersely.

This time, he did better. But when the orchestra suddenly swung into a rendition of "White Christmas," he missed a step again. He swore softly, then said, "Excuse my clumsiness, Kris. It was hearing that song. All my life, I've dreamed of sharing white Christmases with somebody like you. I couldn't have painted a picture of you, but I knew what I wanted. Someone warm and wonderful, someone loving and compassionate to share my life with..."

His voice trailed off and, when Kris stole a glance at his face, he looked away. The hopeless tone of his voice daunted her. All his life, he'd wanted someone like her. He'd just said that, hadn't he? Yet he was acting like he couldn't have her, when in her mind that would be the most marvelous thing in the universe.

As they continued dancing, Kris racked her brains and couldn't even begin to imagine what was bothering David so much. He'd been open with her about everything, totally honest about his first marriage and equally honest about other relationships, none of which, from what she could judge, had gone very far.

He loved her, damn it! He'd said so and she believed him. So why the problem now when they'd managed to resolve so many of the problems that had come between them?

The answer came unbidden.

Jay.

David must have learned something about Jay, something that he didn't want to tell her. From the beginning, he'd tried to protect her, had warned her that the truth could never bring Jay back. But would he sacrifice their love to keep her image of Jay intact? Yes, he probably would.

By the time the music stopped, Kris's anger was beginning to brim. Just the other night she'd told him in no uncertain terms that she didn't want to be mollycoddled. Did he still have no faith in her?

Evan and Marianne were standing at the edge of the dance floor waiting for the music to start again. But Kris had had enough of dancing and suspected David had, too.

Back at their table, he politely held out her chair. The gesture struck Kris as ironic. Usually, David's manners were impeccable. But once in a while he'd do something that would emphasize the rugged nature of his individualism. He was a contradiction in many ways, which made him all the more interesting and attractive. Still, the opposing factors of his personality could be baffling. Certainly, they were baffling her now.

He took his seat and nodded at the silver bucket in which the champagne rested on ice. "More champagne?" he asked.

"Not just now."

He didn't refill his own glass, either. So, Kris thought sadly, neither of them was in the mood for champagne. Here they were in a beautiful setting with David's best friends. Here it was a few days till Christmas. They were supposed to be celebrating the Phillipses' very significant reunion. Supposed to be enjoying themselves immensely.

Kris latched onto that and said, "Let's not spoil the evening for Marianne and Evan, okay?"

David looked startled. "What are you talking about?"

"Obviously, David, my dear, you're not having fun," Kris informed him bitterly. "It shows. I'm just asking you not to let it show so much. I don't know what's on your mind that's causing this attitude change in you. I have an idea, but now isn't the time to get into it."

David looked so miserable Kris nearly felt sorry for him, but letting him off the hook was something she had no intention of doing. When the moment was right, she wanted a confrontation. She'd force one. Because whatever was bugging him almost certainly concerned her.

In a low voice, he asked, "What do you think's on my mind, Kris?"

"I told you," she snapped, "this isn't the time."

At that, David pulled himself together with a visible effort and nodded as if he'd reached an important conclusion. "You're right," he stated. "This isn't the time for anything other than helping Evan and Marianne enjoy their celebration."

"Do you think you can manage to do that?"

"If you can. You're not exactly a picture of holiday happiness yourself, you know."

"I'm willing to make an all-out effort."

"Okay, then, smile at me."

"I'm not sure I want to smile at you."

"Please," he cajoled.

Over David's shoulder, Kris saw Marianne and Evan returning from the dance floor. Then she looked back and met his eyes. The smile he bestowed on her was so infectious, so endearing, her heart flipped.

"You, David Jorgenson," she managed, half cross, half coy, "are going to get it!"

SUNDAY MORNING Dave woke up with a splitting headache and a sore throat. He glanced out the window and saw it was a raw gray day. Perfect for staying at the BOQ and attending to his Christmas cards.

The cards I left over at Kris's, he thought with a groan.

He made himself a cup of instant coffee—his throat was too sore to eat anything—then dressed warmly and headed for the Navy Exchange. Among the thousands of items sold there were greeting cards. Understandably, the Christmas-card section had been picked over. But David was in no mood to leave the base, so he settled on a box that wasn't too bad.

As he walked back to the BOQ, an icy wind was blowing in off the river. It had chilled him to the bone by the time he reached his suite. He got out a bottle of bourbon, filled a jigger and drank it neat—something he rarely did, especially in the morning. Then he tried to settle down at his desk and write cheery little messages inside each card. On the third card, he gave up.

He reached for the phone to call Kris, but stopped short of dialing. He'd walked her as far as her porch last night while Evan and Marianne waited in the car. They'd said a brief good-night, kissed each other quickly and lightly, and that was that. In a way, he was glad there'd been no chance for any further questions from Kris. It had been a reprieve of sorts. But reprieves couldn't extend forever.

David knew he had a decision to make and he had to make it soon. There were just two ways to go. He could be totally honest with Kris at the risk of hurting her terribly. Or he could place the truth in a safe and throw away the combination. In that case, he would have to somehow condition himself to live a lie. He would have to close the door on what he'd learned about Jay and never open it again.

At moments, he wondered if he wasn't overreacting. The story of Jay and Danny was tragic, but there was nothing shameful about it as far as he was concerned. They were two very private individuals dedicated to their work, their families and to each other.

Would Kris take it that way, though?

After a time, David turned on the television. He quickly discovered there was nothing he wanted to see. He felt lousy, totally out of sorts physically, mentally and emotionally, which made for heavy going.

By early afternoon, he gave up entirely and crawled back into bed. Within minutes, he fell asleep...and slept for hours. When he awakened, his throat was sorer than ever, but his head felt clearer. He went back to the Christmas cards, determined to finish them so that he could chalk up one accomplishment on this otherwise miserable day.

ON GRANITE STREET, Kris also tackled writing the few Christmas cards she planned to send out. It wasn't until she put pen to paper that she realized the people who'd known both Jay and herself back in Pennsylvania probably wouldn't know Jay was gone. She'd always hated Christmas cards that conveyed bad news. Yet this was often the only time of the year when people communicated with each other. Catching up on things was practically unavoidable. It was either that or simply sign one's name.

She found it impossible to relate Jay's tragedy next to the words "Merry Christmas." In each case, she wrote a very brief message promising a longer correspondence after New Year's. That she would be able to handle.

As she ate a light lunch of soup and toast, the walls of her apartment started to close in. Funny how they sometimes did that when the weather outside was miserable. She needed to get out. Layering up with a couple of sweaters and her warm wool coat, then adding the red cloche and matching scarf, Kris left the apartment and began walking with no particular destination in mind.

The raw, damp cold was unpleasant. Kris felt it penetrating right through her carefully chosen costume. Shivering, she thought about going to a movie, but knew she couldn't possibly sit through two hours of even an Academy-award-winning film. She was too restless, too edgy. No matter how she tried to block him out of her mind, all she could think of was David.

She had expected—she'd hoped—that he would call her this morning. The fact that he hadn't only confirmed the puzzling notion that he was deliberately avoiding her, and that hurt. Why now, of all times?

The glittering Christmas tree she spotted through the front windows of a classic old colonial house brought an ache to her throat. She hadn't thought about putting up a Christmas tree herself. She didn't even have a holiday wreath on her front door. She would have, had not this strange impasse with David suddenly arisen.

These past few days had drained the Christmas spirit out of her. With only a few days to the cherished holiday, David had said nothing about sharing the day. Perhaps he'd decided to join his brother, his mother and his aunt in Florida. Kris wished she had someplace to go, someone to be with, then told herself to stop feeling so sorry for herself. Self-pity was the worst!

She hadn't intended to do any shopping this afternoon, but as she passed a shop window, a display of music boxes caught her eye. Though it was Sunday, the shop was open. On an impulse, she went in.

She'd been hoping to find something special for David. What, she hadn't the faintest idea. She browsed and, a few minutes later, found herself holding a beautiful wooden box inlaid with a mosaic pattern in Christmas green and red. Raising the cover, she heard the tinkling strains of "White Christmas." And wanted, very much, to dissolve into tears.

It was the perfect gift for David. Something she hoped he would keep, perhaps treasure. Something that, when they were far apart, would forever remind him of her.

KRIS STOPPED AT A CAFÉ on her way home and ordered a cup of hot chocolate and a piece of delicious homemade cake. The cold was draining her of energy, and energy was what she needed more than anything at the moment. Back in her apartment, she wound up the music box and played "White Christmas" over and over. Listening to the melody brought back bittersweet memories of what David had said last night.

Her eyes fell on the thin paper bag that contained his Christmas cards. She'd wanted to give him the cards last night after they'd returned from the Ancient Mariner. But David had stopped at the porch steps, had kissed her quickly, then headed for the car without looking back. That had hurt, too.

Well . . . if he wanted the cards he'd tell her so or he'd come get them, she reasoned. She wasn't about to use them again as an excuse to call him up.

Kris sighed. She took the music box into her bedroom, carefully wrapped it in red and gold foil paper and added a big red bow. Then she placed the present on top of his cards. It added a festive note to the living room, made it look just a little bit more like Christmas. A Christmas she wanted desperately to share with David.

CHAPTER EIGHTEEN

ERIC BENSON STOOD in the doorway of David's office and said, "I've scheduled an appointment for Hank O'Brien like you requested, sir. Eleven o'clock this morning. He wasn't too thrilled about it, but I think I made it sound official enough so he'll show."

Eric hesitated, then added, "Commander Jorgenson, sir...if you don't mind my saying so, you look like hell."

"Thanks a lot," David mumbled. "To be perfectly honest, I feel like hell."

The corpsman advanced into the room and cast an anxious eye at his favorite officer. He felt foolish posing the question, but he asked it anyway. "Don't you think maybe you should see a doctor?"

David couldn't help but laugh, and it hurt to laugh. "Probably," he conceded. "But I don't have time. Don't look so worried, Eric. It's just plain fatigue and a good old-fashioned sore throat. I doubt it's contagious, but I'll keep my distance from today's patients just to make sure."

"I wasn't thinking about your patients, Commander. Can I get you something?"

"If I don't start feeling better pretty soon, I'll prescribe an antibiotic for myself," David promised.

Fortunately, David's patients tended to do most of the talking during their consultations with him. That morning, he was even more monosyllabic than usual. Talking was painful, and he was saving what voice he had for his interview with Hank O'Brien.

Hank arrived promptly at eleven. He was in uniform and looked younger and skinnier than he had at the bar. He could not have projected a more comfortable image as he sat down in the chair in front of David's desk and asked, "You wanted to see me, sir?"

"Yes," David said. He didn't have enough voice to beat around the bush. He asked directly, "Hank, did you ever go to Danny Kalich's sister's house when Danny was living there? Or earlier, when Danny was still in submarine school?"

Hank looked like someone had hit him in the stomach. He shook his head dazedly, unable to speak.

"Look," David croaked, "this is strictly between us. Off-the-record. Off *your* record. You know what I'm talking about, right?"

"I went there a couple of times, sir," Hank allowed. "I didn't want to talk about it because...I'm engaged to a girl who's also in the navy. In fact, she's stationed here on the base. You know how talk travels."

David nodded.

"The thing is, Danny and Jay were both great guys," Hank said unhappily. "Really great guys. Friendly and hospitable. The first time I went over to Danny's place— his sister's place, that is—was when we were still in school. His sister was there. She had us over one Sunday afternoon for a cookout. Me and several other guys.

"When you're away from home, there's nothing like visiting another home, even someone else's," Hank went on. "Danny's sister was a real nice person. I'm sure she knew about Danny and Jay, but she just took it in stride.''

Hank looked up at David anxiously. "I take it you found out about Danny and Jay, sir?"

"Yes."

"Okay. After Danny washed out of school, he moved into his sister's place. He liked to invite a few of us over when we were off duty. He liked to cook. Sometimes we'd have a barbecue down by the river, depending on the weather. Yes, I suppose you could say those were parties, but there was nothing wild about them, Commander. The most that ever happened was maybe a couple of the guys drank too much beer.

"It got around the base about Danny's place, though. Some of the guys who weren't in on Danny's cookouts started stories about those of us who were. You know...they started rumors that we were probably gay, too. That's before I knew Ellen. Anyway, most of those troublemakers aren't even around Groton anymore. I hadn't thought about any of this for a long time...until I met up with you, Commander. Then I got to wondering how it would hit Ellen if even the slightest rumor got back to her."

"I can understand that."

"That's all of it, sir," Hank said earnestly.

"Thanks, Hank. I believe you." David's head had started to throb and his throat felt so thick he could hardly swallow. "Merry Christmas," he managed, giving Hank the cue to leave.

Eric came into the office a few minutes later, took a long look at his superior officer, then disappeared. He returned shortly thereafter to say, "I've rescheduled the rest of your appointments, Commander. Go home, will you?"

David went home.

He forced himself to drink a glass of cold cranberry juice, which stung unbearably, then he crawled into bed. He soon sank into a deep sleep—fever induced, he realized later. When the ringing of the telephone woke him up, he had no idea how long he'd slept.

"Yes," he croaked hoarsely.

"David?" Marianne Phillips queried. "What's wrong?"

"Sore throat, that's all. No big deal."

"Well, you sound terrible. Are you taking anything?"

"Yup," he grunted. He had brought an antibiotic home with him, then had felt so fuzzy he'd neglected to take the first dose.

"Look, I won't keep you," Marianne said. "I didn't realize you were going to Florida for Christmas, that's all."

"Florida? I'm not going to Florida."

"But Kris said..."

"What did Kris say?"

"I called her at the college because I wanted to make sure you both keep Christmas Eve free. Evan and I are having a few people in for eggnog, and we wanted so much for you and Kris to join us. But Kris said you'll probably have left by then."

"She's wrong."

"David, either someone should be there looking after you or you should be in the hospital."

"I'm okay."

"I'm going to send Evan over," Marianne decided, then hung up before David could protest.

Evan arrived within half an hour. By then, David had gotten down the first dose of antibiotic, taken off his uniform—now badly crumpled—and put on pajamas and a bathrobe. He'd also glanced at his throat using a flashlight and a wall mirror, and glumly concluded that he was a mess. Definitely a bacterial infection similar to the one Kris had had.

Evan plied his friend with liquids, made him take two aspirin, then guided him back into bed. Taking a seat on a corner of the bed, he announced, "I'll do most of the talking."

"Fine," David whispered.

"From the way you've been behaving," Evan observed, "I would say you've finally pieced together Jay Sothern's story."

David closed his eyes, swallowed and nodded affirmatively.

"Maybe I should get a notepad and pencil so you can write down your answers." Evan pondered.

"No." The fever was making him too groggy to even think about writing down answers.

"Okay, then. Have you found out everything you wanted to find out?"

The nod was affirmative.

"Have you talked to Kris about it?"

The nod was a violent negative.

"Dave, I'm speaking to you now as both a friend and as a chaplain. You must tell Kris what you've found out. I know I was the one who reneged in the first place, but that was only because I hated to think of her learning about Jay. That was narrow of me, and very wrong. I could go on, but I don't want to preach a sermon."

"Thanks," David managed.

"You're welcome," Evan said dryly. "I'm aware my timing couldn't be worse, but Kris told Marianne she's thinking of booking a Christmas cruise somewhere."

"What!" David couldn't repress the exclamation, though it nearly tore his throat apart.

"You heard me. Marianne asked her where, and Kris said she didn't care. Apparently she sounded very upset when she said that." He paused for a moment, then added levelly, "Look, Dave...Marianne and I already caught the vibes the other night at the Ancient Mariner. I'll give you and Kris A for effort, but neither of you would ever win an Academy award."

David shrugged and looked away.

"Now here you are, sick as a dog," Evan continued, "needing someone to take care of you. And Kris is probably at home, miserable, trying to find some cruise ship she can escape on because she thinks you're trundling off to Florida. If you ask me, it's all pretty stupid."

"No one asked you!" David croaked.

At that, Evan grinned. "At least you've still got some spunk," he observed. "All you need is to develop it and tell Kris what she has every right to know."

David didn't ponder that last statement simply because he felt too rotten to think about much of anything. After a time, Evan brought a carafe of juice to the bedside and advised, "Keep drinking. I'll look in on you later."

"No need," David began, but Evan was already on his way out.

Sleep came again, and when David awakened it was dark. His throat felt parched. He poured a glass of juice and drank it, checked the clock and saw that it was time to take more medication. He wobbled his way to his kitchenette, spooned out the medicine and grimaced as he swallowed. It was much easier to be a doctor than a patient, he concluded.

Evan returned with a thermos of chicken broth and a quart of vanilla ice cream. David did his best to oblige his friend and managed to consume some of both, but it was still very difficult to swallow.

Evan stayed around till nearly nine, and admonished as he left, "If you need anything don't hesitate to call."

In the morning, David felt slightly better. Still, he was ridiculously weak and knew he was in no shape to see patients. Lounging around his apartment, he had plenty of time to think. And Evan's remark about Kris's right to know came back to him.

Evan made it sound like a moral obligation, and David couldn't quite buy that. It was a judgment call, in his opinion. A judgment call based on deep concern for Kris's psychological welfare. And no one was more concerned about that than he was.

It was something of a shock when she phoned him early in the afternoon. "Marianne says you're sick," she stated immediately.

"Just a sore throat," he allowed.

"Like I had?"

"I guess so."

"You probably got it from me."

"It's going around, Kris."

"If it's like what I had, I know how you feel," she commiserated. She paused, then said softly, "I wish you'd called me yesterday. Marianne said you left work early, you felt so bad."

"Marianne talks too much."

"David...is there anything I can do? Something I can get that might hit the spot?"

"No."

"Do you want me to come over?"

"No," he repeated. "Your resistance..."

"Don't try to talk," Kris said. "You were only going to tell me my resistance is still low, that I could get sick again, right?"

"Uh-huh."

"I'm a lot stronger than you think."

Maybe his mind was hazy, but that statement seemed to have a lot more than surface meaning. David had the impression Kris was telling him something, trying to make him see something. He was just too groggy to figure it out.

"The college is closing for the holidays," she said. "There's a staff party a little later on this afternoon. I should be home by four, though. Please...if you need anything, call me, will you?"

"Okay," he managed.

He took another nap, and this time when he awakened he felt stronger. Not strong, but better. Well enough to reach a very painful decision. He put on warm clothes and made his way downstairs and out to his car. He felt steady enough to drive if he took it easy. It took him twice as long as normal to reach Granite Street.

Kris came out into the front hall a moment after he pressed her buzzer. She peered through the leaded-glass door with wide eyes. Then pulling it open, she demanded, "David, what in the world...are you insane?"

"I need to talk to you," he said soberly.

His voice was so hoarse it hurt Kris just to hear him. She watched as he moved past her into the living room, then slumped into the armchair by the fireplace. His dark hair was tousled, he needed a shave, his color was ghastly... and he looked more wonderful than anyone she'd ever seen in her entire life.

"Would a drink help?" she queried. "A bourbon, perhaps?"

He shook his head. "It would burn so much it would destroy me. Anyway, I'm on medication."

"Well, I'm glad to hear you're doing that much for yourself. How about some tea? Or maybe a soda?"

"Tea sounds good."

Kris thought it would take forever for the kettle to boil. She added milk and honey to the tea and hurried back into the living room.

David had slumped down even further into the chair and his eyes were closed. Hearing her, he opened them and yanked himself into a sitting position. "Look, Kris," he said, forcibly trying to gain control of his voice, "I can't stay long. But there's something I have to tell you."

Kris drew up a hassock, sat down and surveyed him thoughtfully. "Does it have to be now, David?"

"Yes."

"I can wait, you know."

He shook his head firmly. "No."

"It's about Jay, isn't it?"

"Yes."

"You know why, don't you?"

"As much as anyone will ever know why."

"David, I've lived for eight months now without knowing the answer. Another day or so won't make any difference." Kris said that for his sake, while inside she was frantic and fearful to hear what he had to say.

She watched David sip his tea. "Helps," he mumbled.

"I hope so, but you've still got to be careful about talking. Every time you say something I can hear the way it's straining your voice."

"I'll live."

"I don't doubt that," she agreed. She smiled faintly and added, "If you don't watch it, though, you may be left with a permanent case of laryngitis."

As she spoke, Kris felt her pulse beginning to thump. The dark cloud was descending again. She could feel its ominous edges brush her. There was only one way to ward it off, she realized. She had to question David.

"David," she asked, sounding almost as hoarse as he did, "did Jay do something terrible?"

He shook his head.

"He didn't steal anything?"

"No."

"Cheat in submarine school?"

"No."

"Was he into drugs?"

"No."

"What, then?" She groaned.

"He loved too much," David told her.

"Loved too much?" Kris frowned, more mystified than ever.

"He loved another man, Kris."

She went rigid, blank. Then the fire flared in her eyes. Her instinctive reaction was anger toward David for his daring to suggest such a thing.

"What are you saying?" she demanded. "How can you say something like that?"

"Because it's true."

David gingerly cleared his throat and took another sip of tea. "A long time ago," he said slowly, "Jay had to deal with some very difficult feelings. It must have been very hard for him. No one to tell. No one to share with. Considering the type of family you were raised in, he decided you'd feel...well, he really had no idea *how* you'd feel."

Kris got to her feet, clenching her hands into fists. "I can't believe you're saying this!" she challenged.

"Didn't want to say it. Didn't ever want you to know," David croaked. "But Evan said it was your right to know...and it is. You said you're stronger than I think you are. I think that's true. You'll get past the shock. After that, maybe you'll understand."

Kris's eyes were ablaze. "What makes you so sure you're right?"

"Evan told me, for one thing. But I also found out from other sources. Cal Demott would know, too. He counseled Jay. Haven't talked to him, but there's no need to now. Then, there were other friends..."

"And, I suppose, Jay's...lover?"

"A sensitive, intelligent young man named Danny," David said. "I knew him. I counseled him. That's how Jay must have heard of me. Danny had the house by the river. It belongs to his sister. But somehow Jay must have gotten the impression that I owned the house. Danny might have been joking, or protecting his sister for some reason. Jay simply misunderstood him. It no longer matters, anyway."

"I suppose you've spoken to this Danny?"

"Danny died last April...of cancer. Jay was with him. His grief was too much for him. Much as he loved you, Kris, he didn't want to go on living without Danny. Try to understand, Kris. Please, try to understand. I...I wouldn't want to go on living without you."

David looked up into her lovely face as he spoke and, in the intense moment that followed, wished he'd remained silent. She could have been wearing a stark white mask, her face was so void of expression. Except for her eyes. Those turning, tearless eyes. If only she could cry, David thought miserably. If only she could let it all out.

Suddenly Kris swerved and bolted from the room. David heard the bedroom door thud shut, then there was total silence. After a while, he got up, walked down the hall and listened. Nothing. He turned the knob. The door was locked. He called her name. This time, she opened the door. Standing on the threshold, she looked like an exquisitely carved statuette. Marble...all the way through.

"Thank you for coming," she said politely, as if he were a casual guest. "But please go now, will you?"

"Kris," he began to plead, but she only shook her head.

"Please go, David," she said, and quickly shut the door.

THE TWO PSYCHOLOGISTS in David's office assured him they could handle any patient emergencies that arose between now and Christmas. "Take it easy while you can," he was advised.

It was good advice, but the last thing David wanted was to take it easy. His suite was comfortable. Normally he welcomed the opportunity to lounge around, read or watch TV. Now, he felt hopelessly cooped up and incredibly lonely. Everyone who could get away had gotten away by Christmas Eve morning. Those who were still on base were there because they'd drawn duty over the holiday, plain and simple.

It had never occurred to him that he and Kris wouldn't be spending Christmas together. He'd long since decided that whether he discovered the truth about Jay's fate, he would somehow convince Kris to put the past behind them on Christmas and live that one day solely for each other.

What a travesty!

As he shuffled around his apartment, turning on the television then shutting it off, picking up a book then putting it down, David couldn't believe how weak he felt. His trek over to Kris's in the bitter cold hadn't done him any good. Physically and emotionally, dealing with Kris had taken a surprising toll.

Well...he'd leveled with her. For better or worse, he'd told her the truth. But because she didn't want to accept it, she'd made him a scapegoat. She'd transferred her anger and frustration about a truth she couldn't bear to cope with.

Not unusual psychological behavior, David reminded himself. Then suddenly he took a book he'd just picked up and hurled it across the room. This was no time to be clinical, damn it! Despite his powerful ability to rationalize and his expertise in the workings of the human mind, every fiber of his body was hurting. Hurting like hell!

DAVID WAS DOZING that afternoon when he was suddenly awakened by loud banging. He rubbed the sleep from his eyes and fought off the grogginess that still persisted even with the fever gone.

"Hold it," he called irritably, realizing someone was knocking persistently on his door. He shuffled across the floor and was surprised to discover Eric standing on the threshold.

"I'm checking out for the holidays, sir," Eric told him. "I wanted to stop by and see how you were doing before I left."

"I appreciate that," David said sincerely. "I'm doing much better."

"You still look a little green around the gills, sir."

"You should have seen me yesterday."

Eric laughed. Then he said, "Oh . . . there's something else, Commander."

"What?"

"Well, there's this lady downstairs who says she has a Christmas tree to deliver to you. I told her I'd help her with it. Be right back."

David stood in stunned silence as Eric disappeared into the elevator. A moment later, the miracle happened. The elevator door opened again and Kris stepped out into the hallway.

She was wearing her heavy coat, the red wool cloche and the red wool scarf. David rubbed his eyes again, wondering if he was hallucinating. How could Kris possibly be here on the base? But then he saw her turn, heard her call, "Need help, Eric?"

"Got everything under control, ma'am," came the muffled reply.

Kris, David saw, was carrying two large red bags brimming with bright packages. Over one arm, she'd slung a large Christmas wreath. "I have to finish decorating it,'' she murmured over her shoulder as she brushed past him and entered his suite.

Speechless, David followed her and watched as she stood in the middle of his living room, surveying the surroundings with a calculating eye.

She said judiciously, "I think maybe the tree should go over in that corner. What do you think? It's big enough to stand by itself."

She was holding her breath as she spoke, wondering how David was going to react. She wouldn't have blamed him if he told her to get lost, Christmas tree and all.

But he didn't say a word.

Eric appeared in the doorway, struggling with a beautiful fragrant spruce. The tree was a good six feet tall, with branches so thick Eric could hardly get it through the door.

He leaned the tree against the wall, then said, "The stand's downstairs. I'll be right back."

"Great," Kris answered quickly.

Eric returned in what seemed like seconds. Then, for several minutes, he and Kris worked to secure the tree in its stand, making sure it was perfectly positioned.

"Fantastic," Kris said. "Now, if you don't hurry, Eric, you're going to miss your bus."

"Plenty of time, ma'am," Eric said easily. "Are you sure you don't want me to get some water for the stand?"

"No, no. I can do the rest myself." She gave him a luminous smile. "Thanks, Eric," she said. "Thanks for everything. You've been terrific."

"It was my pleasure," Eric said.

Eric actually blushed as Kris leaned over and kissed him on the cheek. "Merry Christmas," she said.

"Merry Christmas to you, too," Eric told her. He nodded to David. "And to you, Commander."

The door thudded behind the corpsman, and Kris turned to face David across the length of the living room. She felt as if she were harboring whole colonies of butterflies inside her. Desperate, she tried to read David's expression and couldn't.

She said, tentatively, "David...maybe it will seem funny to you, but I wanted so much for you to have a Christmas tree. Eric told me his name when he dropped off the crystal jewelry you gave me. I managed to locate him, and he fixed things so I could come on the base."

When David didn't answer, she pointed to the red shopping bags. "I have all the ornaments in there. Plus tinsel and the trimmings for the wreath. There are also a couple of little things for you..."

She broke off as he continued to stare at her. "For God's sake, say something!" she blurted.

David hesitated, then managed, "I don't know what to say."

Kris swallowed hard. He looked so pale and tired and miserable. Probably as much from learning the truth about Jay as from his sore throat, she realized abruptly.

"Look, David," she said carefully. "I owe you a lot of apologies. I know that...and I'll give them to you, in time. I just had to work through all the things you told me. I had to look back on my life, as well as Jay's. You can understand that, can't you?"

"Yes."

"David, please. Try to understand. In addition to the shock of hearing what you had to say, I was terribly angry at you for being so hesitant about telling me."

"What are you saying, Kris?"

"I told you I'm not a weakling. I never have been. I wish you'd believed that. When I thought about the problems Jay could have had, what you told me was almost a relief. Except that it had such a tragic, tragic ending."

She hesitated. "You know," she said finally, "there's an old saying about it being darkest before dawn. In my case, the entire *day* before dawn was my darkest time. It took me a while to work my way through those uncertain hours. But dawn has come for me, David. It's incredibly beautiful . . . and it's here to stay."

"How am I supposed to interpret that?" he said quietly.

He was still eyeing her warily, Kris saw, nor could she blame him. She smiled wryly. "I guess you could say I've learned a great deal in such a very short time. About life, about people, about motives and values and love."

"Love?"

"Yes."

David's silver stare softened ever so slightly, prompting Kris to say, "I know the reason you didn't want to tell me about Jay was because you love me, you wanted to protect me. We all want to protect the people we love. Perhaps we want to protect them too much."

"Very true," he agreed huskily.

Kris gazed across at him and thought her heart would burst. She reached for one of the shopping bags and dug out a small present wrapped in red and gold foil. Moving to stand in front of David, she held it out to him.

"Open this, will you?" she said softly.

David's fingers were trembling as he untied the ribbon and pulled away the wrapping paper. He took out the little music box and slowly, carefully, turned the key. The lilting strains of "White Christmas" punctuated the silence between them.

It was Kris's turn to be unsteady. She said, her voice faltering, "I've dreamed about white Christmases, too, darling, and about sharing them with someone I loved...forever and ever. Are we going to share our white Christmases, David Jorgenson?"

The romantic carol was slowly winding down. David turned the key again, then set the music box on the coffee table. In the next instant, he took Kris into his arms and embraced her with all his heart. Kris clung to him, knowing that the dark clouds of yesterday had vanished forever.

He cupped her chin in his hand and gazed down into her eyes. "I'm past the contagious stage, darling," he whispered.

"Even if you're not," Kris told him, "I have a doctor in the house, don't I?"

"So...you finally believe that psychiatrists are really doctors?"

"Oh, David!" Kris exclaimed, as tears of joy filled her eyes. "This is going to be such a wonderful Christmas. The best of my entire life. Do you know that?"

He kissed her mouth gently, then moved back just enough to tease, "What about the cruise?"

"What cruise?"

"Marianne told me you were booking a cruise over Christmas."

"Marianne talks too much. Besides, if I'd gone and done that, my tears would have swamped the ship!"

David lovingly surveyed her, and a tender smile curved his lips. "You exaggerate, Miss Sothern," he decided. "But we psychiatrists have a way of dealing with that."

"Are you strong enough to handle your own prescription, doctor?"

"Maybe not today," David admitted. "But tomorrow..."

"Tomorrow and forever," Kris told him, reaching up to return his kiss. Tomorrow and forever.

MAIL-IN-OFFER
OFFER CERTIFICATE ✂ - - - - - - - - -

I have enclosed the required number of proofs of purchase from any specially marked "Gifts From The Heart" Harlequin romance book, plus cash register receipts and a check or money order payable to Harlequin Gifts From The Heart Offer, to cover postage and handling.

002

CHECK ONE	ITEM	# OF PROOFS OF PURCHASE	POSTAGE & HANDLING FEE
	01 Brass Picture Frame	2	$ 1.00
	02 Heart-Shaped Candle Holders with Candles	3	$ 1.00
	03 Heart-Shaped Keepsake Box	4	$ 1.00
	04 Gold-Plated Heart Pendant	5	$ 1.00
	05 Collectors' Doll Limited quantities available	12	$ 2.75

NAME _____

STREET ADDRESS _____ APT. # _____

CITY _____ STATE _____ ZIP _____

Mail this certificate, designated number of proofs of purchase (inside back page) and check or money order for postage and handling to:

Gifts From The Heart, P.O. Box 4814
Reidsville, N. Carolina 27322-4814

NOTE THIS IMPORTANT OFFER'S TERMS

Requests must be postmarked by May 31, 1988. Only proofs of purchase from specially marked "Gifts From The Heart" Harlequin books will be accepted. This certificate plus cash register receipts and a check or money order to cover postage and handling must accompany your request and may not be reproduced in any manner. Offer void where prohibited, taxed or restricted by law. LIMIT ONE REQUEST PER NAME, FAMILY, GROUP, ORGANIZATION OR ADDRESS. Please allow up to 8 weeks after receipt of order for shipment. Offer only good in the U.S.A. Hurry—Limited quantities of collectors' doll available. Collectors' dolls will be mailed to first 15,000 qualifying submitters. All other submitters will receive 12 free previously unpublished Harlequin books and a postage & handling refund.

OFFER-1RR

PAMELA BROWNING

...is fireworks on the green at the Fourth of July and prayers said around the Thanksgiving table. It is the dream of freedom realized in thousands of small towns across this great nation.

But mostly, the Heartland is its people. People who care about and help one another. People who cherish traditional values and give to their children the greatest gift, the gift of love.

American Romance presents HEARTLAND, an emotional trilogy about people whose memories, hopes and dreams are bound up in the acres they farm.

HEARTLAND...the story of America.

Don't miss these heartfelt stories: American Romance #237 SIMPLE GIFTS (March), #241 FLY AWAY (April), and #245 HARVEST HOME (May).

HRT-1

GIFTS FROM THE HEART

from Harlequin

FREE BY MAIL

With proofs of purchase
plus postage and handling

A. Hand-polished solid brass picture frame 1-5/8″ × 1-3/8″ with 2 proofs of purchase.

B. Individually handworked, pair of heart-shaped glass candle holders (2″ diameter), 6″ candles included, with 3 proofs of purchase.

C. Heart-shaped porcelain keepsake box (1″ high) with delicate flower motif with 4 proofs of purchase.

D. Radiant gold-plated heart pendant on 16″ chain with complimentary satin pouch with 5 proofs of purchase.

E. Beautiful collectors' doll with genuine porcelain face, hands and feet, and a charming heart appliqué on dress with 12 proofs of purchase. Limited quantities available. See offer terms.

HERE IS HOW TO GET YOUR FREE GIFTS

Send us the required number of proofs of purchase (below) of specially marked ''Gifts From The Heart'' Harlequin books and cash register receipts with the Offer Certificate (available in the back pages) properly completed, plus a check or money order (do not send cash) payable to Harlequin Gifts From The Heart Offer. We'll RUSH you your specified gift. Hurry—Limited quantities of collectors' doll available. See offer terms.

501R

GIFTS FROM THE HEART

ONE PROOF
OF PURCHASE

To collect your free gift by mail you must include the necessary number of proofs of purchase with order certificate.